02/2012

AUTO-EROTICA

Stacia Saint Owens

Livingston Press

The University of West Alabama

Copyright © 2009 Stacia Saint Owens
All rights reserved, including electronic text
isbn 13 978-1-60489-025-9 trade paper
isbn 13 978-1-60489-024-2, lib. bind.
Library of Congress Control Number 2009920495
Printed on acid-free paper.
Printed in the United States of America,
Publishers Graphics
Hardcover binding by: Heckman Bindery

Typesetting and page layout: Joe Taylor
Proofreading: Margaret Walburn, Tricia Taylor, Asa Griggs,
Creed Robbins, Allie Ellis, Shelly Huth, Aubree Hudson, Stevi Bolen,
Jamareé Collins, Ivory Robinson, Terry Kennedy, Shelly Huth,
Joe Taylor

Cover design and art: James Graham
www.jamesgrahamartist.com
Cover layout: Jennifer Brown

This is a work of fiction.
Surely you know the rest: any resemblance
to persons living or dead is coincidental.

Livingston Press is part of The University of West Alabama,
and thereby has non-profit status.
Donations are tax-deductible:
brothers and sisters, we need 'em.

first edition
6 5 4 3 3 2 1

For my mother

Sandra Ayers Owens

who gave birth to an oddity,
and instead of panicking,
recognized that her child was a writer.

CONTENTS

AUTO-EROTICA

LURID DETAILS

AN URBAN LEGEND FOR THE YOUNG AND NEW

This story could only take place in Los Angeles. It has to be somewhere high-crime and danger-loving where a door would plausibly be left unlocked. It requires an exceptionally pretty, pathologically ambitious, and wholly disposable girl. A city full of people who believe so fiercely that they are going to die rich that they take the sort of risks only a billionaire could survive. Equal parts high profile, under the radar, and off the map. Sex, drugs, and getting killed for being too nice. Sensationalism as the local religion. And the sun has to be shining while all of this is happening. Remember that. It's easier to believe that the girl would be so stupid if you picture the sunshine.

She called about the studio apartment for rent because it was only one block from her office and even though she hated this job, answering phones all day was relatively un-taxing so she thought she would keep it until she finished writing her screenplay in the evenings.

Her screenplay wasn't going very well. It was about a girl like her from the Midwest who moved to L.A. to work in movies. The heroine kept meeting a lot of outrageous characters: an elderly, tobacco-stained Mafioso who had spotted her at an all-night grocery store and constantly brought her foot-high tiramisu cakes curlicued with the names of unknown couples; a snarling girl

1

with blacklight violet hair who wore crawly plum velvet thrift store capes and described herself as a drummer but spent most of her time reading tarot cards for free, laying out the deck then chuckling darkly, refusing to voice her disastrous predictions; a guy who arranged twigs in his Amish beard and stood in front of a coffee shop, hat on the sidewalk, hoping to be appreciated as a performance artist and subsidized with loose change; an excitable little golf caddy who went out at night with a can of baby blue spray paint and large stencils, branding the freeway off-ramps with such cryptic messages as: YIELD TO THE DRASTIC VOID TEMPLE.

Despite all of these colorful characters—Life in L.A. was surreal! You couldn't make this stuff up if you tried!—nothing much was happening in her screenplay. If she could eliminate her commute, she would have an extra hour and a half per night to write.

The extra hour and a half would slip down from the craggy hills that ringed the city, in the shape of a scraggly, world-weary urban coyote. The coyote would leap through the window of her new apartment and sit at her feet, slurping cappuccino from a saucer, her witch's familiar. She would sit with concert pianist posture, raising her stiff, alert hands over her keyboard. The extra hour and a half would poke its wet grey snout against her ear, telling her what should happen next.

The girl had a very good imagination, but the things she imagined didn't really belong in a screenplay. Screenplays have to be both fake and stubbornly realistic at the same time. She was new at it. It was all foreign to her.

The realtor didn't bother to hide her disdain for a person who could only afford a studio. "Yeah," the realtor snapped into the phone, "It's open. Let yourself in and look around."

"Thank you," said the girl. She had been brought up to think that good manners would open many doors.

"Yeah," sighed the realtor, then coughed cigarette phlegm into the girl's ear, then hung up.

The girl called her boyfriend before she went to look at the studio.

"It's not a good idea," he said. "Wait for the weekend and I'll come with you."

"Someone'll get it by then."

"No one wants a studio. How much they asking?"

"1050."

"I'll talk them down to nine. We'll look on Sunday. I've got to work late with Marilyn again."

"That's fine. I'll be writing."

"Love you."

"Me too. Bye."

She was still going to look at the studio at lunch time. She thought she should tell someone at the office where she was going, just in case. She wasn't really friendly with anyone at work. It was a top entertainment law office. Very well known people called and screamed at their lawyer, who then called and screamed at six other people. It was not clear if this ever accomplished anything. The very well known people did not seem to understand that the stacks of papers they had signed had the final word, even if the papers were dull and soberly formatted and never screamed.

The more the girl saw of Hollywood people, the more she thought of them as bats, travelling in swarms, laying siege, always flapping and screaming, never wandering far from the pack because on their own they would be reduced to a peculiar little rodent, no real threat at all. The screaming was essential. They screamed and screamed, pushing it, testing how far their sound waves could travel before they hit something bigger and the screaming bounced back at them. It was how they gauged their position in the world. She was sure that they all slept badly, suspended upside down, never at ease, miniature dragon wings pulled over their faces like leathery baby blankets, twitching through the non-working hours with the paranoia of reviled creatures until it was time to scream again.

All of the Assistants were much older than the girl, and got paid a lot more. She had recently discovered that the office's monthly expenditure on fresh flowers exceeded her salary. The flowers could never quite mask the pervasive funk of stress and antacids. The scents clashed disastrously. All those towering bouquets ended up smelling chemical, like floral-scented disinfectant, and they looked like bleeding ulcers. Guests always left with a headache.

The Assistants talked non-stop about shopping and kids, two subjects the girl was not interested in. After the weekend, there would be breathless accounts of items purchased and things said and done by their kids. Even the lawyers participated in these Monday morning exchanges, though they downplayed the shopping so their underlings wouldn't get jealous of them, and inflated the amount of time they had spent with kids, so they wouldn't get jealous of their underlings. When someone asked the girl about her weekend, she would say, "I was writing." They would nod and think, *Stupid girl.* They had all abandoned their screenplays years ago.

Lorraine probably would have been interested in the fact that the girl was going to look at a vacant property that had been left open for anyone to just walk inside. Lorraine's desk was nearest to the reception area, where the girl sat brooding over day-old trades, trying to memorize faces so that visiting clients would be spared the slight of having to announce their names. Lorraine had frosted hair and nails and the arrestingly symmetrical facial features of a leading lady, only she was 50 pounds too heavy. She called it her pregnancy weight, even though her only child had now started college. If the girl had told Lorraine where she was going, Lorraine would certainly have put a stop to it. She would have told the girl that empty properties were hideouts for rapists, that L.A. was not a place to take chances like that, that girls like her disappeared every day of the week. Lorraine had moved to L.A. from Minnesota when she was 18, came all the way by herself on a Greyhound bus, not knowing a soul, her stomach bulging with what turned out to be a hysterical pregnancy, and she could tell you plenty of stories like this one that would make your blood curdle. Afterwards, she told this story over and over, especially to her son's girlfriends. She didn't want her son getting mixed up with any careless women.

But Lorraine was in the bathroom when the girl left, slathering more pink frosted lipstick onto her still-gorgeous head, glowering at her flabby body. As Lorraine looked in the mirror and contemplated becoming a Satanist if they could rid her of the weight, the girl took the elevator down twenty-three floors and walked out onto the bright, magnolia-scented streets of Santa Monica.

She walked briskly along toward the studio for rent. Even the quieter, residential side streets in L.A. seemed excited, on the brink of something. The green grass bristled. Lawn sprinklers chattered like monkeys and doused her ankles, stinging a little. She had to mentally pause and ask herself what time of year it was. Summer year round! She decided it was fall.

She felt guilty about going against her boyfriend's advice. She hadn't actually lied, but she had been misleading, leaving him to think that she would wait for him before looking at the apartment. Where she came from, lies were always found out and liars were always punished.

If she moved into this studio, she would live about an hour's drive from her boyfriend. She imagined writing to her mother: *We only live in two different neighborhoods in Los Angeles, but if this were home, he would live as far away as two towns over!* She was beginning to understand that although her mother didn't like her living in Los Angeles, she was there largely so she could report interesting things to her mother, unbelievable things, magical things. Her mother had told her lots of stories as she was growing up, and it gave her a taste for the extraordinary. Her mother's life hadn't turned out as planned. Her father barely acknowledged her mother anymore and with the kids grown and gone, her mother had frayed into loose ends. The girl felt an obligation to feed her mother interesting reports, as vital as a nutrition drip down an I.V. tube. Of course, many of the goings-ons here alarmed her mother, but the girl was unsparing in her reports. She thought of it as an EKG machine shocking her mother back to life, forcing her heartbeat to go on a little longer.

The girl's boyfriend was untroubled by family ties. He was a mover and a shaker. He had grown up poor, despised everyone he had known before moving to L.A., and was determined to succeed. He kept moving up, up, up. He had started out as a runner, a faceless grunt in a motorcycle helmet delivering scripts and contracts and baskets of soy-based pastries around town, and already he had moved up to Assistant to one of the V.P.'s at a production company.

The girl's financial and career prospects kept getting worse. Each job she took was more ill-paid than the last, and her responsibilities kept diminishing. She told herself she just wanted a mindless day job so she could work on her screenplay, but she knew this panicked her boyfriend. She kept meeting people who could do nothing for her career. She tended to befriend unattractive people prone to frizz and acne who rapidly told her outrageous life stories, rife with abuse and fleeings and psychotropic misfortunes, then asked to borrow her car. This enraged her boyfriend. "Who comes to L.A. without a car?! It's like these people want to fail!" He didn't say, "It's like *you* want to fail," but this was implied. He didn't understand that she was gathering stories, that her life had been very sheltered and unerringly stable, that this placid, clear-horizoned existence was what was killing her mother, the same as living too near a radiation factory. Exposure to eccentric dysfunction was a kind of life-saving nectar to her. These self-deluded losers were giving her something very precious, something he—with his circled sports car ads and savings for a pair of the right exorbitantly priced shoes and plans to eventually walk her down the aisle with an announcement blurb in *The Hollywood Reporter* listing them both by job title and company—could never provide for her.

She was sure her boyfriend loved her. Her certainty was based mainly on the fact that he told her so repeatedly. And she loved him, or she wouldn't have said so.

She shouldn't have worried so much that her boyfriend was going to bring fatal predictability into her future. He was already trying to leave her. He had identified the most powerful female in his company and was fucking her using an illegal, half-herbal, three times as powerful version of Viagra sold by the insomniac interns at UCLA med school. The girl's boyfriend swallowed the little moss-colored pills and gave the V.P. of Business Affairs the impression that he was perpetually, painfully hard for her, that he could not exist without banging her five to seven times a day, that this was all new to him, no one had ever made him feel this way. He was only 23 years old, but already he had figured out that in Hollywood, it's best to be young and new. He behaved like a 17-year-old in as many ways as possible.

He had a genuine affection for the girl and he didn't know how to break it off. He kept saying things like, "I have to work late with Marilyn again," and waiting for her to question him, to check his phone bills, to get fed up and barge into the office while he had Marilyn's angular body unfolded beneath him across her desk, flat and compliant like assembling a kite. But the girl had no experience with romantic strife and she kept believing him. Even when he started leaving used condoms in the back of his car, she accepted his mumbly-mouthed, shifty-eyed explanations that the valets must have been taking wild liberties. He couldn't stay with the kid because she was too much of a liability. She never, ever lied, and she couldn't grasp that everyone else in this town was lying, always, about everything. She never watched her back. He had a nagging feeling that she was going to come to a bad end. If he were a character in a movie, this would make him determined to save her. In real life, it made him want to get away from her, fast. Everything in L.A. is contagious.

But time was up. It was a very short walk. She was now standing at the door of the apartment she thought she might want to live in. It was a high pollen count day and the air was teeming with reproducing irritants mixed with reflective droplets of smog. There was something thick and sexual about breathing it in, something close to blacking out, to losing yourself. The sun was of course beaming down at 82 degrees, so dependable that it verged on obstinate. No one knew she was there.

It was a first floor studio. She tentatively twisted the doorknob, and sure enough, the cream-colored wooden door swung open. She stepped inside, backward. She stood just inside the threshold, facing the rectangular patch of sunny, bird-twittered public space, her hand still on the doorknob. She decided it was best to close the door behind her, so no unsavory types happening by would wander in. She pushed the door closed.

She turned and faced the studio. *The whole place is only as big as our kitchen!* she imagined writing to her mother.

She tightroped heel-against-toe across the room, trying to measure the dimensions. The brown carpet was long and furry and matted like a favorite stuffed animal. The girl imagined the last occupant sleeping peacefully on the floor, clutching a handful of the carpet while saliva pooled over it. Or maybe the saliva came from the coyote. A lot of people in this city would spend their extra hour and a half fast asleep. This was incomprehensible to her. She was too new. She didn't even think of it.

She slid open the closet that ran the entire length of one wall. It was reassuringly empty.

She looked out the little window above the steel kitchenette sink. There was nothing to see, just a narrow alley blocked by two illegally-parked cars with out-of-state plates. Michigan and Oregon. She was squinting hard in an attempt to read the state motto of Oregon when something shifted in the bathroom.

She went rigid. Not just her body. Everything about her. All the rules she relied on in life snapped to attention and formed a steel cage around her, like a deep sea photographer in shark-infested waters. Her mind raced through cold calculations. She would have to walk past the bathroom door to get out of the apartment. The bathroom door was cracked open and it was dark inside. If there was someone in there, he could see her, had been watching her. Had the advantage.

If she had left the front door open, she could have made a run for it. Now she would have to pause to grip the doorknob, hope she didn't fumble, move backward into the tiny room to allow the front door enough space to open. She estimated that this would place her right in front of the bathroom door. Perfectly positioned to be pounced.

She eased her cell phone out of her purse and flipped it open. The rectangle stayed black. It matched her last look through the car window at her unlit homeland the night she drove off for L.A. She hadn't charged her phone. Her job had made her hate phones and people who were always yelling into them. This was a big mistake.

She made the sign of the cross and mentally raced through a Hail Mary while holding her breath. She could hear panting inside the dark bathroom.

"Hello?" she ventured. Trust the rules. Try to be civilized. Give friendliness a try. Don't jump to conclusions. Give the other person the benefit of the doubt. *I relied on my wits like you always taught me!* she composed to her mother.

A hiss erupted from the bathroom. She couldn't make out the words, but it had the intonation of a command and seemed to be desperately restraining a burst of motion. It reminded her of a muted train whistle. Or a signal for starting a race.

She strode across the room, thrust her hand into the bathroom door's open crack, slapped at the wall inside until she flipped on the light switch.

She stood back, staring at the illuminated strip between the door frame and the bathroom door. She held her hand tightly at the wrist, as if it had been severed and needed to be re-attached.

"I'm leaving," she blustered. The empty room had a tiny metallic echo.

As she walked past the bathroom, she didn't hear anything at all and her fear got the best of her. Adrenaline surged through her. She kicked the bathroom door with all her might.

The door hit someone who was standing behind it. Another someone was huddled on the lime tiled floor, his cheek balanced on the open plastic oval of the toilet seat. He had dark skin and pungent black hair tied back with a rubber band, curling out this way and that like the dandelion stems she used to slice then soak in cups of water when she was growing up someplace where entertainment did not require darkened rooms. His clothes were studded with meandering rows of silver metal, as if some sloppy corn-cob eater had bitten him up and down, embedding teeth fillings. The fabric had originally been black, but was now charcoal-colored from sunlight and lack of washing. He was very young, probably a teenager. He was shivering terribly, constant tremors pulsing through his body, his slack face wracked by repeated contortions, his teeth chattering, a telegraph machine stuck on the same urgent message.

She had seen shivering like this once before, when a runty asthmatic boy from her brother's Cub Scout troop had to be sent home from the winter camping trip. Instead of delivering him to his house, the Scout Master had him transported to the school gym, where everybody was at Saturday basketball practice. Living examples were considered very valuable where she came from.

The adults made the boy inch into the gym on his shaky legs and sit shivering and hugging himself on the bleachers, waiting for his parents to arrive. The squeal of rubber soles and springy echo of dribbling stopped for a few seconds as the other kids held their basketballs and watched him, an ancient feeble man at age 10, a boy who didn't have the stuff to survive.

"Howdy," a second male teenage head popped out from behind the bathroom door. Once blond, now yellowed, skin like the dehydrated transparent tape holding down photos in a grandmother's album. Teeth varnished a golden hue. Blue irises peeping out from jaundiced eyeballs. The same once-black death metal clothes, more aggressively stained than his companion's, a lot of the marks blood-colored.

Two homeless drug addicts were hiding in the bathroom! she imagined writing to her mother.

"I'm Phoenix," drawled the Yellowed One. "This here's Injun."

"Hello," she said. But did not offer her hand. And stood wondering if she should.

Injun went on shivering. The Yellowed One didn't volunteer any comment on his friend's state or what they were doing there.

She came from a part of the country where drugs were evil, the tools of thieves and child exploiters and college dropouts who wasted their parents' hard-earned money and squandered their opportunities to escape their small towns. There was absolutely no distinction between marijuana and heroin. Both would get you hard time and bring ruin to your family. Her knowledge of drugs consisted of "Just Say No." This shivering boy draped over the toilet of a vacant apartment struck her as a graphic validation of her clean-living choices. But wasn't he fascinating? How did he live? What did he dream about? Had he ever been in love? She wanted his background, his daily schedule, his vocabulary, all his lurid details. She could use them.

If she had lived long enough, she would have one day found it absurd, equating toking a joint with shooting up. If she would have lived long enough, she would have blushed at her righteous naïveté when she first moved to L.A. If she had survived this era, she would have one day shaken her head at her own foolishness and tipped a glass of red wine down her throat and looked her poignantly frail, cross-dressing Filipina lover dead in the eye and said, "It's a wonder I wasn't really taken advantage of back then."

Her lover would have answered this with a half-smile beneath the brim of her black bowler hat, re-crossing her yoga-sculpted legs so the long tuxedo jacket rode up her thighs, flashing the lacy tops of her sheer stockings and the tight garter straps, distracting the girl, making her lose interest in nostalgia and ghost stories. If you stay in L.A. long enough, you learn that all the dire details and disappointments can be eclipsed if you just concentrate on the sex.

The Yellowed One slouched down against the side of the tub. He seemed satisfied to carry on as if she weren't there, doing nothing, hiding from someone else.

"I might rent this apartment," she announced, hoping to exert some ownership.

"It's damn small," observed the Yellowed One. "There's a house over off Los Feliz? Vacant for four-five months now? Wicked fucking dream crib, man! Me and him and my ho stayed up in there—It's like you got your hot tub, Jacuzzi, six showers, three bathtubs, whirlpool, sauna...." As he listed each bathing fixture, he pointed his index finger at the ceiling then chopped it down toward the floor, a charismatic minister at his pulpit. She found it interesting that someone so grimy would get so excited over methods of washing. This was the sort of realism that people living in other, safer places wouldn't be privy to.

"Now that asshole's showed up from Ken-tuck," he continued. "But I told her not to worry. I'll scrub that boy out. We'll be back. You ain't gonna tell the realtor lady, right? This place gots running water. Man gotta keep clean, you know."

She felt a bit braver. She gestured at Injun. "What's his story?"

"Same story all round, man. Hard luck, good times, street life, high life, low life, got-to-go life. Straight up. You a doctor?"

She realized he was staring at her clothes. She bought her work clothes at discount warehouses in the Valley, and they were usually marked IRREGULAR due to some manufacturing flaw, an uneven seam, a mis-positioned pocket, button holes sewn into a zippered garment. She bought grudging imitations of office wear because she really didn't belong in an office and after she sold her screenplay, she would shop on Melrose. She had already chosen the stores she would patronize. She didn't have the nerve to go in and look at the prices, but she knew which window displays appealed to her. After she sold her screenplay, she would totter along in tall shoes and convincing fake fur and total block-out black Italian shades that made the whole city look like tranquil film noir. She would buy all her clothes a few shades too bright because everyone in town was wearing sunglasses all the time. Wannabes would come trotting up beside her, offering to carry her shopping bags so they could pitch her their screenplays-in-progress. "Sounds good!" she would say. "Keep writing. Don't ever give up!" She couldn't wait to say this to people. She would mean it with all her heart. Getting to say this was going to be the best thing about being successful.

But to the Yellowed One, she already looked like the picture of professionalism. Unlike New York, people here didn't crush into subways or crowd into parks or pack the streets with foot traffic. He was almost never this close to a person who slept in a bed every night. "I mean, you look real serious and all, so I thought you must be a doctor or somethin."

"Are you hungry?" She wasn't scared anymore. It occurred to her that if she fed them, she could get them to talk about themselves and she could write it all down for her screenplay. She might even come back several times with her little tape recorder. She wasn't one to miss an opportunity. Plus feeding the hungry was the right thing to do.

"Starvin Marvin, man. You got $10, me and him can both eat real good."

"I'll go to Ralph's. What do you want?"

"Ohhh, god. Coke. For sure, Coke. Snickers. Pop Tarts. Cinnamon. He loves them Lucky Charms, but I ain't sure he'll eat it just now. Marlboro

Lights. Anti-crush pack."

"I'll get a couple of sandwiches."

"No mayo, man. Can't fucking stand mayo. Mayo makes me crazy."

His lack of gratitude confused her. She kept stalling, asking more food-related questions. It didn't seem like she could leave until he said, "Thank you." The inherent order of the universe was being disrupted and she felt slow and dizzy. Maybe it was her who was saying the wrong things.

"You sure you ain't got 10 bucks? You look like you got 10 bucks."

"I'll just get the sandwiches."

The front door banged open, letting in a blazing flash of sunlight. A broad, heavy girl stomped in, slamming the door behind her. Her lank shoulder-length hair had been dyed platinum, crowned by two inches of black roots. She was barrel-chested, squeezed into a faded thrasher band t-shirt and a hot pink vinyl micro-mini skirt. Her legs were spindly and marbled by a bright red hair-remover rash. She reminded the girl of the stripy pudding her mother used to set in clear parfait glasses, wide at the top and tapering to the bottom, a different color and texture on each layer. Parfait Girl was slurping from an enormous bucket-sized fountain drink and her ringed nostrils were flaring.

"Who the fuck is she?"

"She's goin for food." The Yellowed One was clearly afraid of Parfait Girl. He put his palms out when he spoke to her, as if expecting her to rush him.

"What she gettin for me? Huh? What you gettin for me, bitch?"

The girl didn't like answering to "bitch." She thought she should concentrate on leaving. She suddenly remembered hearing stories about some homeless kids who thought they were vampires and needed to drink blood. A gang of homeless youths somewhere had trapped a boy in a closet and tortured him for days, sodomizing him with a hot curling iron. Also, the girl noticed that Parfait Girl smelled horrendous, salvaged cigarette ends and rancid suntan oil and lowest-rung, junkie-pimped, bargained-down, against-a-dumpster sex. The worst things the girl had ever smelled before were locker-rooms and baby diapers and vomit, things that would soon go away. It was like coming upon a bush flowering with poisonous sap. The girl thought she should go back the way she had come.

"I'm getting sandwiches for everybody." The girl took a step toward the door. She did this more timidly than she meant to. Sure enough, Parfait Girl blocked her.

"Why you macking on my man?"

The girl was at a loss. She didn't think of the Yellowed One or Injun as men. She didn't even think of her own boyfriend as a man. They were all too young. She didn't know who Parfait Girl was talking about.

Injun whimpered, still staring into the shadowy grey cavern of the toilet bowl. He had a finely-tuned antenna for violence.

"She's the realtor!" screeched the Yellowed One. "She'll call the five-oh, man! She gots folks comin!"

Parfait Girl pivoted mightily toward the girl, a pierced-faced kabuki actor. "You the realtor?"

The girl gulped. "No. No, I'm not. I'm just a girl. I'm writing a screenplay."

The Yellowed One reached over wearily and flipped off the bathroom light. He closed the bathroom door. He and Injun sat in the dark. They couldn't say for sure how it all happened out there. They knew the girl never said anything more, never made another sound, even when she had time. Her silence seemed to be frowning.

The girl was right, the rules had changed. Her honesty and generosity went unrewarded.

Three days later, another girl came by alone on her lunch hour to view the studio apartment. She was ordinarily a nice, normal, balanced person. But she was fantasizing about abducting her husband's mistress from the Venice Beach volleyball court and dragging her to a place like this and really showing her what pain meant. She imagined the bitch tied up in the middle of this brown carpet, imagined her olive face raisining into a thousand creases of excruciating pain. Let her know what it feels like.

This girl slid open the long closet. What she found inside scared her straight.

This story is told over and over in Los Angeles to young new girls searching for their first or second apartments. The villain changes. Sometimes it is an elderly man she finds sitting in the dark bathroom, shaking with rheumatism, a sinister gummy-mouthed rapist. Sometimes it is snuff filmmakers lying in wait and they already have another girl tied up in the bathtub. Sometimes it is an impressively dressed career woman in her 40s, soft spoken but driven to homicidal lunacy because her boy-toy lover moved out of that apartment and left no forwarding address. There are plenty of villains and they should all be feared. They are the truest part of the story.

The young new girls usually laugh it off when they first hear this story. But it does leave an impression. They may shudder when they see FOR RENT signs. When they are assaulted by the strangeness of the city, when they find themselves brushing against one of the wink-quick episodes of meaningless violence that dapples life in L.A., somewhere in the back of their minds they think of the girl in this story and they try to do the opposite of what she would do. The opposite of what their parents taught them. The opposite of what would be considered good and right almost anywhere else. The opposite of what their sister, with her two grinning children and her nights full of sleep and her big porch with the endless back yard in Topeka, would do. The rules from home will get you socially ostracized, backstabbed, swindled, left for dead in L.A.

The old rules are relentlessly channeled into movie scripts because they are something every successful Los Angelino has lost. The old rules have become unattainable fantasy material, like youth and car chases and sex with people who are both gorgeous and sincere and who find mediocrity to be a turn-on. Hollywood has ripped off everything under the sun, but it did create one original mythological creature: the whore who, underneath it all, isn't really a whore. The young new ones must be taught that this is only a myth. Anything with a soft underbelly won't survive L.A.

It takes awhile for this to sink in. One day, years later, when the girls are no longer new and not exactly young anymore, they will be stuck in clogged traffic on their commute home, cars bobbing forward like corks floating in a bathtub. They will be swallowing exhaust and leaving terse voicemails and punching through radio ad after radio ad. They will be visibly harder by this time, fast-talkers, axe-grinders, ball-busters, strap-flashers, heart-breakers, but they will still have that little roll of ingénue fat, they will still be writing the same screenplay, they will still yearn for the extra hour and a half to nuzzle up against them and tell them million dollar bedtime stories.

At that moment, a coyote will come limping across the eight lanes of traffic. It's something to look at and everyone will watch as the coyote takes finicky steps around the creeping vehicles, constantly looking back over his hunched shoulder instead of watching where he's going. Everybody will see it when he comes to a dead halt in the lane just past one of the not-so-young-or-new girls and looks back directly at her, luminescent yellow eyes asking, *"Where have you been?"* The sports utility vehicle next to her will idle forward, blinded by the sun, claiming its two yards closer to home. The enormous tires will smash the coyote into a sauce of blood and fur, though not as much blood as you would think. Mostly he's just flat and untroubled. Watching this, it will hit the not-so-young-or-new girls that they will never, ever finish their screenplay. Because they've played it smart and lived through it all and nothing has happened.

Only now does the real point of this story hit them. Now it will all make sense. That girl would have been much happier and lived a lot longer if she had taken an interest in shopping and kids.

Suddenly, they are not in the same hurry to get home. Outside the car, the shrillness of the city mounts. They all give up and blend in, become screamers.

***

THE HUNGER ARTIST'S AGENT

They have both ordered lettuce. There are certain roughage foods—lettuce, celery, parsley—that expend more energy chewing and swallowing than the food itself contains, which means you can eat it and end up with negative calories. The usual contest is silently raging to see who can nibble the least lettuce, who can leave the most leaves on her plate. Ordinarily, Sondra would let her win. It's part of the job, making them feel comfortable. Today she's irritable. She talks a lot even though she knows it puts her at an unfair advantage as far as not eating. She sips her ice water and its refusal to taste like anything only urges her on in her cruelty.

She's been doing this for a long time. It's best to take an instructive tone. The newly thin are like freshly-hatched zombies. They thirst for commands, for an opportunity to show off more diligence, more discipline. The world has never patted them on the head before and now that they know the formula, there aren't enough chin-ups in the day. Never assume that they won't want dessert. Always linger over the tray, pretending you're on the verge of selecting the Mississippi mud pie. Ask graphic questions about the chocolate. Tantalize them. Give them the opportunity to trumpet the glorious "no." Quashing temptation is their favorite sport. The only sport they have ever played and won.

Sondra gives this woman strict instructions, maps, itineraries, tips for the photo shoot. She lends her a pen to take unnecessary notes. She tells her how to trick jet lag, how to tea bag away dark circles under the eyes. They love statistics. Their new lives are all numeration and subtraction. She tells her that this commercial will run during prime time. Over 30 million people will see it. At least 20 million of them will be jealous of her. Ten-year-old girls are already sizing themselves up, scheming for bikinis. The mentally unbalanced will write her iambic death threats and free verse sonnets, undaunted by having no address to send them to. She will appear in the dreams of people she will never even pass on the street. Things have changed for Davilina. Not just because she lost all that weight. Because she manages to look sweet and understanding and next-doorish and doesn't have too much of the turtle expression that afflicts so many of them, folds of extra skin and an infantile perplexity over whatever happened to their shell. Davilina came through it all and somehow kept her good hair without intaking all the fats and oils usually required for an exceptional coat. She also had the foresight or, let's face it, calculatedness to save her huge yellow gown, the one in the snapshots of her at her prettiest little sister's wedding, staring ruefully through humidity-fogged glasses at a lump of white cake. The first thing Sondra did when she signed Davilina was get her into contact lenses. It's the oldest trick in the book. Nobody fucks with their glasses on, therefore nobody wants to see glasses on TV.

The yellow gown sits in its own chair, a third guest demurring, denying her appetite. It's not on a hanger, but folded like a parachute, a stout taffeta square, covered in transparent dry cleaner's wrap. Sondra loves spreading out these garments of shame, the yards of billowing cloth representing the inverse potential of the human body, the monstrous proportions that can be overcome through rigid denial. She longs to rip open the thin plastic covering and unfurl the yellow tent. She wants to turn every head in the restaurant, confront them with the evils of unused energy. But she has to be polite, professional. She runs through her usual quips. How she measures weight in British stones so she can stay in the single digits. How there ought to be a system of weights and measures where if you're really really good, your weight could be in the negatives. Davilina nods, chews her shreds of lettuce with disquieting regularity. Someone has told her to chew every bite fifty times and Sondra can see her counting, a prayerful twitching of her eyes.

The headache is worse today, a long-neglected child mimicking all her bad habits. She has to keep talking, instructing, because they always try to talk about the weather even though there is none here, or about the slick reflective hotel fortressing the edge of the Universal Studios lot where the ad agency puts them up, a soul-sore embarrassment that the natives won't even acknowledge. Instead of discussing the weather, the natives fill the time by flirting, and she's often tempted to give her clients a crash course in sex appeal and the art of idle seduction, two subjects in which the newly thin are as unprepared as hormone-deficient freshman boys. But they are almost all Southern housewives, with uncoordinated children and feckless husbands sporting cop-staches, unapologetic guts spilling over their name belts. Davilina's husband Tobey is drifting around Universal CityWalk, a fake street representing a Hollywood Boulevard safe from inexact prostitution and homeless kids with their Tourette's Syndrome and zip guns, a retail-ready Boulevard removed from any sort of luck or possibility. He is bewildered by it all, feels extraneous for the first time, but never self-conscious. He stands on the artificial corner, giving cunnilingus to a twist cone, his mustache soggy and matted, watching the goose-pimpled tourist legs. Davilina should get back soon, and the only way to return to him is without any working knowledge of her new allure. Sondra spares her.

She pries open her phone and checks her messages. The young grandmother in Shreveport has reached her ideal weight, so she'll be sending photos, side angle, tummy sucked in, the attempted smile more of a vengeful grimace. Her contact at the Plus Size Warehouse in Savannah has a woman who's dropped four dress sizes already, and she's only 19, so when it's all over, you can stick her in a cheerleading skirt or a wet suit and it won't be going too far over the legal limit on promises of happiness. She should jump on that one, but she's leaden today. It's one of those days when her job is not fulfilling her. It's not because Brandon is off shooting in Maui. He's only a sound guy, nothing chiseled about him. Only the most exquisitely abused model would ever give him the time of day. Focus on her career. Women all over the country are melting down, whittling away, redefining the variables of physics instead of its laws, always been good at the details. She should be reveling. Everyone deserves to see the results, Before and After, a Cinderella story, ugly ducklings, bootstrap pulling, hot little engines that could could could. This trend will last as long as there is an audience, which is to say, forever.

She announces that it is time to go, that she will keep the yellow gown to insure that nothing happens to it, that it arrives at the shoot on time, steam pressed, ready for the most difficult job of all, that of illustrating a point. The ad agency would kill her if they knew what she did with their invaluable fabric, the crown jewel of their intellectual property, but you can't get through life without cheating somewhere. She settles the check. Davilina goes haywire and tries to sneak a whole cherry tomato into her mouth. Sondra has to pretend not to see. It's annoying, surveying the scenery while her companion gags on red yolk. At another table, the waitress asks an elegantly tarnished fellow if he is a musician. "No," he answers. "I'm a rock star."

And the night just got longer. There will be something to distract her from the constant pining for sustenance. She's been hungry for so many years that there is a static in her head, unpredictable as popcorn and grey as the perfect interview suit. It is impossible to do a crossword puzzle, read beyond the headlines, pretend to save the world or the animals like everybody else. Watching television is out of the question, its parade of the unachievable goads her into neurotic envy, plants a seething insomnia never experienced by even the most faithful speed addict. Who can watch TV these days without getting drunk first?

She does a quick professional assessment. He's eating some kind of eggs, methodically scraping the platter bone-clean, his hunger attacking the far edge of the plate and locusting in toward him. He has the self-congratulatory smile of the new boys in this city. He's aware that he's waiting for something, but he doesn't realize that he is hunched over the last bit of his food with the posture of a jackal.

She flicks on her sunglasses and hands him a card on her way out. Not the one that says HUNGRY ARTISTS at the top. The other one, the pied piper's overture: SONDRA SINCLAIRE, PERSONAL MANAGER. Her cell phone number. Her home address. He watches her ass ping-pong off the premises with an appreciation that goes far beyond the physical. No, she was not born "Sondra Sinclaire." Don't be stupid.

She speeds the yellow dress home, menacing other drivers with the urgent self-righteousness of an ambulance transporting an expiring heart. The house is moping without doughy Brandon, and no messages from him on the machine. His loss. She has devised a thousand cruelties for him—trapping different flavored cookies in the same airtight container so none of them can taste quite chocolate or vanilla or oatmeal raisin. He hasn't noticed her deceptions. He takes cookies by the handful. If she weren't around, he would poke his snout in like a bear and wag his head at the sky while he chewed.

Brandon needs to be disciplined, she thinks as she straightens the living room, hides his man clutter, and sometimes the bondage wasn't enough. She isn't one of the cowering ones that let the grinding defeat of her pursuit of physical perfection interfere with her sex life. Denial of sex makes you into a sociopath. She did have specific tastes. She would lace herself into a black latex corset with copper ribbing, so stringent and beautiful that breathing became a choice—had to be placed somewhere on the list of priorities, had to be traded for something else. Wearing it, she felt streamlined, well-engineered, mechanical at last. He liked the shackles, but wouldn't wear the mask, even though his face in these situations was among the most redundant she had ever seen. The authentic boys' school thrashing rod, ordered all the way from a private collector in England (RULE WITH AN IRON FIST!), still shivering with the sweat of countless whining pasty heinies, was used only three or four times before he got bored of it. He played at pain on weekends only.

She places Davilina's hefty yellow relic in the exact center of the bed. She pats its sturdy belly, hot with anticipation, but not allowed to open it yet. She goes to the kitchen and whips up an enticingly correct creme brulee. She does not lick her fingers (35 calories in a teaspoon) but she does stir in a rophee, already powdered. You can get drugs in this city without having to drive out of your way. They just arrive and accumulate, like junk mail.

DING DONG. And there is the moment of coquettishness, of triumphant girlhood as her choice walks in the door, her anonymous rock star. This boy who drove here from Southern Missouri—no, hitch hiked with that smile. Who now lives in a two door car near the Hollywood Bally's, where he spends his days working out and showering. He's gorgeous—lithe and muscle-textured and moving with the cavalier ease of someone whom everyone has always wanted to touch. He's done this before—come on, he has to eat—and he knows to be attentive but not sycophantic, to be slightly surly but sit extra close to her. To make her pour the rum and fetch the refills, but to rub the knots out of her neck without being asked. His hands are not appendages. He is a marvelous machine, every part essential and integrated. When his lips touch his drink, she sees a flash of violent phosphorescence, electric flow meeting liquid. He feels the shock. He likes it. He grins disarmingly at the wall.

She offers him creme brulee. This is where free will gets its chance. If he doesn't accept, if those muscles are hard-won badges of glory instead of fortuitous accidents of birth, if he flashes her just a flickering instant of discipline, taps his toe on common ground, she will pay him for his time, let him go. This never happens. "That anything like ice cream?" he drawls, trying to pretzel the question into an innuendo, trying to earn his keep. Creme brulee is not for the hungry. It's for the indulgent.

She starts singing in the kitchen, a blowzy folk tune, as fond of her own desperation as Janis Joplin was. He throws back his pretty head and croons with her, not knowing that this is the former fat lady singing, marking the end. She spoons the deceitful creme into a crystal goblet and thinks of a childhood humiliation, the time she got stuck out at recess. But it's not *her* humiliation. It happened to a tragically obese child in her mother's third grade class. Sondra has never endured true behemothy. She never got to experience the purification of multitudinous pounds dripping away like whale oil, revealing a gleaming multi-purpose skeleton, the excess caught in a vat and lit for decades, an eternal flame of both homage and warning. She is merely one of the typical paranoiacs. Her weight is pesky, puckish, attracting and repelling as hairy grey iron shavings to the red horseshoe magnet of her dignity. She is singing a dirge with this glorious boy, and she needs humiliation to get her through, still the best motivator in the world. So she re-plays the tragedy of Little Darlene Somebody from her mother's class, who got stuck in a stump during recess and abandoned with the cockle burrs and the low-growing huckleberry, still chuckled over some fifty years later, forever expansive of ass, forever freckled, forever baby-toothed, forever betrayed by her own backside—*Et tu, Bootie?*

When she smoothes Davilina's voluminous yellow dress over his dumb-luck body, he is docile and drowsy. He thinks it is an expensive sheet, another gift. He does not know the word "shroud."

She feels energetic as she prepares him, straps him in, the same high she gets from over-exercising. She doesn't have to cover her tracks, remember details. She can do this in a frenzy, which is part of the fun. They never call the police. They don't want to admit that they are fucking brittle women with 13 year old bodies (from across the room, anyway) and prematurely 50-ish heads for 100 bucks a pop. It means their smile didn't get them enough commercials this year. Talking to a cop, they are nancy-boys again, the heart-throb dew hosed off, too fine-boned to play football, dance a little too well, own a hair drier. Still getting women the expensive way, using charm instead of brute pheromones. None of this should be reported or written down because their lives hinge on the anticipated unofficial bio, the ever-upcoming self-facted memoirs. Nobody can afford to lose subsidiary rights. She knows this and she swings the rod like she's tearing down drywall. There is a danger that blood will soak through the yellow dress, ruining tomorrow's photo shoot, halting the entire campaign. But danger and pleasure are always in lock step when you are on the endless diet. Their rigid marching is a craving that won't cost you a single calorie. No blows to the face, though. In her business, you have to have a healthy respect for orthodontics.

This rod was built by people who knew what they were doing. He is one of the electric ones, jerking and jolting instead of writhing and flailing, the yellow covering twitching and rumpling, but the cloth is ultimately serene, all indignities paling in comparison to its memories of attending an outdoor July wedding stuffed with an enormous lady, blighted by sweat stains and dried icing and the bemused *hubba-hubba* of a hundred raised eyebrows. "Swing away," chirps the dress, and she does. Her arms ache. Her hand *does* become iron. She hopes this will build more muscle mass, convert her body into a fuel-burning mechanism, rigidify this shameful inflatable skin she is cursed with. The atoms in metal move at a divinely slow rate. To be metal, to be forever one size, to have your weight equal strength.

She sleeps on the couch, blanketless, luxuriating in perspiration, but there is no sleep. The hum of transformation fills the house, rattling the shelves and pressuring the windows, an earthquake aperitif. Something has shifted. The photo shoot is tomorrow morning at 10 in Universal City. The yellow shroud must be peeled off his corpus nuevo, the unveiling of her work, a startling career of bruises and welts and luminous little scar-lettes. She will free him gently, try to spring open the shackles firmly but slowly so it won't even sound like metal, unlace the mask as if she is cradling the injured heel of a marathon-running lover, dig the shredded wad of cloth out of his clenched teeth with no more fear of being bitten than a valiant mother during wartime. She will dress him, his clothes inevitably a little looser, that's exciting, the day beginning with a victory. She will help him limp to the door, swing it open, gesture grandly at the concrete steps jumbling down to the road. Traffic will already be hissing down there. The rest of his life will be what he makes of it instead of what he was born with. The scales are not even a little bit more equal. She's not deluded. But watching his newly inadequate legs stumble out into the world, she will find the strength to skip breakfast again.

Did this really happen? For about three weeks, he will think so, as he is forced to skip work-outs, to hobble along the sidewalk under the assessing stares of both men and women, everyone measuring his injured body against their own, quickening their pace and rushing past him, feeling not fortunate but basely superior. Then he will heal if not rejuvenate, and it will only be a few chronic marks and occasional pain in the clavicle, and he will count it as just one of his attempts, one of the usual tariffs imposed upon those who dare to present themselves in this picture-perfect city. Don't worry about him. He is not the hero.

***

VIV THRAVES GOES MISSING

Mel has stopped waxing her bikini line. Soon we won't match at all. I smack her ass extra hard. She's supposed to moan now, but she just keeps staring at the drapes like she's choosing a flavor.

Afterwards, he lies on the big bed, naked, sticky white, and Mel and I lie on the floor, panting more than we need to. It's a good idea to stay entwined in case he looks at us, but Mel is hugging herself, and he's talking to us but looking at the ceiling. The usual wife-talk. She's such an intellectual that she neglects her body, doesn't see to his physical needs, never lost the baby weight. He has one of those accents. He's from London, on business. "Over from London," Mel will say later, doing the accent perfectly. She's the one that needs the drama. All the games we played were for her. I would have played it straight, kept my mind on the money. He orders strawberries from room service. "Please," Mel imitates later, "are you sure you won't have a berry, Viv? They're quite good."

* * * * * * * * * *

ALIASES: Octavia Orange, Trudy Fletcher, Tiff Mercury, Veloria Van Pelton, Frances Key Scott, Immaculata Invitigo, Peggy Organza, Rosemary

Snow, Mandy Becky Bird, Wellsley Wellington, Sara Rule, Skye Lesser, Prominence Locke, Martina Cadillac, Lana Under, Tori Kingdon, Twyla Tee, Shirley Christchurch, Penny Frock, Easter Vigil, Colleen Savage, Ann Marie Kozcelny, Lady Zam, Jeannie Goodjeans, Dominga Kurtz, Dinah Eyre, Amy G. Dala, Vivian Thraves.

* * * * * * * * *

I always keep one card. I'm not the sentimental one. It's for Mel. I get the collection out on long Sunday nights during January and February, the months when it rains and I realize that I haven't gotten my hands on any of the money in this city, not really, and begin to suspect that I'm wasting my life and should go to New York where the weather is bad and the men are hunchbacks-in-training, but they roll big. If it were up to me, I wouldn't be interested in remembering. I keep it all present tense. But Mel loves those cards. She has a story for each name, doing everyone's voices, making me look foolish for getting too wasted and telling off the bouncer or following some luscious Latino right into the men's room before I could even make eye contact with him. I have to admit, I laugh. I only used the Vivian Thraves card once, so it's funny that that's what they ended up calling us.

* * * * * * * *

In the elevator, I tell Mel she has strawberry juice on her chin. I could also tell her that her hair's not even brushed. I spend literally two hours blowing out my curly hair and setting it so we can look the same, but Mel has stopped caring. I reach over to rub the red juice off of her face, and she swats me away. "What the hell?" I demand, but she's back to her zombie contest with the wall. "What do you think her name is?" I ask.

Mel perks up in spite of herself. She carefully shrugs her shoulders. "Juliet Trusley-Hall," I announce. Trusley-Hall is actually his last name. I saw it on the room service bill. We work on a strictly cash basis, so they think we don't know their names, but I have my own game of finding out, and there is no creature so sloppy as a man who's just come. I prefer a touch of reality, but I play it off to Mel as if I made up the name.

"No," Mel says. "Vivian Thraves." Then she makes the remark about the strawberries. She answers herself. "No, no, Julian. You know very well I'm watching my figure lest you go off hiring a pair of whores to wank off to." I let Mel win. She lets me rub the strawberry off her skin, but makes a face like

I'm hurting her.

* * * * * * *

Melody and Melanie. I know it's a coincidence, but Mel takes it as a sign. I want to come up with new names, but Mel insists that we both go by "Mel."

* * * * * * *

I make the cards right away on the computer, to make Mel happy.

VIVIAN THRAVES

Mel is unhappy with the font, so I change it. I ask her what time she wants to go out. She says that Viv Thraves doesn't go out on weeknights, and certainly not without an escort. I tell her as far as I'm concerned, Viv Thraves will be going to Spaceland tonight at 11, and she can come or not come. I stand in my closet looking for a good Viv Thraves outfit, something in that school-marm-whose-hair-you're-dying-to-take-down look. I realize I'm shaking because I'm afraid Mel won't come with me. I divide the stack of cards and put Mel's half on the dresser. Mel comes in and puts on a wide-brimmed black hat, still not talking to me. Then she spins around and says, "Fancy me, do you, love?"

* * * * * * *

"Where the fuck did you get this?! Huh?! Think I'm playing?" The Cop is waving around the Trudy Fletcher card. It's his wife's real name, which was admittedly stupid, but you can't be in this business if you think you're ever going to get caught. I could tell him that her name was printed on the order form sticking out of the family-sized bottled water delivery on the front porch of his ratty little Manhattan Beach house, where Mel and I wouldn't have been caught dead if he hadn't forced us to meet him there. *And what the hell happened to your "protection"?* I could ask him. *I seem to be sitting in a jail cell.* He comes at me, smacking his billy club into his open palm. My cellmates raise their dark eyes and stare at The Cop just long enough to let him know they're all potential eyewitnesses, but they remain lurking in the corners. I'm nobody's sister. I'm not used to this. I grew up in the suburbs, Orange County. If I was ever abused, I don't remember it. My father loves me. I came to L.A. to go to college. I just wanted more money than I could ever earn. I wanted Mel to have nice things, too. That's not what I call using someone. I told her she was going to starve, studying Drama.

I tell The Cop that no matter how many times he hits me, I will drag myself up to testify, and maybe he should think about that. He stands there, a bad dog not quite associating the slap on the rump with the behavior problem, still thumping his stick. "I'd sure as fuck hate to have a friend like you, Mel," he sneers. Now that Mel is missing, he's decided she's a damsel in distress, the reason he went into law enforcement, forget the free drugs and bear claws and blow jobs. Before, he couldn't tell us apart.

I think about the rough piece of trade I picked up at Aftershock in the Valley the night we were both Trudy Fletcher. Mine says he's into S and M and tries to wire me to his guitar amp. "A mild shock," he says, and Mel and I use this phrase for comic relief whenever a customer asks for something scary-ridiculous. Mel picks up an actual cop that night. She is so good at being their wives that it's eerie.

* * * * * * * *

Mel's mother's. Utterly dismal. No matter how much money Mel gives her, she won't quit her just-shoot-me-in-the-head job as a dispatcher at a shipping yard. She lives in San Pedro, which was even farther from L.A. when Mel was growing up than it is now. All that flat freeway just to get anywhere. So grindingly bleak and so close to the oasis of L.A. that only the most frightened people in the world choose to stay there.

Mel's mother scrimped and saved, sewed her own polyester outfits, stuck with a black and white TV, to send Mel to UCLA, then Mel defied her by studying acting. If Mel hadn't been so terrified that she was going to go broke and let her mother down, she never would have agreed to work with me. We sit in the front room with the ceramic elephants and sip Lipton tea. Mel's mother isn't sure why she doesn't like me one bit. She's the only person who hasn't noticed that Mel and I look alike. I never wear make up when we visit her.

Mel slides her mother an envelope full of cash and tells her she got the money from being in a gum commercial that's only shown in the Midwest.

* * * * * * * *

I'm not sure why Mel and I sleep in the same bed. It was my apartment first then she moved in. Neither of us likes to be alone.

* * * * * * **

"There's the girl that looks like you," and Susan Somebody points out Mel across the cafeteria. We only look similar at that point. Our hair is wildly different and Mel has brown eyes while mine are blue. With our hair that different, men would never equate us. I don't have a business plan at that point. I just stare across the room at Mel and see the first woman I ever liked at first sight.

* * * * * * *

Our second or third week out, driving home from the Encino Hilton in my new Mustang which I convinced my father to co-sign for. I want those monthly car payments hanging over my head to force myself to make our business venture a success. Mel is meek and moody like she always is after. I try to talk to her about the money, wondering out loud if we can raise our fee, calculating how many appointments we'll have this week, if we should risk a photo ad without the black strips blocking out our eyes.

"What do you think her name is?" Mel blurts out.

"Who? Whose name?"

"You know. The one he was talking about. His wife."

"God. Who cares?"

"Do you think she knows what he does?"

"I don't think about it, Mel. Why would you want to think about that?"

Mel is silent but blinks her eyes very fast. So I add, "That's between him and her. If it wasn't us, he'd just be paying someone else."

"How does he hide the money from her?"

"They're probably rich. He gets bonuses from his company or something. He's in sales and he gets commissions and she never knows exactly how much he's earning." Mel trapped me into playing the game, I can see that now. She's the quiet one, but she's very good at getting what she wants.

"Honey, I want you to have this set of pearl earrings. Take it, now. I just sold another jet ski machine. Don't Daddy always take care of his sugarpussy?" Mel does him to a T, raspy fake Southern twang, a sleazy good ole boy act.

"You are my mountain of love fo' sho'," I say in the strained high register of Monty Python women, doing a Southern accent even though I suck.

"No, no. She's not Southern. She's from Idaho and she's the only one who doesn't know he's faking the accent. 'Beauregard, a man called from the credit card company. Our account's over the limit again. I sure as hell haven't been out charging anything. Stuck here all day in this heatbox. When are you going to order that part for my car? How long am I supposed to sit here?'"

His name isn't Beauregard. It's Nelson. Nelson Orange. It was engraved on his brass key ring. But I don't tell Mel. "Wall, sugarpuss," I drawl, "you just let me worry about the money."

"Finances," Mel corrects me. "He would say 'finances.' Ayyaaak. He's so gross." Then she's back to the wife. "I swear to God, Beau, one day you'll stumble in late like you always do with all those excuses on your breath, and you'll get a big surprise from me. I still know how to draw and quarter a calf, Mister."

I bust out laughing at that, but Mel has a dark, concentrated look on her face. "What's her name?" she demands.

"I don't know. Mrs. Orange."

"Octavia Orange." She was our first.

* * * * * * * *

In the news, they're calling us "Viv Thraves" and also saying we're both madams, which is completely untrue. We always work alone, from day one. We don't make arrangements for anyone else. We aren't anyone's hos. We are small business entrepreneurs. We set our own prices, never have to split our money with anyone but each other. We never get threatened or beat up. I did my research beforehand. Voyeurs are the harmless ones. It's all a show. They watch us and pay us for it. How is that different from this simpering anchorwoman on TV? I can answer that one: she's eating at The Ivy and Mel and I never got out of my one bedroom in Miracle Mile. I expected to earn a lot more money, and on paper, we should have. The problem is, it's a profession with a high burn-out rate, and sometimes you just have to say fuck it all and not work again until the rent is due. And, okay, Mel's drugs ate up a lot of our profit. Not to mention the rehab. I try to look out for her, but when we go out, she likes to stay as far away from me as possible so people won't see that we're the same. Personally, I can't really imagine being dependent on anything, so I didn't see her addiction coming.

Viv Thraves. The picture they're showing is Mel dressed up as Lady Zam, very mod and Continental, someone in a Felini movie. Viv Thraves would never make such a spectacle of herself. Since it is the L.A. news, Viv is the lead story, before whatever happened in Washington today, and all the other world disasters. Nobody in the jail common room recognizes that I am a dead ringer for the girl on the screen.

* * * * * * * *

"Are you actually twins, then, girls?" He raises himself up on his elbows as we're getting our stuff together to leave, lewdly slurping strawberries through his bad teeth.

"That's right," I say. Almost all of them realize that I can't actually ask for the money, and sometimes they fuck with us at the very end. There's way too much info on TV these days. Too many vice cop shows.

"Ah. I was just curious, you see, because you, darling, have got blue eyes, and—look this way, dear. There's our girl. Your 'sister' has got brown, hasn't she? And that, ladies, is genetically impossible." He smiles that tight lipped smile that men who think they're good looking learn in countries without dentistry, smug times one hundred. I wonder if I can somehow get him deported or lift his passport or plant drugs in his suitcase or something.

He holds up our envelope and I go over to grab it. He holds firm. "Not that it matters, dear. Your whole city is built upon third-rate imitation, isn't it? I'd have to be well daft to expect the real thing here. Give us a kiss, then, you nasty little fakey." I stab him with my tongue, remembering how tightly he'd screwed shut his eyes while we were performing. If he wasn't even going to look at us, why did he need us there? Some kind of warped loneliness, or a need to pay a fine for masturbating. It's not like me to think about this stuff.

He lies back and keeps his eyes closed as I take the money. I quickly lift the sterling platter of strawberries so I can get his name off the room service bill. Simon Trusley-Hall. I don't know why I memorize their names. It seems like it might come in handy someday.

"Do you want a business tip, love? Totally gratis, of course." I freeze with the heavy strawberry tray in the air. My arm shakes as I try to ease it down without him catching me snooping. But he doesn't bother to look at me. "Choose a partner with a bit of enthusiasm about her. Someone cheery, right?

It's the mistake I made in choosing my wife. And look where it's got me, dear."
Then I know why he keeps his eyes closed. He knows he's white and soft as
a glowworm, passion doesn't fit him and never will, he looks ridiculous, and
no matter how much of a snob he tries to be to me and Mel, in the end we're
going to take his money and leave him with one less secret. He's pathetic but
I don't feel sorry for him or scornful of him. I don't have time. The hour's up.
We got paid. He's over.

I'm all set to lay into Mel for not wearing her colored contact lenses, but
she looks so glum it's not worth my breath. She has strawberry juice on her
chin and she's hunched inward. She looks like a girl that no one's ever looked
at twice.

* * * * * * * *

"Mrs. Octavia Orange drinks two sea breezes at home," Mel says, mixing
our drinks on the cluttered coffee table in the living room. "She borrows her
girlfriend's car and drives too fast over Mulholland to Sunset Strip, but she
doesn't have the guts to go into any of the clubs alone. She ends up going
downtown to Park Plaza because she's read about it in the *LA Times*. She's
wearing something with flowers on it."

"Okay," I say. "We can wear the red rose dresses with our black boots."

"No," says Mel. "We'll each wear a different outfit. Octavia Orange is
nobody's twin." She tilts back the cup and downs her drink, then slams it on
the table. Every once in a while, she does things too big, and I am reminded
that she is an actress.

* * * * * * * *

Mel didn't know their real names, and I sure as hell never wrote them
down, so where did the cops get this list? Was somebody following us? The
Cop? It's entirely unlikely that someone who spends all day following his dick
around with flashing red lights would have the patience to lay low and track
us all those months. Maybe some figure of justice came galloping into town
and struck them all down. After the rehab, Mel was convinced that she had a
guardian angel named Melvin. They told her she had to choose a higher power,
but that never made sense to me, because she already had me.

My only hope now is if another one of them bites it while I'm locked up
in here, which will prove I didn't do it. But no, they're all alive and well, out
ramming their cocks into the soft give of a hotel mattress while some other

team shows them the professional writhe and moan. And Viv Thraves is still At Large.

* * * * * * * *

Me and Mel and that bitch Simone at the Beverly Center Hard Rock, the end of freshman year. My original plan is to be their manager. Simone doesn't look as much like Mel as I do, but she's in the Theatre Department and she likes costumes and adoration. I present it to them in a highly professional manner over burgers and fries and fuzzy, persistent music out of Seattle which is supposed to be so new and full of stubble that it's revolutionary.

Mel is quiet. She won't look up at either of us. She's engrossed in scraping the cruddy hard ketchup remnants off the neck of the bottle. Simone speaks up. "Hell, no. I'm not a prostitute."

I give the figures: the amount she can expect to net this summer by temping or waitressing or working retail, versus the amount she'll net, in tax-free cash, in just a few hours working with me.

"God," Simone uses her whole body to express her outrage, flailing around in her chair, "where are you from? Money isn't everything."

"But it's very useful if you want to eat," I say, plunking a wad of cash down on the check. It's mostly ones and all the money I have in the world. I'm bluffing. If they won't do this, I'll have to spend the summer in OC, hostessing at a family steak restaurant, letting all those overfed assholes ogle and flirt for minimum wage.

"Forget it, Melanie." Simone is already onto the next thing, some shellacked glory boy at the bar she's locked eyes with, probably not a single credit card in his wallet.

Mel and I sit alone. I chain-eat my fries one after the other, not registering the synthetic taste. I ask Mel if she wants a malt, even though I'll have to scrape for loose change if she says yes. She shakes her head. We can hear Mr. Pretty flirting with Simone at the bar.

"Introduce me to your friends over there. I fucking love twins."

Mel looks up at me quickly. We both have our hair pulled back. "It's a lot of money," I say, and somehow I know to say it softly. Mel nods. Her face doesn't harden slightly like I thought it would.

* * * * * * * *

Oh Christ. The news is playing that fucking porno video. The beginning where Mel and I are both dressed in schoolgirl uniforms, holding a portrait of two bald babies, saying something stupid about how we were born in the Appalachian Mountains just after midnight on a night with a full moon. We look like dumb cows. I never, never, never, never should have done a video. Worst business decision I ever made. Mel is just out of rehab so we haven't worked in a while and bills are flooding in through all the earthquake cracks in our dumpy apartment. That tape is the beginning of our troubles. I've always been able to eat whatever I want, I don't think about it, and half the time I forget to feed myself. Mel spends a lot of time imagining the taste of chocolate. She's always sitting still and gaining five or seven pounds which she then has to starve off. That porno had no lighting, no stage make-up, it was supposed to look "real." Mel was just off the meth and compared to me, she came out looking chubby. She acted like I tricked her.

"Viv Thraves," the news anchor is saying for the thousandth time. They've cut the video so the frame ends just above Mel's breasts, and I'm not in it at all. Mel gazes off camera while I say my line. For a split second, I see a look of hatred flicker across her face. She keeps her eyes vacant, but there's a tightening of her nose and a posture of ravenous hunger fleets over her mouth. I'm not even sure if I saw it. I'm dying to rewind the tape, but this is a newscast in the Sybil Brand common room, and a woman with orange hair and a scar that looks like someone held her down and poured battery acid over her cheek, then relented and tried to wipe it off, switches the TV to a re-run of a game show.

* * * * * * * *

I have a real sister, five years younger than me. We're not close. She's studying to be a dental assistant. Who in the free world would do something like that?

* * * * * * * *

"If you're Octavia Orange, who am I?"
"We're both Octavia Orange."
"But we're dressed in different outfits."
"People can be more than one thing at a time, you know."

* * * * * * * *

Here's how it will end: Years later, I will happen to run into Mel in some supermarket in the Valley. She'll have two fat kids, each singing a different commercial jingle, a midriff-baring top, sunglasses too dark to see her eyes, and a pitch-perfect Valley inflection, all of her sentences rising up at the end like the muscular outstretched arms of a synchronized swimmer. She will be playing somebody's wife for good, no little cards to hand out. Her shopping cart will be crammed full of meat and sugar cereals. And what will I have in my basket? Medicine and yogurt. Dirty pigeon feathers off a useless archangel named Melvin. A secret hole left by Viv Thraves, who couldn't be bothered to say goodbye.

* * * * * * * *

"If you know where she is, you should tell us. She's really selling you out."

The lawyer sounds ridiculous trying to use street lingo, and it's hard to tell her apart from the cops, with her uniform of cheap navy suits, and her eagerness to be the hero who puts Mel and me back together, Superglues the broken toy so they can wind us up and see how it works. Viv Thraves would never turncoat on a friend. She went to public boarding school where she learned a strict code of honor. It seems I am not Viv's friend.

* * * * * * * *

Before we start taking appointments, we actually have arguments over which music to use, what color to wear, we choreograph as precisely as cheerleaders or thieves. About 90 seconds into our first time, I realize that they couldn't care less about this flashy stuff, it's something they endure as politely as their kids' piano recitals. They put up with it because they think *we* like it. I would have chucked the whole routine, but this is the part Mel gets into. I think she needs something to keep her mind on. We keep up the big show until Mel gets too twitchy with speed to keep it straight in her head. She's the one who notices that we're still using the same alt rock music we chose when we were in college, and the radio is now calling it "retro."

"How long do you think we can keep this up?" she asks, her trembling hands moving compulsively back and forth over her pants as if she's erasing something. I'm not sure which part of it she's asking about. I haven't noticed that we have gotten any older.

"Tell people your name. Say 'Octavia Orange.'"

"That sounds—you don't give your last name in a club. You just say 'I'm Octavia.'"

"She's old fashioned. She's from a potato farm in Idaho."

"But still. It sounds retarded."

"She has those little—calling cards. Beauregard gave them to her after they had a fight. He told her all the ladies in the South use calling cards. She hands them out because she can't hear over the music. Use your computer. We'll cut the paper into little cards." Mel clip-clips the scissors in the air, happy as a castaneta player.

"What about her phone number?"

"No phone number. Just her name. It's mysterious."

* * * * * * * *

At home we never touch each other.

* * * * * * * *

"You bloody daft cunt," she mutters under her breath, while we are drinking our morning coffee.

"What?"

"Oh, sorry. Yes, sorry. You see, those words aren't nearly so ... shocking where I'm from as they seem to be over here. But even so, yes, we're eating, and I did speak out of turn. I didn't mean to be nasty at all. I do apologize."

"I'm sick of Viv Thraves, Mel. Come off it."

She doesn't answer. Then: "We usually have tea with our breakfast, but coffee's rather nice, too, don't you think? One mustn't get too set in one's ways."

* * * * * * * *

My Intro to Econ professor at UCLA. He invites the top boys in the class to his house to have dinner with some president of a Wall Street firm who is in town. I confront my prof about why I wasn't invited. He shuffles some papers indignantly. He still has a typewriter on his desk. The worn keys stare up at him expectantly, neat rows of mannerly scholars with distinct hair parts and hats on their knees, crowded into a lecture hall.

"I can no longer afford to have female students over to my home, Miss. Sexual harassment policies. Speak to the administration."

I begin to argue. He cuts me off. "And quite frankly, Miss, I'm not convinced that you could have held up your end of the conversation. If you want to force me to speak to you man-to-man, I'll tell you that I find your manner to be abrasive. Now. Report me if you will. When you're older, you'll find that some things are worth running afoul of the officials. Good afternoon."

So fuck him and fuck Wall Street and fuck those cloying toad-like boys. Some people call me hot-headed. I call it being decisive. I decide then and there to start my own business.

* * * * * * * *

"Octavia, listen. I don't say this to many girls. You listening?"

"Yeah."

"Okay, listen. You're the type of female I could see spending time with. What do you say to that, Ocatvia?"

"I'm married."

"Yeah, but you're out at a club by yourself, aren't you? That right there tells me something."

"What does it tell you?"

"I've got a condo in Santa Monica. You can almost see the beach."

"Almost?"

"Don't bust my balls, Octavia. I'm opening my heart to you here. I'm— damn. Isn't that you?" He shifts unsteadily and points out Mel at the other end of the bar, cozied up to a surfer trapped in a suit.

"No. I'm right here."

"She's your sister, isn't she? What's her name—fucking—Oct—no— Rrrr—Rocktavia? Hee hee hee."

I could go for a threesome, for the added security. The bar scene is dangerous. But Mel won't even look over at me.

"I don't know her. Are you taking me home or not?"

* * * * * * *

Mel never went out on a single audition that I know of. She never even got headshots made or looked for an agent. I don't know why.

* * * * * * *

Viv Thraves is sighted everywhere. The Mint, Dragonfly, Bar Marmount, Red Rock, Eden, Molly Malone's, Giant, Bang, Cane's, El Coyote, Cherry, Sinamatic, the late night line outside Pink's Hot Dogs. People trying too hard to have a good time parade across the news, flashing little Viv Thraves cards they claim she handed them after ordering a Cape Cod or a mudslide. Viv Thraves doesn't go for sweet drinks. Her drink is straight vodka, and she calls it "vodkar." Only one of the cards on the news is in the right font, and that one could be an accidental match.

People are warned not to approach Viv because she is considered armed and dangerous. There is a shot of two girls standing in the line outside Make Up in Viv Thraves wigs, their torsos bare except for two calling cards taped over their nipples. They notice the news camera and lift their arms and open their mouths silly-wide, giving hoots of victory at the feat of being spotted.

* * * * * * * *

"We're never going to be anybody's wives, are we?"
I snort. "We don't have to be anybody's wife. Thank God for that."

* * * * * * * *

That British guy is the first to go. There is no forced entry. The wound is neat like the killer has been practicing for a long time. The hotel lobby security cam shows a grainy black and white image of a person who looks like Mel and me, entering alone then leaving alone one hour later. The desk staff say they've seen us there before and they could have sworn they saw two of us again that day.

* * * * * * * *

We never spend the night. Even if we don't wake up until five a.m., we each call a cab. We crank down the window and toss the rest of the cards out into the deserted early morning streets, streets that don't look tired but like they are napping with all their might, vigorous babies that will pop up at the appointed hour, wide awake and cheerful.

No matter how late it is, we meet up back at home. We make it back to our big bed and tell each other the story of what happened to Mrs. Octavia Orange or Mrs. Rosemary Snow or Mrs. Frances Key Scott after she left the club.

Viv Thraves is already asleep when I get in, and when I shake her awake, the accent is already slung up like a slingshot. "Leave me to my bloody rest," she snaps. I tell her how Vivian Thraves went to a spread in Hollywood Hills with a studio marketing V.P., how he comes up with those one liners you see on movie posters: He's back and he's mad. He rubbed massage oil all over my thighs, went down on me, then passed out. I laugh, but she doesn't join in.

"And what did Viv Thraves do tonight?" I ask.

"Ah, but a lady never tells, does she?" She rolls over, giving me her back.

She hasn't thrown out her extra cards. They are sitting on the dresser, spread out in the shape of a fan. Two weeks later, Viv Thraves leaves the Polo Lounge with a record label exec and never comes home.

* * * * * * * *

I scan the Want Ads for jobs I could conceivably do, but I don't want to do any of them. Wouldn't do that if you paid me.

* * * * * *

Then someone finds Nelson Orange's house in Encino and his wife finds him tied to the driver's seat of his yellow Corvette, carbon monoxide darting around the garage, his stiff fingers just inches from the ignition keys that he couldn't quite reach to turn off. His wife's name is Tracy and I want to see a photo of her, but the paper doesn't print one. I'm sure she's not the type of person Viv Thraves would associate with.

Nobody witnessed anything out of the ordinary. The cops found Polaroids of Mel and me locked in his safe. We don't allow photos or videos, but this was when we were new at it and scared of them all and somehow he did it without us seeing. On the back of one of the photos, he scrawled: "PHOTO RIGHTS $500 PAID IN FULL." Then there's supposedly a signature, but I was there the whole time and nobody signed and I sure as hell never saw any of the money.

"Is it possible that your girlfriend was also working alone, on the side?"

asks the lawyer. No, it's not possible. Mel didn't enjoy it. She did it for me. I had no idea being a lawyer was so tedious. It makes me glad I left college after freshman year.

* * * * * * *

Herr Zam is killed in his mansion in Pacific Palisades. Well, it's close to a mansion, if it's not one technically. The wound is identical to the one that killed the Brit. His housekeeper says she saw two girls run across the lawn, but she can't say what they looked like, and she has been watching the news reports about the two Viv Thraves.

I am at home eating wheat toast and wondering if it's worth it to go to Trader Joe's for jelly since I ran out. But I don't like to leave in case Mel calls. The cops pound on the door and when I open it, they shove me inside and pin me against the wall.

It's stupid to think I had anything to do with killing those people. I haven't even thought about them since I last saw them. What kind of businessperson would I be if I wished harm upon my customers? I've lived in L.A. for ten years, and at least once every six months, I come outside to find my car window smashed in, piles of round green glass pebbles glittering on the curb. Nothing's ever done about it. But somehow it's important to keep people from paying me to watch me lick my best friend's pussy. What kind of fucked up world is this? I tell the lawyer I want to say this on the stand, but she says absolutely not because most people wouldn't agree with me.

* * * * * * *

"You could at least try to be tender, Mel."

What is she talking about? I look at Mel, and she's a little fat these days. I think it's cute, but I have a business to run. I realize she must be reading and doing things that I don't know about. *Tender*? Where did she come up with that word? Why does she think it should apply to me?

* * * * * * *

Mel's never been arrested, so they don't have her fingerprints.

* * * * * * *

Am I in love with Mel? She's my partner. Learn a tapdance with someone. Do it together for years and years, until you have a perception of when the other person will move, until you can instinctively fill in for her tired leg or distracted arms. See if you can keep from crying when you're sitting alone and you hear that music. It's the reason people still tear up when they watch Fred Astaire and Ginger Rogers. To become truly great dancers, they would have had to dance on their own. It's heartbreaking that they don't.

* * * * * * *

"We found her." The Cop is not supposed to discuss my case with me without my lawyer present. As usual, he's too thick with gloating to care. "Naked. In a dumpster. On Venice Beach. She left a suicide note. Said all she ever wanted to be was a actress but she didn't succeed. She didn't mention you at all, Mel. Looks like you're on your own." Where was the suicide note if she was naked? Under her tongue? I don't believe a word he says.

Later, the lawyer says that Mel's death is what will save me, because now the whole truth will never be known, and as the defense, I don't carry the burden of proof. She sounds disappointed.

* * * * * * *

I imagine Mel tracking down the real Viv Thraves, Mrs. Trusley-Hall. They meet on Rodeo for coffee, and Mel convinces her that her husband is a philandering pig.

"I see. Thank you very much," says Mrs. Trusley-Hall, and without me there, Mel doesn't think to charge her for the info. Or does she? Maybe she's picked up a few tricks along the way. The security camera in the Brit's hotel shows a statuesque, glacial blonde woman entering and leaving that afternoon, but no one focuses on her. She is one of those people who fits in too well to be noticed.

Then Mel gathers together Mrs. Tracy Orange, Mrs. Lady Zam, Mrs. Trudy Fletcher, and all the rest, in a conference room at a hotel by the airport. Over complimentary Continental breakfast, she tells them what pricks they're married to. They butter their croissants slowly and take their domestic troubles into their own hands. Mel has thrown her little drama queen fit, and now she will come home.

* * * * * * *

Our very first time. We've rehearsed for weeks. We're wearing short, tight green dresses that make us look like whores, but we're young enough to pull it off as UCLA girls who watch too much TV and don't know any better. We pull up to the condo high rise on Millionaire Mile. Red uniformed guys rush to open our car doors. I don't want them to touch me because minimum wage is unlucky.

We announce ourselves at the front desk, and the concierge is too discreet to say anything, but he gives off that little flutter of excitement people get when they see a praying mantis or a rainbow or twins.

Mel's new contacts are bothering her and in the elevator, she keeps tilting back her head and squirting in drops of saline, smudging her mascara and giving her eyes a deep-set, purplish, desert nomad look.

"Here," I say, grabbing the saline bottle. I drip some into my raw eyes and smear my mascara so we can match.

"You look beautiful," Mel says suddenly.

"You look hot," I say. We're both eager to laugh, both staring only at ourselves in the elevator's mirrored panels.

"Mel?"

"Yeah?" I'm arranging my cleavage with one hand, balancing the mini boom box against my hip.

"So, are we actually—Do you think—I mean, when the time comes, do you think we'll actually have to…."

"Violate each other?"

We both howl with laughter. I notice that Mel really is a knock out and I figure in three years we can retire and go our separate ways. And right up to the last possible moment, we both believe that it's only going to be an act.

***

SOMEWHAT FUNNY

In the next instant, Misty looked down and saw that his legs were useless pine shavings and he was sitting in an oversized silver wheelchair which didn't fit under the little café table. His crippleness didn't deter her. She had always had bad luck with men. The scaly Armenian standing behind him glared at her and gripped the wheelchair handles as if she had triggered a disaster drill he had rehearsed many times, but now he had forgotten what to do. She smiled wide, her teeth glinting mating signals, and strode toward them like a Texan. She had just stepped out of a test screening at the Roosevelt Hotel, and there on Hollywood Boulevard, considering his iced tea, she had spotted the man she was going to marry. She just knew.

His heroin habit didn't throw her off, either. Leighton lived in a foul little studio overlooking the Boulevard, full of pungent cat smells that actually came from the waste of disloyal humans. The Armenian lived there, too, for all intents and purposes. The apartment was dislocated from time. Misty had to leap to get into Leighton's apartment, from a place where people demanded beginning, middle, end, and wore watches and lined up so they could get good seats. Things up at Leighton's were irregular. He slept or not, kept Stravinsky's "Rites of Spring" on repeat for days or played half of a Hank Williams Jr. song then sat in silence. He rarely ate, but would sometimes crave a chicken fried steak and would viciously berate the Armenian for dietary incompetence until the Pink Dot delivery arrived. Food started to rot as soon as it crossed the threshold, a victim of supreme indifference. This was part of the smell, a moldiness from forgotten remains which were allowed to lay there until they grew fantastic green and white hair then mummified in a pathetic grey attempt at a dignified end. Roaches ran the place. They scuttled all over, different sizes and shapes, big ripe black ones and dainty brown dots, but they all stuck together, and if one of them saw Misty's shoe coming at them, they all scattered. They could survive anything, Misty knew, because none of them tried to be special. The whole atmosphere at Leighton's felt like when Misty's mom would go out for the evening and Misty and her sisters would try to get the babysitter to do all kinds of wrong things, and sometimes she would. They once coated the bathtub with chocolate syrup, and another time they cut up her mom's sparkly gold pageant dress into squares, and wrote "Happy Birthday" on the underside with felt tip pen and stuffed the pieces of material into envelopes labeled Granma, Kermit the Frog, Teacher, Lassie, and on like that. "Why?" her mom kept saying. "Why?" And Misty remembered playing house with her little friends, how godawful dull it was, because they all wanted to go by the same routine: "I'll go to work and you watch baby, then when I come home, we'll eat dinner." "No, I'm a dandelion," she would say, and float all over the garage, upsetting the ironing board and banging into the deep freeze until her playmates got so frustrated they pulled her hair and she could go home. A lot of remembering went on over at Leighton's, because it never seemed to be any particular day or year.

There was a balcony, and after Leighton shot up, the Armenian would wheel him out onto the concrete slab so he could watch the traffic patterns. He peed into a plastic gallon milk bottle which the Armenian kept at the ready. He had body lice because he was far too vain to let the Armenian lift him into and out of the tub very often. His remarkable genes enabled him to look battle-torn instead of derelict, blond and berry-stained and resigned to some tragic fate. Misty got the sense that he hadn't created his abject living conditions, but had been exiled there and was enduring it with a royal spine. He had been raised as a Southern gentleman and would not scratch, point, or buy foreign whisky no matter how wretched his circumstances. It was the smell that made him a deviant. Even in the open air of the balcony, Misty had to hold a red bandana spritzed with Love's Baby Soft over her nose and mouth. Leighton noticed her discomfort but would not acknowledge it. The three of them sat looking down at L.A., a city with the spaciousness of a sound stage and the traffic snarls of a European capital. Misty got bored and ended up watching the night shift people from her survey company, taking photos of tourists' mammoth feet beside the elfish concrete imprints in front of Mann's Chinese Theater, then broadsiding these folks into agreeing to view a test screening of a new sitcom across the street at the Roosevelt Hotel.

"You don't even see the pattern, do you?" drawled Leighton.

"The cars?"

"Binary code. They teach you that in Texas?"

"I've heard of it."

"Ones and zeros. Repeating patterns. You can build anything out of ones and zeros. But they're looking in the wrong place, staring into their computer screens. That's a mere distraction. Look down there. That is what we've created. These patterns of movement. Do you think that's about transportation? Tell me where they're all going. These cars sit at a dead stop half the time. It's a pattern and we're all of us complicit. You can read the day by watching over the streets. Answer me this, Missy Texas: which is more crucial, the stock market report or the traffic report?"

By this time, he was worked up and losing focus. Putty-colored drool was hanging off his chin, but the Armenian quickly sopped it up, so neither of them noticed. Misty's eyes watered up. Nobody had ever talked to her this way. The problem was, she was a big bad blonde and she kept her hair long in the tribal Texas tradition, smooth and flowing to the small of her back. Even in Texas, she was disproportionately large, a giantess. People got the impression that she was advertising something, a symbol glorifying all the real girls next door. Everybody stared openly at her, but most thought it would be foolish to speak to her, as immature as talking back to the TV set. The only men who ever approached Misty were those with out of control egos. Race car drivers, lead guitarists, airline pilots, surgeons, evangelical ministers, wanton stockbrokers working for daddy, stand up comics, and lawyers. Misty didn't appreciate being chosen by these types with their quick tempers and double parking habits. She decided she wanted a boy with an outstanding vocabulary, which was a little strange since she wasn't a particularly strong reader or speaker herself. It was the same doomed peevishness that made paunchy comb-over men insist upon dating only models. She wanted someone who would tell her stories not about himself, but all the smart boys scattered when she entered the room, glancing nervously at each other more times than they looked at her, and if she spoke to one of them, they all grew defensive and he would make a snide comment designed to confirm that she was stupid. So she numbly dated exciting men, baking side by side in the guileless Texas sun, and she felt herself solidifying until only her marvelous mane was free to flip and swing.

All of her boyfriends had encouraged her to become a stewardess. She went through the entire training course, then flew her first assignment to LAX and never re-boarded the plane. It was the right choice. In Los Angeles, everyone made a play for her. Even the underfed brown boys bagging her groceries had enormous egos and gushing full-time lust. They all wanted the big prize, and being too large for the landscape was suddenly an asset. It sort of knocked her off-kilter, the thought that she wasn't going to scare people anymore.

"See the movement there? See it?" Misty thought Leighton was talking about the roaches scurrying across her feet, poking industriously into the eyelets on her tennis shoes, but he was going on about the traffic again. She waited for the day Leighton would collapse. She would let him pulsate and lose his shape like a beached jellyfish, then she would knock that clingy Armenian out of the way and CPR him back to life. Then he would fall in love with her.

He didn't love her now. He was constantly pointing out that she was Texan, not Southern. "Texans," he would say, "are the types who smack their gum and use too much tape." Leighton's family was in South Carolina, and they were Old South aristocrats. He had a modest trust fund, but to finance his habit, he lent his name to be listed as the CEO of record for a Japanese home video porn company. He got 2% of the gross and the Japanese got to keep their family names respectable.

Jason the CPA had set up this deal. Jason was from Tennessee and he was a horse jockey, too, but he was as bloated as Leighton was withered. He had thinning blond hair, an obstinate double chin, and he drove an absurdly small Porsche which his white doughy body filled with the expansiveness of a harvest moon. The little car was always dragging its belly along the road, straining under the weight of Jason, protesting sparks flaring out. Jason didn't possess the large personality to support his girth. He was one of those people who used drugs because it provided an instant paranoid solidarity which he could insist was friendship. He picked up the baggies downtown and faithfully delivered the pony to Leighton several times a week, always presenting his big shaggy head for a love pat which never came. Misty kept expecting Jason to shrink. When he pricked the needle into his thigh, she imagined that he would puncture and fly around the room like a relieved balloon.

The Armenian hated Jason. When Jason came by, Leighton would banish both Misty and the Armenian off the balcony. They would have to sit side by side on the unmade, sheetless bed enduring the degenerate stench and flicking at elusive roaches. The Armenian would turn purple with rage as he watched Jason's big round back shudder with incontinent laughter. Out of sheer frustration, the Armenian would tell Misty stories about himself, spitting the words at her as if she were supposed to be taking notes but had stupidly forgotten a pen. "We met at UCLA film school. I used to work at Blockbuster Video. I would cry myself to sleep every night. You don't get it. You couldn't get it. There is nobility in servitude. Every day I accomplish something. I contribute. When he finally does it, that will be my glory, too. He doesn't like you, you know. After you leave, we make fun of you. He imitates your ridiculous lisp. Why do you think he's never slept with you?" Misty would slap him, hard. Because she didn't want to admit that he knew all the details, that every time she had succeeded in getting Leighton into bed, the Armenian had stood just outside the glass balcony door, a slighted dog.

It was true that Leighton was not sexually interested in her. Misty spent her days recruiting for the TV test audience company, trolling Hollywood Boulevard, striking up conversations with out-of-towners who were all punch drunk on the immortality underfoot, so she was inundated with offers. She could have sampled the world. But Leighton was the only one that tickled her interest in the least. He had to develop a taste for her because she was convinced that they were going to be married. He had used his hands, twice, but had stopped suddenly, while she was still light years from Nirvana. She told herself that it was amazing, that he had perfected phenomenal manual dexterity, but even she knew she was making this up. He was manipulative, and probably impotent. Except what about his other women?

"We're going out," he would announce, always after dark, in that weird reflective charcoal night of inner L.A. It was just a matter of someone moving his chair to another location. He made no preparations, no shower, no change of clothes, not even fingers run through hair. He always wanted Misty along for this part. "The most powerful man always enters the room with a lady on his arm. And you, Missy Texas, will have to do." They only went to tiny Hollywood dives without handicapped ramps, so that Leighton's entrance would have dramatic sweep and hold the room hostage for a few minutes as everyone had to wonder if he was going to get stuck in the narrow door or topple the bored candles on the table tops. His wheelchair was an ancient non-electric model, so every move was cumbersome. His strain and suffering were all part of the show.

It still shocked Misty, his pick up routine. Not the perverse risk of it, but the proof that there really is someone for everyone, sometimes several someones. In Texas, beauty and conformity were lifelong pursuits. She couldn't believe that a twisted, smelly little cripple could ignore the statuesque blonde who was in love with him, and actually go out and succeed in picking up strange, less-attractive women to fuck. It seemed like an evil fable written in some foreign language they had made her look at in high school, drained of its lyricism because she could only pick out the nouns.

Every single time, she thought he would fail. But there was always someone up for it. Freckled girls from Iowa, Eurotrash princesses with prancy foal physiques, middle aged barflies gone thick around the middle with bleached out moles sprouting on their upper lips. Leighton was staunchly heterosexual in his exploits, but she suspected this was only since her arrival, the right blade for the severest stab. She was so certain that he was going to fail that she even helped him, smiling at any women who glanced their way, striking up non-threatening conversations about which movies she should go see, before introducing them to Leighton. The Armenian could only glower and was restricted to fetching drinks.

Leighton would hold court, detached and charming, complimenting the girl's body until she became uncomfortable, then seamlessly switching to intellectual flattery by comparing her to a great heroine from literature. "But you know who you remind me of? Dreiser's Sister Carrie. Oh, yes, you've got that spark in your eye. You don't know Sister Carrie? Well, you ought to. You're the spittin' image." Misty suspected that he was actually insulting these girls, but no one ever knew the books. It was a bold move to mention books at all in an L.A. bar, and the girl would be hooked in. At some point, Misty would clutch the girl's knee, as if to make a statement about solid legs, and whisper, "He's magnificent," although she knew the girl would take it as a sexual verdict and an open invitation. She didn't think anything could possibly come of it. She was just playing along. And Misty would melt down to soap suds as she watched Leighton tell the girl, "Let us go then, you and I," and the girl would bite her lower lip and nod.

When Leighton brought the girl home, Misty would have to wait on the balcony with the Armenian and sometimes Jason, too. Jason didn't have one-tenth the self-confidence required to talk to a girl like Misty, but she would sometimes catch him making lecherous inquiries with his eyes at the Armenian, as if to say, "But if we gang up on her, one of us might have a chance." There was never any danger because the Armenian refused to acknowledge Jason.

Misty would look down at the Walk of Fame and picture cutting the girl to shreds with the points of one of those pink glittering stars. The girl would inevitably be louder than necessary, which Misty took as a sign that probably Leighton wasn't trying very hard, or had nothing to contribute. She never once turned and looked through the glass door at her future husband and the one he had chosen.

The girl always left immediately. The smell was overwhelming, and she needed to get away in order to start convincing herself that she had been really smashed or she'd never have done it. Leighton would lie on his back and call out, "Mimosa!" The Armenian would dampen a wash cloth and wipe him down, mopping up all traces of the girl.

Misty would walk to the corner market for o.j. and cheap champagne. This was a dangerous walk and she would hope to be kidnapped so her fate would be altered and she wouldn't have to marry Leighton. But without him, her life would be reduced to sure bets: a job involving a filing cabinet, single motherhood, and an ocean view apartment. The problem with the middle of the road was that she could see it all coming miles in advance. She would hope that a witch of some kind would step out of one of the cutesy display windows of hooker clothes and block her path, someone tan in white vinyl thigh-high boots, with the wide-brimmed benevolence of a mushroom. "Honey," the witch would purr, "you deserve better." Then the witch would crack a hokey fake leather whip. But didn't Misty deserve, just this once, to get exactly what she wanted, even if it was bad for her?

It was Christmas time and the Boulevard was tinsel-encrusted. The Scientologists had set up a garish Santa Claus display, many times larger than the department store versions, to match its larger hidden motives. Christmas decorations in L.A. always looked forced and sheepish, the birthday boy's good-sport smile caught in the flashbulb as the drunk guests leap forth and scream "SURPRISE!" Misty walked past the spots where she had approached tourists that day, smiling and wheedling, and saw where a buzz cut frat boy from Maryland had pressed his face next to the Michael Jackson star, then told her she was hot and he'd come to her screening if she'd sit next to him. She had laughed her flattered laugh and he told her he didn't mind going down, he did it all the time, he had a hotel room and some friends she should meet. It always deteriorated so quickly, the swing from friendly to lascivious. She was always caught off-guard. She wished she had a boyfriend who could pound those rude little freaks. She had an H'd-out, crippled boy who insulted her and picked up other women right in front of her. But surely one day he would run out of willing victims, and she would still be there, the only one left standing. Please, girl. Misty knew that the one thing Hollywood would never be short of was willing victims. One day he would grow up, come to his senses. Change. "T" is for Texas, and "T" is for tenacious. Misty had never been devoted to anything before, and if the object of her desires was imperfect, oh well. She would fight forever for her chance to be the chooser.

Inside the little market, she had to wait for a shivering jockey who was leaning despondently against the drink cooler, killing time in the fluorescent light, his black jeans marbled grey and petrified to his skin. *There, Mr. Leighton, is where you'd be without me*, thought Misty, but Leighton never noticed his fellow flotsam on the Boulevard. He only looked at the stream of cars. The jockey could tell that Misty wanted in the cooler, and that the Egyptian behind the counter was about to throw him out, but his insides were being microwaved and all he could manage was one pinkish eyeball rolled in her direction. After he had been chased out with a ball bat, the bat making fast, angry jabs, the jockey pouring away like a slow leak, Misty stepped up to the cooler and slammed her hand in the sliding glass door to test if she was a masochist. It hurt like hell and she immediately wished she hadn't done it. Plus, she instinctively chose her non-writing hand, which must prove some level of mental health. Nope, she had no excuse. She was just in love. She chose the orange juice with the pulp pieces in it because it seemed more nutritious, and hurried back to Leighton's.

Sometimes Misty was allowed to sleep at the foot of his bed, like an electric blanket he didn't use but couldn't quite throw out. Or maybe it was only on nights like this, when he passed out and couldn't protest. She looked up at him, and his small, girlish features seemed to be coated in something thinner than wax, the clear mucus on a glazed donut. She had the stark realization that he was going to die first. There would never be a moment when he stood in front of her satiny coffin and felt regretful and was bitten by a twinge of deepest affection for her. He would cheat her out of this.

The next day she had a headache and she was suddenly afraid to approach the strangers on the Boulevard. Even the children looked ravenous. She couldn't smile at them anymore. A seven year old boy, whose every article of clothing was emblazoned with large company logos, pointed at a star and started shrieking, "DAD! HAN SOLO! HAN SOLO!" Then he looked dead on at Misty and she imagined him cataloging her to come back to when his ego grew as oversized as his t-shirt.

The 3:00 test screening was only half full. Luckily no supervisors showed up for a spot check. Her manager, Jed, was consistently brokenhearted over his stripper girlfriend, and was holed up behind the one-way mirror, hissing into his cell phone that he didn't give a fuck if she was onstage, hand her the phone or they would all be sorry, they had no idea who they were fucking dealing with.

The network reps called from the car to report that the 101 was impossible, they couldn't make it, the clog dance of four different cell phone conversations clattering on in the background as each of them tried to set up the feature deal that would rescue them from TV, insulted and bearish at being stuck inside a car with other people, they knew they should have driven alone.

This freed up Misty's other manager, Crestla, who had won all kinds of company awards for recruiting the most viewers, until reeling people in became a compulsion she couldn't shake. She paced the Roosevelt lobby on brittle heels, unable to loosen her shoulders until she had picked up at least four strangers and convinced them to meet her in room 421 where they did things which fulfilled her only because these people hadn't planned to do them, and the fulfillment was only temporary anyway.

Hollywood was built on self-imposed twists and turns, the childish dismissal of the direct route from A to B, the lingering and loudly announced belief that the earth was more exciting if it was flat and unchartable. So sometimes things worked out that had no logical right to. Misty wasn't caught for not recruiting. The task of running the screening was left to just her and Tenille, a crafty wannabe actress with a hideous South Boston accent. The new sitcom pilot was about some beautiful people who meet at work in New York and first fight but end up going to bed in king-sized Manhattan apartments. The test audience of Midwestern families politely swallowed their distaste and earnestly pushed the buttons when they could tell something was supposed to be funny, and cooked up nice things to say about the show on the comment cards, always ending with *Thanks!* Tenille sat behind a prim baby blue Samuel French script, mouthing the Stella part for her scene study class that night. Misty filled out fifty comment cards for the people she had failed to recruit. On every question, she marked: Somewhat Funny.

After work she went back to Leighton's. He got high and they watched the traffic. "I'm gonna marry you one day, you know," she announced quietly. "I don't care if I have to wait til we're both eighty."

"You're a numbskull," he said. "Have you noticed how the birds fly these days? They're following the cars. I wouldn't be surprised if the stars were re-aligning. The clouds have been penetrated by smog and linked to car exhaust. It's done a one-eighty. Nature is under our control now."

"I'm gonna marry you," she repeated.

"Cut off your hair," he commanded, out of nowhere. She would later swear that he had said, "If you love me, cut off your hair." Misty's hair was her ticket out, her trapdoor back to Texas, the link back to an ordinary life. Alright, she would commit to him. She was more afraid of being sent back than of losing her way back.

"Fine," she said. "Do it."

The Armenian's eczema hands grabbed her hair at the nape of her neck and he hacked at it with a pocket knife, deliberately slicing into her skin.

She bit into her perfumed bandana, sucking up the bland alcohol. She had a moment of panic when she noticed that Leighton wasn't even watching. Some deviation in the traffic had him transfixed. The Armenian threw her long blonde curtain to the ground, where it stayed for years afterward, the wind never liberating more than a few fussy strands at a time. The melodramatic hunk of hair lent the balcony the air of a staged murder scene, until Jason the CPA masturbated into the furry mass one night, after which it just looked like something disposable had died, or maybe like something the roaches had built, according to their unanimous plans.

Misty immediately felt different without her hair, unmoored. She reached out to stroke Lieghton's cheek, but he reared back. "What am I gonna do with you now?" he asked. "You're pug ugly." Then, "There! There! That'll shake things up!" He lurched forward to get a better view of a left turn accident. "How much you wanna bet there's a corresponding nebula? Telescope!" The Armenian smirked and loped off to Hollywood Toy and Costume to shoplift a telescope.

Misty looked up at the sickly slug trail of a jet plane. Her hair re-attached itself to her head with a thick red ribbon to match the flight attendant uniform. It was her first assignment and the other two girls stood straight, but she had to hunch since she was too tall for the plane. The other two knew each other and the partridge plump one was showing the dehydrated one her new engagement ring. "How'd y'all meet?" asked the dried out one.

"We looked at each other across the room, and we just knew. It's like I knew the waiting was all over. There he was."

"That won't never happen to me."

"Yeah, it will. It'll happen to everybody. There's a perfect soulmate for everybody."

Then they politely asked Misty if she had a boyfriend, and cooed over the fact that she was dating a neurologist who treated all the Cowboys' head injuries. "You'll be next," the plump one said sagely, then winked her glistening puppy eye.

The pilots came through with their commanding white hats and succinct luggage, and one of them made an off-color remark comparing the tight fit of the luggage compartment with a vagina, without actually saying *vagina*. The other two girls managed to smile tightly in an off-putting way, but Misty guffawed loudly, and the pilots looked at each other.

When they were over the scraped red plateaus of Arizona, the pilots buzzed for service and Misty volunteered to go. The cockpit nearly blinded her with its crowded black minutiae. "This your first flight?" they asked. They both had the same hat and kept their eyes forward, so Misty never could tell which one was speaking when. "We have a lot of fun on these flights. You like fun?" She nodded, but they seemed to be talking more to each other than to her. "You want to steer the plane?" She reached around their shoulders and touched the black joystick and she was directing all those lives, just for a minute because now the pilots' hands were climbing her legs and squeezing her ass, and she looked out the big windshield at all the ground they were covering so quickly and calmly and she wondered why she had been the one to walk stupidly into the cockpit while the other two girls sat safely out there sipping Diet Pepsi and talking about gold karats and drapes.

She didn't move away, so the pilots probably thought she didn't mind, but really it was because the room was so tiny and she was afraid to let go of the wheel and find out that she wasn't actually controlling anything. The plane wasn't going to crash. It was just going to go on like this, smooth sailing, with her accidentally inviting all sorts of average insults, until one day they would chase her into the middle of the road and she would be too worn out or confused to dart back out of bounds.

She swiped a fat, crunchy roach from her bald neck. Leighton was going on about the repercussions of the traffic accident, making conjectures about the trade winds and the upcoming governor election. Misty sat with him while he talked on and on and his words got heroin hazy and his neck flip flopped to the side. Eventually she felt at the back of her hacked-off hair. She tried to feel outraged, but here she sat with the one she had picked out of all the world, and she felt blessed. She thought Leighton had passed out, but he looked at her and mumbled, "It surely is a shame, Missy Texas. It surely is a shame."

There was a low, vast rumble and an insistent, tinkling little shake. It could have been a minor earthquake, but to Misty it was a jet airplane taking off from Dallas Love Field. She saw herself steering the plane with one finger, and if she wanted to crash it, she could.

***

KIDNAPPING LESSONS

Marjorie wrote her own version of her daughter's diary, but it didn't help because she kept getting stuck at May 5, 1982. "Just write it in your own words, the way you would like for it to have happened. You're completely in control of the events," the therapist reiterated weekly, in a voice that was starting to wobble into pleading. The rest of the entries were easy.

Mom is such a bitch. She never pays attention to me, she's so busy getting high.

Mom brought home two strange men last night and they fucked her out in the open on the vinyl lawn chair by the pool. One of them had a full beard, and the other one was Guatemalan. The height difference alone was obscene.

We went out for fro-yo and mom left me sitting there and went out to the car with the redheaded teenage girl from behind the counter and traded her a line of coke for a thorough licking in the back seat. This wasn't right, even if the girl did have for-sale eyes and soon after she became a teen movie star, proving that no matter how fucked up my mother was at the time, she still had good taste.

Marjorie noticed that the diary had an unlikely focus on herself, and didn't sound like Che at all. But why shouldn't it be all about her? Marjorie was the one who had to endure the therapy. Che's real diary got burned when Che renounced all her worldly possessions, heaping it all in the drained swimming pool—including several CD's and lipsticks and finer undergarments which actually belonged to Marjorie—dousing it with gasoline, then chanting while the blaze charred an indelible black circle onto the pool's serene blue concrete. "Crop circle," Marjorie would tell her guests. "Even the aliens can't get beach access in Malibu." Marj was known for being dependably acerbic. This is why they let her into the industry, though they made her write and produce sickly sweet TV movies for the women's networks. They wanted someone who could be funny in meetings, even though they intended to scrape all wit out of her scripts, leaving a banal nutshell that wouldn't exacerbate their professional paranoia. Watching scene after drably-shot scene of her projects, she would see the specter of her father, fastidiously dressed in his tailed tuxedo, his thin moustache a finishing stroke by Miro, facial muscles clutching a monocle to give him an excuse not to smile. "But buttercup," he would say, "at the very least, make them add some colors! Take a risk, do pastels." This latest round of therapy had made Marjorie discover that her father was gay, that her fashion model mother's body stayed so Peter Pan perfect largely because it was so seldom used. Her father's live-in male secretary with his blond Muscle Beach ineptness and nasty hysterics took on a whole new role in her memory. Here was the wicked stepparent she had always felt she had grown up with! Her ravishing mother had a passion only for three way mirrors. She would spend her days dressing in Marjorie's father's sumptuous costume designs, gazing at herself with a choked sensualism while her husband fluttered about, making prissy adjustments, tugging and pinning his wife like a tailor's dummy. Marjorie's compulsive nakedness—all her flashing and stripping and skinny dipping, her immediate disappointment when introduced to someone clothed—could be just typical rebellion against her parents. And now her own daughter had rebelled against her. It could be that simple.

Marjorie was obviously close to some kind of emotional breakthrough, something that would smooth her crow's feet and make her name start popping up on summer feature short lists. Something that would free her from her over-extended teenhood. It was imperative that she talk to Che. She hid out every afternoon near the campsite where Che's cult lived, hoping to catch a glimpse of her daughter.

"Let me have the binoculars," Marjorie said to Rav, her good man hard found. Rav was kind and faithful and wore Italian suits and enjoyed stalking Che, which was a requirement that had ruined all of Marjorie's other halfway promising relationships. But she didn't quite trust Rav. He was ordinarily very accommodating, but when he did get mad, it was over the wrong things, like an American watching a soccer match. He had rutted through three marriages, scarred wives and discarded children, and she thought of him as not so much good as worn out. He had gotten rich by producing straight-to-video action movies which were used to launder weapons money for his native Israel. Now he was tired of pretending to work, and rarely went into the office, even though he still paid to have his name in red letters on the outside of his Wilshire Boulevard building, obscuring the views of all the middle management drones on the 26th and 27th floors. Rav went around all day with a high-end still camera, zoom lens like an aardvark's snout, taking pictures of ghetto girls' panty lines. He used black and white film and tilted the camera just enough so that everyone was forced to call him artistic rather than perverted. On the infrequent occasions when he felt up to sex, Marjorie was positive that he was imagining all those bus-stop-waiting behinds which he was too tired to chase. Afterwards, he would show her his latest bootie photos, which Marj supposed was his attempt at intimacy.

She looked at the unshifting brown dust of Topanga Canyon through the twin circles of the binoculars. Nothing stirred. This was drop-out territory, the hills above Malibu where people came to reject Los Angeles without actually weaning themselves from it, to establish cults and horse farms and nudist colonies that someone with industry money could finance. Marjorie kept the binoculars pressed to her face even though there was nothing to see. The double circles reminded her of breasts, but therapy had taught her that she should picture chocolate chip cookies instead. She thought of the now-defunct nudist colony nearby, which she had been thrown out of in the late '70s for aggressive tactics in the sauna. Maybe other people could pretend that seeing naked bodies everywhere only diffused their sexual urges. It had made Marjorie damn hot. She didn't really talk about her sexual addiction. She was as instantly revealing as everyone else in Hollywood about her personal traumas, but she had learned to focus on the drug habit. People had a morbid fascination with her nymphomania and would corner her for hours on end, asking breathless questions that missed the essence of the matter, asking: "But how could you screw that many people?" which was like asking an actor: "How do you learn all those lines?", completely misunderstanding the skills involved. It wasn't the indiscriminate acceptance of hundreds of partners that posed a challenge. It was conquering them, making them do things her way, devising ever more outrageous demands. She once tied a uniformed nurse face down to a pigeon coop, and almost couldn't go through with the sex because she was so overjoyed at having gotten away with this set-up, which was not a carefully guarded fantasy but a flighty whim that didn't occur to her until they reached the roof and she saw the coop. Marjorie relished writing about that incident in Che's diary, including it even though Che had been at school or somewhere and had no knowledge of that event.

As tyrannical as she was with her many lovers, Marjorie had been such a lax mother. She had always let Che do whatever she wanted, but Che showed an alarming lack of gratitude for this. For all her nutty religious posturing, Che was an ungrateful person. She sent back all of Marjorie's birthday presents, and Marjorie used to let the spa certificates sit there and expire until therapy taught her to stop punishing herself and use them. Marjorie wrote in the diary at length about that black day when Che was 10 and sulking about some relatively minor offense of Marjorie's—she hadn't shown up for some ballet recital or talent show, something with a costume. She had sent Che with an adult, someone who didn't hate kids' stuff. Bella Bergman's mom, whom Marjorie used to make out with whenever Mrs. Bergman was getting over her divorces, soft pet on the sofa with a video playing, high school scenario, Marjorie playing the flushed, uncertain virgin who cruelly doled out her affections and never let Mrs. Bergman get as far as she would have liked, retreating kisses tasting of burnt microwave popcorn.

> *I got so mad at Mom that I wouldn't speak to her. I also wouldn't eat, as the IRA was doing this at the time and hunger strikes were all over the news. My mother had a bulbous hangover and a genital itch from too much hot tubbing, but she sat me down for some straight talk. "Che," she sighed, "you can't ever doubt that I love you. When I found out I was pregnant, I quit the hard stuff. All of it. For nine months. My fingernails were bitten to the quick and I couldn't orgasm. But I stayed clean so you wouldn't come out retarded." I made it clear that I wasn't impressed, that I actually expected these types of monumental sacrifices from my mother as a matter of course. Realizing this, my mother had never been so frightened in her life.*

"There! I see someone!" Rav was looking through his zoom lens, using it as a telescope. Here they came, dripping over the hill, ten bald disciples in sunny orange robes, rotund Leader Pete bringing up the rear, a watchful shepherd. It was getting harder to recognize Che as she got older. She mimicked her cult's beatific smile, but it never sat well on her face. That dopey grin looked to Marjorie like a Japanese theatre mask, painted happy but meant to signify the villain. Marjorie still pictured Che with her adolescent scowl. Che had always seemed to have old typewriter cross-out marks all over her face, angry and encoded.

Right after Mom had me, everybody kept saying: "Don't you want to hold the baby? Don't you want to hold the baby?" But frankly, my mother was in shock over the pain and the fact that her vagina felt stretched and torn and she was surrounded by nurses in white panty hose but she couldn't find her sex drive. The baby looked bald and generic, and it seemed mad about something, and no she didn't want to hold it, she wanted someone to French kiss her until she felt like herself again, to fuck her in this room with the unlockable door. Later, when she hobbled out to look at the nursery, all the babies looked exactly the same and she couldn't find me. On the way home from the hospital she stopped at Beverly Center and got my ears pierced so she would know me. It was the first time she lied about my age.

Rav was already out of the car. "Take the right! Take the right!" He pointed urgently toward the flock of baldies, but Marjorie still couldn't find Che. Rav rushed at an unattractive beanpole woman and locked his burly arms around her waist in a wrestling hold. The other cult members scattered, but they didn't go far. They clucked and twittered over this display of violence, and chanted in a disorganized manner. Leader Pete held his palms up to the sky. Marjorie hated that guy. Not just because he had brainwashed her daughter when she was only fourteen. There had been an all-consuming round of child endangerment charges, but it was so dispiriting dealing with the police, they were all so eager to be handcuffed to her bedposts, and Che kept running away anyway. Marjorie took the battle into her own hands. Her background check on Leader Pete, a.k.a. Peter Paul Steinberg, proved that he was a harmless crazy from Toledo, Ohio, minor convictions for trespassing and panhandling, no sociopathic tendencies, half a college degree in Theology from some crackpot Bible basher school in Orange County. She resented Leader Pete for his plainness, his overall lack of charisma that assured that his flock never increased past twenty people (there wasn't even a website for the distraught mothers of his followers), his bald-faced rip-off of the Hare Krishna costume, and most of all for his condemnation of sex, which is what gave Che the courage to call her mother unclean.

Mom heard me in the garage getting my camping equipment. It was around two in the morning and she snuck up on me with a flashlight. "Baby," she said, "Why don't you move back into your nice room and grow your hair back? I have plenty of college money for you, you know."

"You're unclean," I muttered.

"What?"

"You're a fornicator. I feel sorry for you." But actually, I didn't. I had to pretend not to hate her, the same way she had to pretend to be glad to have a child.

Rav flipped over onto his back. The Olive Oyl woman, who must have been Che, had pulled some kind of martial arts move, turning Rav's weight and conviction against him. The flock wasn't allowed to cheer, but they took up a warbling song in some nonsense language devised by Leader Pete. Che, adrenaline-fueled, ran in circles around Rav, then swiped his fallen camera and took a few touristy snapshots of her pogo-hopping family. Leader Pete made a trilling sound and everyone shut up and turned to him. He shook his head almost imperceptibly at Che, who lowered her shining eyes and placed the camera gently on Rav's chest. That fucking killjoy! Who was he to keep her daughter virginal all these years, hastily shorn and frighteningly naïve? If she could ever get Peter Paul Steinberg away from his devotees, she would have him flat on his back in no time. She would make him wear spike heels and garter hose and frilly ribboned panties. She dreamed of mounting her nemesis the same way battered women dreamed of knives and poison and the witness protection program.

"Marj, help me up," rasped Rav. He sounded perfectly calm. Che had flipped him before, and he spent a lot of time drawing charts strategizing how to overcome her, without doing any physical training. Che offered her skeletal hand and he took it, lumbering to his feet and examining his damaged camera. He wasn't upset over the breaking of his favorite toy, but when one of the baldies handed him a blue photocopied pamphlet describing enlightenment with many misplaced apostrophes, this set him off. He shook his fist and fake charged at everyone, as if demonstrating his wrath to a tribe of monkeys.

Everyone retreated a few yards, and even Leader Pete sprawled on the ground in his non-violent resistance pose. Only Che stood her ground, and Marjorie was proud of her. Che crossed her arms defiantly over her flat boy chest, which Marjorie was sure she wasn't supposed to do under Leader Pete's rules. There was still enough of Che left inside that loopy stick body to get some answers out of her.

Bella Bergman's mom and all the other mothers—whose names and faces I cannot remember because they are not in any way interesting, they exist to carpool and rent helium tanks for birthday parties and ask if there are peanuts in the food—have hired this lady from the PLO to give us kidnapping lessons and teach us how to fend off attackers. A lot of wealthy kids from Malibu and Beverly Hills get snatched and it's a big headache for their parents getting them back. Rasha comes over on Saturday mornings and teaches me to flip her and to hide in small spaces like under the bathroom sink, the way Charlie Manson used to do it. She says to never go along with a kidnapper. Fight him tooth and nail because once he gets you to his own environment, you have no chance.

Rasha had been delightfully military in bed, wore her boots and sweated profusely and had a discernable moustache and all that hardcore butch stuff. Marj asked Rav about her years later because he knew all the Middle Eastern players in town. "Her? She's a total fake. Israeli draft-dodger bull dyke." But she hadn't faked her orgasms, and apparently she had really taught Che to overcome men three times her size. People were too quick to call each other fake. Some people were genuine chameleons.

Che was staring at Marjorie, expecting her to say something. She had her old accusing frown, face smudged with inky indominatable anger. Marjorie finally recognized her daughter, and immediately felt shy. She wondered why she didn't hold enough allure for Che to cross the six feet or so of scraggly grass between them for some sort of greeting.

Marjorie's cell phone rang. Rav politely stopped raging and waited for her to answer. The interruption snapped him back into neutral and he returned to calmly fiddling with his camera. Marjorie shuddered as she answered the phone. It was the director calling from Montreal, where daylight was already gone and he hadn't gotten the outdoor skating rink scene. "Are you aware that they don't speak English in Canada?" he demanded.

"But they do, sweetie. You must be in an ethnic neighborhood or something. I've got to go. I've got people waiting." It wasn't worth explaining it to him, making him feel stupid. Marjorie could make everyone else feel good, be happier, just not her own daughter. Marjorie hoped that Che would be impressed that she cut short an important business call for her, but of course Che was still beading her eyes and pouting. Leader Pete raised his head in a weasel-like move. Marjorie had to speak up before he whisked Che off into the cult's tumbledown white van which squatted in the bushes looking unemployed.

"Che. It's Mom. We need to talk."

"I have nothing to say," Che's voice was froggy from disuse. Marjorie thought of all the sick days she had resented having little Che at home, all the cups of honey tea and lemon she had been too stir-crazy to provide.

Mom rubbed up against another maid and she quit. These people aren't even attractive. I clean up all her spills and ashes, even though she told me I didn't have to and she borrowed Mrs. Bergman's maid until she can find a new one. Mom walked by my bedroom and I was whispering to Mrs. Bergman's maid, or she thought she heard me whispering, and I told her I was just telling her where we keep the clean towels, but she could tell it was more than that. It is a big house and my mother has given me a suite of three rooms to myself, rooms that she won't enter without knocking. I complain and complain, whining like a girl who lives in a hut with a dirt floor. The house is never clean enough for me.

"Well, you have to talk to me. I'm in therapy." Another point went unscored. Two baldies tugged Leader Pete to his feet. He swept his hands toward the van, and his children happily climbed inside, eager for their field trip to the laundromat or the bulk discount club. Leader Pete stayed where he was, pointedly allowing Marjorie a supervised visit with her daughter. She was supposed to be impressed by his benevolence, but she wasn't. She walked closer to Che. She could see the gummy red nicks in Che's skull from her mirrorless home hair shaves. Looking at Che, so reduced and unwomanly and out of synch with modern life, Marjorie saw her own bony corpse, forced into a smile by the undertaker. She gagged and looked away.

"Your mother's not well," Rav offered gravely, an intentional misrepresentation. Or did he really believe there was something wrong with her?

"I have feelings of guilt, Che. It's holding me back. I can't go on writing these sappy disease-of-the-week, woman-wronged, save-my-daughter scripts forever. I want to write romances. Something with kick. Something I can be proud of and leave behind with my name on it."

Che shook her head. Marjorie was getting through to her. "Che, I feel like—maybe I drove you to this somehow. I feel bad that you left home so young and you haven't really progressed in life—"

"You only see what is superficial. I can go twenty-three days without eating. I can put flames on the soles of my feet and not feel a thing. I can communicate with squirrels, as equals."

"Yes. Regardless of all that. I've suspected for a long time that some pivotal event happened on May 5, 1982—"

"I don't measure time according to your calendars."

"The year you were twelve. Cinco de Mayo. Your teacher came over. Remember that? You overheard us."

Mom took me out of the experimental co-op school because I wasn't making friends. She put me in a Catholic school run by radical nuns who have seceded from The Vatican. My teachers are soulful women in page boy haircuts and neatly laundered denim whose hands are always smeared with day-glo paint from rally signs. Mom is smitten. She is pretending to have a major crisis of faith, and has tricked my Language Arts teacher, Sister Felicity, into long, passionate discussions which always end with Mom mournfully hinting at suicide. Now Sister Felicity comes over to our house on Wednesday nights and I cower in my room with my Paddington Bear and my books that I really like—Ramona Something and Sweet Something High School with its photo covers of soap model girls with sweaters and excellent complexions and tottering virginities, the girls I should have grown up to be instead of running off to make myself ugly and ridiculous and angry at my mother for life. Downstairs in the living room, with the picture windows thrown open and the muted roar of the Pacific making the house feel full, Mom goes to work on Sister Felicity. But Sister Felicity is very devoted to her vows. She accepts one glass of wine. When Mom scoots closer to her on the sofa, she sits cross-legged on the floor. When Mom strokes her short glossy brown hair, she takes Mom's hand kindly but firmly and sets it down in Mom's lap, as if she is returning an elderly relative who likes to wander off with her robe gaping open. Sister Felicity goes on talking about Descartes and Martin Luther and Martin Luther King, and when Mom gets dead drunk and starts masturbating beside her, Sister Felicity merely gets up and kisses her fingers and rubs a cross sign into Mom's forehead and leaves. I know about all these things. Somehow I have been watching. The kidnapping lessons taught me to curl up in tiny corners undetected. I hear every manipulative word my mother utters, and feel the thousands of rejections from Sister Felicity, her shield of honor chiseling my mother into a grotesque gargoyle, wings open and tongue too long for her mouth. This is when I begin to truly hate my mother, to plot ways to escape from her house. I pour red wine in her face one afternoon when I come home from school and she's asleep on the couch with an aged sun-dried surfer snoring into her crotch. I quit going to school and hang around Santa Monica Beach, shyly watching tough homeless kids who mistake me for the lost penniless daughter of Midwestern tourists. Sister Felicity keeps coming to see Mom, and she tries in vain to make Mom take an interest in my bad behavior. But all Mom can see is a glorious medieval chastity belt diapering Sister Felicity, the sacred lock giggling, the dark keyhole winking at her. Then it is Cinco de Mayo and Mom blends margaritas and dresses up in a conflicted costume, like a cowgirl with a sombrero and a bikini top. Sister Felicity comes over. I am home, hiding under the dining room table, balancing on the rafters there, a female spider, waiting. Sister Felicity is very upset because the Archdiocese has filed a lawsuit to reclaim the land the school is on, even though the renegade nuns paid for it. Mom massages Sister Felicity's neck, then she reaches up under Sister Felicity's off-brand red polo shirt and finds a bra from the '50s, more like a spinal brace than a piece of lingerie, fortress gates. Sister Felicity closes her eyes. "Marjorie," she says, "I cannot keep fighting you on this. You use your sexual desires to distract yourself from your real problems. Putting your hands on me will bring you only momentary satisfaction." Unaware that this is bedroom talk at its best, sweet sincere girl. Into the armor and Mom has a brush against one plump, bon-bon-like nipple, which hardens dramatically,

Stacia Saint Owens

and so does the other one, little explosives leaping forward in time like the first few sentences of Genesis, rushing toward an inevitable bang. "Marjorie—" Then Sister Felicity spasms and pushes Mom and all her longing to the floor. She jumps to her feet and stands with her red shirt bunched up over one defiled breast, and she looks taller and thinner, rigid with a new bitterness. She points toward the dining room. One long brown braid dangles from beneath the table, a green velvet bow swaying. Sister Felicity is shaking with repulsion. Mom lies flat on her back for a minute, parenthood weighing down her chest like Inquisition torture bricks. Wanting to say to Sister Felicity, "But it's just us, darling, just us. Don't you understand that if you just lie down with me, everyone else will disappear, and if you hold me afterwards it will prove that I am safe at last, because we are the only ones alive and you are my only potential adversary, conquered and sleepy with your head on my chest?" Mom gets to her feet and calls my name. And then ... And then ... And then....

"Che, please. I've blocked it out. What happened? Your teacher disappeared, remember? They never found—"

"MOVE FORWARD! MOVE FORWARD!" screeched Che, in a very unenlightened tone, commanding a sailboat in a squall, the real skipper dead and the compass smashed. "Quit dwelling on things!"

Leader Pete walked up to Che and put his hand over her bald head. Marjorie wanted someone to touch her, too, but Rav was busy calculating if he should bum rush Che from behind, and Che wasn't allowed to touch non-family members. Leader Pete looked seriously at Marjorie and spoke some gobbledygook that meant, "She's had enough." He took Che by the waist and led her swiftly toward the white van, where the whole family sat stewing in the happiness of self-denial.

"Che, please! I need to know! Where did—"

"Marjorie! I'm going to follow them. When they cross the border I'll get her. I'll bring you that bastard's head on a stake. It's lawless down there. I have friends. You, pal, you!" He pointed at Leader Pete and dove into the car, starting the engine and idling with barely-contained excitement, all set to chase the bouncy white van all the way down to Rosarito, where he theorized they had a compound. It was more likely that they were going to Subway to dumpster dive for food. Marjorie had the sudden therapeutic discovery that Rav was carrying a loaded semi-automatic, that he always carried a loaded semi-automatic, in an ankle holster. People were such complex creatures when she tried to deal with them outside of bed.

Leader Pete was unfazed by Rav's threats. Marjorie didn't move toward Che. The only time she had ever laid a hand on her daughter was on Cinco de Mayo the year Che was 12, when she dragged her out from under the dining room table then blacked out. When she came to, it was two days later. There was a nun missing and her daughter had gone for good though she hadn't found the cult yet and so would still sleep in the house more nights than not. Marjorie realized it was time to clean up her act. She quit cold turkey, tossing the drugs and paraphernalia into the ocean and settling alone into the dreary cave of her bed, stroking the luxurious sheets, trying to find comfort in thread count like a normal single mother. Che never noticed that she had changed. Or maybe she thought her mother was being fake.

Che turned back toward Marjorie before she climbed into the white van. "Check the crawl space!" she yelled. Leader Pete was visibly taken aback. He tapped Che's shoulder in his version of *Don't make me ask you again to get into this car, young lady*. Che was only startled for a split second, then she turned and leapt into the van, long jumping toward the strange estimation of domestic order that her evangelical bald family provided. The van sputtered then sidled off snake-like, side to side as much as forward. Rav's Audi followed menacingly, well-engineered and half-cocked.

Marjorie stood for awhile in the clearing by herself. Her cell phone rang and she checked the caller ID, but didn't answer. She tightened and released her buttocks and thought of seeking out some stable boy from one of the shabby horse farms, but she forced herself to picture the horse, until its flanks turned her on, then the stirrups and bit, but that was no good either. She persisted until she hit upon red hot horseshoes being pounded into rough, flaky hooves. She had never been able to get off on feet.

There was a crawl space under her house, a narrow, sand-encrusted opening beneath the imposing ocean view deck, a tiny space Che had probably learned to squeeze herself into during kidnapping lessons, a space that she may have been able to stuff a small woman's body into, far back in the shadows where her would-be assailants would never find her. Marjorie wasn't going to check the crawl space. The police had searched the house at the time and found nothing, though they were distracted by Marjorie's distress and her cleavage and the way her bedroom seemed full of wild risks. None of them went in unarmed. If Marjorie found any remains of Sister Felicity, so much as a tatter of red shirt, the old longing would hit her and she wasn't sure she would survive it. And she could not bear the thought that Che hated her so much she would make up a story designed to drive her crazy with the hope that she wasn't truly alone in that big crypt-like, well-behaved house, that the things she saw darting down blank hallways out of the corner of her eye might be a haunting born of some residual longing as unkillable as her own, seeping into her hollow house from an unmarked grave, requiting her with little pricks and pinches that were the valentines of an otherworldly, eternal devotion, not just the complaints of aging and insomnia.

Instead of checking the crawl space, Marjorie spent the next week chewing up pens, writing an ending for Che's diary. She had never told Che any fairy tales. Still, she fooled herself that one day, Che would read this one.

It was difficult to write. She wanted to teach her daughter that bad people do not always have to be punished, do not always end up faded and alone and inconsolable as Marjorie had. She wanted Che to fight tooth and nail against old age and flat shoes, to flip deathly respectability onto its back and hide in the crawl space with a busty Scandinavian scuba instructor and a waterbong until it was safe to come out.

Marjorie's therapist called the end of the diary closure. But Marjorie didn't want to close anything. She wanted to throw open the case file, to force Che to explain step by step how she should solve this mess. Los Angeles is a city full of people enjoying an extended adolescence. Marjorie didn't want to end hers. She regretted all the puddles of maturity she had allowed into her life in an attempt to appease Che. She just wanted to be treated like a grown up sometimes, like someone her daughter had to be nice to. This would be a good start.

There were always alternate endings. It seemed like a good time to start lying again. Some strangers offering candy are just nice people who like to give out candy, but you can't tell your kid that. That's why parenthood is such a fucked-up endeavor. You either scare your kid too much or not enough. And when it's over, you scare yourself, not believing the damage you have done, shocked that you ever had that much power over another human being, that you didn't know this at the time. You spend your old age growing kinder when it's too late, wondering how things could have been different.

And then my mother fainted from the alcohol and the disappointment and the general trauma. Sister Felicity left the house and tears got into her eyes and she accidentally drove her order's red Le Car off the canyon road and it fell 50 feet into a remote patch of foliage where she was never found. I ran away and joined a cult for reasons which I cannot discuss. My mother cleaned up and got a long term adult male boyfriend. Sister Felicity doesn't know she is dead. She believes she is the giant maple tree that her car crashed into. During winter months, she loses some leaves and she feels coy and provocative and longs for someone to carve initials into her bark. In the spring she becomes lush and fertile again and all of her leaves are well-nourished. She attracts many insects and newts and squirrels. They tickle each other and she takes care of them all and in her branches lies the perfect embrace.

***

INHERITANCE

Bobbie doesn't know how to be nice to the kid. Doesn't want to. She's rich enough to last three generations, but her mother will never be impressed till she's married. Has to make an effort. Her therapist, sister, stay-at-home girlfriends told her. Get a puppy. Let your car break down. Smile at children.

I watch her try this female stuff. Doesn't make her softer. Makes her weak. A hard-boiled egg with runny yoke in the center. Better hope no one gives her shell a hard whack.

Half the dating prep she passes off to me. Describe her face to a make-up artist. Read her horoscope chart every morning. Write up a three sentence synopsis. Draw up lists of vocabulary words. Positive words. For what? How will she fit these in? These words will throw her off-balance. At an agency, you have to talk in spurts. You always sound like you're on the phone, being interrupted. Because you always are.

She tried the puppy. I inherited it after a week. I'm not a dog person. This job only leads upwards if you put in extra.

Bobbie frowns at the kid. Rushing around. Late for lunch. Can't think of a single nice thing to say. Wants to scream at me for letting a kid wander into her office. If she had more time. If she wasn't trying to re-package herself on the side as someone's wife.

"Give her some of the—. No, no. The candy. Don't leave the fucking phones. Order in. Connect me through. Chadwick. Plus one. Bev on cell. I'm 15 late." Bobbie lunges past the kid. Doesn't look. Kid looks at Bobbie. Scared. Round brown eyes without much pupil. Look better on a cow. Frizzy black hair. Grease at temples. Dirty red bow passed out drunk on top of her head. She's what? Six? Nine? How do I know? We don't handle juvies. Janitor's kid. Mexican. Round Tinker Toy girl. Too fat to sell anything.

I do Bobbie's commands in order. Give the kid a candy. Italian. Gourmet. Watercolor fruits on the wrapper. Jelly—no, marmalade inside. Watch her chew it seriously, like meat. Send an intern out for a cap and salad. The pink girl. Raw. Sensitive. A little toe. From some Catholic school in the South. Is she kidding, talking that slow? Smiling brave like a crybaby. Blue copy toner marks on her forehead. Three stripes. Claw marks. Don't tell her. Don't give her money for my lunch. Let her figure these things out.

Call Bev's assistant. Tell her Bobbie is running 10 late. Flirt. Butter. Talk screenings. Stab that Harvard imbecile at NBC. All those fucking brains and he can't pick the right tie. Doesn't confirm lunches. Isn't buying anything, *nada pinata*—passed on the cowboy Mafia thing, the blind gymnast, the historical thing about what's-their-names who won the Grammy then had to give it back because they were lip synching. Tried books. Still didn't buy. You should have seen the number of pages she had me read. French stuff. Slooooooooow. How long? Before they axe him? Two months, three. Seen the ratings? Guy better start prying the earthquake tape off his diploma. Go back East. Try Wall Street. It's easier. You know he's only 26 years old? This shuts us both up. For a second. Watch the kid spit out the candy. Not into her hand. Slobbery lump of yellow rolling down her tight, pilled-up sweatshirt. Faded fuchsia. No color sadder. Color of a bull's eye. A billboard: KICK ME. Chewed up candy plops on the floor. Christ. Kid wiping at her mouth with her plump brown paw. Holding her tongue outside her mouth. Looking at me on the phone. Why? For help. For instructions. To blame. "Mini-crisis," I tell Bev's assistant. "Christ," she says. Not commiserating. Gloating. Glad it isn't her.

"Bobbie give up the Vanity Fair tix?" Schulman enters. "No? She toss you to E.J. and Dave? Trade me for Gov Ball? Up. Let's see your moves. Come on, strut the red. You ready to cure some AIDS?" Schulman is macking on me? No. Schulman is using me for target practice. Anything in a skirt and his asshole blows out musk. Schulman took me to his temple. Once upon a time. Bev Hills, but outer. Congregation half industry. Half wannabe. No elderly, which is something. Brought me along to meet people. Anywhere else, this would be touching. Sweet. A sign of interest. Schulman's eyes were popping during the service. Didn't know when to sit, stand, mumble. After, Schulman got digits from two 17 year old JAP cousins. Hancock Park. Too dumb—young?—to realize that Schulman would call them both on the same night. Convince them both to meet him at the beach house. Mai tais with grain alcohol. Even has them both wearing yellow tank tops. Schulman's good at arrangements. Stood around after the service. Didn't introduce me to anyone. Slipped his arm around my waist. Murmured that my suit wasn't doing my hips any favors. Patted my ass one too many times. A sadistic older sister. Powdered sugar around his mouth from the donut. Chalk circle in a football play. Loathe Schulman. Dying to kiss him. Tackle his mouth. Bite his lip. Draw blood. Schulman played Run DMC loud on the way home from temple. Mercedes. Daddy Warbucks. USC. Works 10 minutes from where he grew up. Learned to walk, read, fuck right here.

I don't date. Always working. Got my eye on a bigger prize. Can't get sidetracked. Can't stand the type of men who like me as I am now. Be honest: can't compete with the actresses and the strippers and the surfer girls. Attract men only because I am 22 and obviously from somewhere else. I talk Hollywood and dress Hollywood but I keep being surprised by how they act. Keep flinching. Never before went to a party where the host got his wife to fuck both a jockey and his horse. Saw this woman a few days later. Sitting in reception. Reading the trades. Humming. She looked up. I shifted my eyes away. Couldn't help it. "Hey!" she chirped. "*You* were at our party. Did you have fun? Did you get home okay?" It gets better. A woman I'd never met grabbed my arm. Told me she's sure I'm the re-incarnation of a serial killer. Insisted that I confront my demons. All of this in the WGA lobby after a screening. Eating cold shrimps. People milling around behind her dying to talk to her. She's not just a raving nut. She's a rich, successful raving nut. People impressed that I know her even though she's telling me how I dismembered an eight year old. The President of the agency called me into his office. Closed the door. Asked me to describe my panties. What was the right answer? Sometimes at a loss. Mouth not fast enough. Yet. Later I'll be in a better position. I'll pick someone then. I'll be luckier than Bobbie. Already I'm laughing at her mistakes.

Schulman dates. Not just fucks. Hunts. Promises. Fields tearful phone calls. Doesn't distract him. Not in the slightest. Hard to give the local boys hard-ons. They grew up seeing their mothers in string bikinis. Locals at a huge advantage. Nothing shocks them. Don't miss a beat. High school classmates mobilizing. Schulman & Pals will rule this town in ten years. Five. Seven. Schulman's trying to slow down on the coke. Makes it hard to get out for breakfast meetings. Sniffles. Constantly. Thinks it's charming. Sniffs toward the kid. "Story?"

"Janitor's kid."

"Magda has a kid?" Okay. Pathetic. Also using the janitor as target practice. "Introduce me."

"Take her to Sid's office. You got toys."

"What's your name, Princess? Huh?" Says it like he's talking to an old crippled dog. An iguana. Schulman could no more keep a pet alive than Bobbie. Doesn't count against him. Still gets plenty of tail. Luck is a lady, but all the females in Hollywood are girls. It's tough luck being female. No more you can say about it. Fatal to whine. Be thankful if it isn't you.

"Cat got your tongue?" Schulman doesn't have to be nice to the kid. Doesn't lean down. Can see the choke leash in his hand. So can the kid. She hobbles in a confused circle. A roach sprayed with poison. She lopes up to me. Grabs a handful of my Stella McCartney skirt. I lived off screening food for three months to afford it. Cubes of cheese and strawberries. War rations. Kid smells like a rotting rind.

"You'll make a great mother one day, Cassie," Schulman sniffs. Winks. Smug motherfucker.

"Let go," I command. The kid makes a whining sound. Hangs on. No English. Of course.

"No hando el dresso," says Schulman. Laughs at himself. Laughs hard. Even a person who has never been anywhere should know better than to do that.

The janitor bustles in. Short. Squat. A raisin. Young and plump but dried up. Grey uniform. Unbuttoned. T-shirt underneath. GUATEMALA. Letters flaking off. Several mounds on her body besides her breasts. Same ratty black hair as the kid. Yelps, "Aiyeee!" You'd think it's a joke. She runs for the kid. Winds back her hand. Way back. Like she's going to bat all the piss and vinegar out of the kid right here right now. Slows it down. Gives the kid a tiny swat on the head. Kid lets go of my skirt. Howls. The janitor is saying, "Sorry. We are sorry. Sorry." Schulman slinks out. Bored. Had enough practice for one day. Not a man to go the extra mile. A climber, not a champion.

"Your kid shouldn't be here," I say. Snap. "Why isn't she in school?"

"Vacations," mumbles the janitor. She's scared. White girl. We all have speed dial to Homeland Security. We cruise East Los at night, looking for wetbacks to turn in. That's what we're laughing about when we meet for lunch and keep pestering the bus boys for more ice water with a lime wedge. Please. I could care. I'm going to need a gardener someday.

The kid coughs. Hacks. Gags. Throws up a watery pile of yarn. On Bobbie's carpet. Harvard's coming in at three. Shit.

The janitor spits Spanish curses. She drags the kid off the floor. "I will take care. I will fix."

"GET OUT OF HERE!" Not a bad scream. Loud with just the right hint of psychosis. Not shrill like a girl. From the diaphragm. A studio scream. The way Jesus yelled at lepers. The janitor is crying along with the kid, but no soundtrack. Just tears. Rain down a dirty windshield. Dear God, don't let her quit. The see-saw is creaking. I went too far? I'm going to end up scrubbing that human waste off the floor myself. How to get the cleaning supplies without Schulman seeing? Dammit. How to keep her here? Stare? Smile? How much money? I realize I am humming. Frank Sinatra. Pure nerves. I am still an amateur. I make myself sick.

The janitor takes the kid out. Comes right back with a bucket. Scoops up her daughter's vomit with brown paper towels. Sprays green stuff on the stain. "Air freshener," I demand.

"Yes, yes. I am cleaning." No idea what air freshener is. I dig into Bobbie's bottom desk drawer. Find the plastic baggie of sage from that New Mexico project. Dump the pens—medium point. Black only. Bobbie's rules—out of my DGA mug. Light the sage. Bitter smell. Not ambitious. Not shaking hands and meeting people. Not trading up. No seduction. Can't see the point of this stuff.

Janitor on her hands and knees. Scrubbing. Crying. Big big stain. Birthmark. Persian rug. Fuck. I'm going to catch hell. Goddam brat.

Janitor feels me seething. "Ahm, ahm, dry. Is drying. Drying. This—"

"Bring me the kid."

"No, is drying. Wet. Wet."

"The kid. Now. Pronto." Two years of Spanish and when the time comes, I can't remember a goddam word. *Me llama Cassandra*. Once you start at an agency, you find out that everything that came before is useless. I've been through city college. Poetry. Wars. Woolly mammoth teeth. So what? That won't keep you safe in here. No one's ever heard of that stuff. Not in the Directory. Didn't sell over the weekend. This is square one. Ground zero. Learn to survive. Make a plan. Thrive. Fuck over enough people and The Next Big Thing will grow between your legs in a fat plastic panty hose egg.

The janitor sighs. Shuts her eyes. Putts out a few more tears. Silence. She pants. Puffy little chest heaving. A gerbil worn out on the wheel. I wait. What can she do? She's in no position.

She nods. Eyes down. The way she would greet the Virgin Mary.

"Hokay."

Comes back with the kid. Brown paper towels plastered to the kid's forehead. Eyes swishing. Same kid but drained. This kid will be very very old by the time she's eleven. Growing up in the same city as Schulman. The luck of the draw. Hard knocks. One of us has to win. The kid, Schulman, or me. Bobbie's good, but she peaked a few years ago. If she wants to walk up the aisle, she'll have to take off her ass-kicking boots. There's no reason to choose an average-looking ball-breaking bitch in this town when you could have a gorgeous one. Look at the movies. There's four female roles. Girlfriend, Wife, Mother, or Whore. Women like Bobbie tell themselves, "I'm not liking any of these. Fuck this. I'll invent a new role." Hasn't happened yet. Can't get financing. When I'm up there, I'll figure out how to do it.

One of us will inherit this office. This Persian rug. The Lichtenstein on the wall. Israel, Costa Rica, and Iceland with someone else carrying your pack and talking to the waiters. Tickets fixed. Tables reserved. Wrinkles zapped. Convertibles. Mocha ice cream and a platinum teaspoon at 3 a.m. Delivered. One of us. I'm the most grounded. I can see all sides. I dress like an insider and plan my attack from this island.

"Goodbye," I say to the janitor. Even I know *adios*. Tired of globalization. This is America. I am here to sell. For a split second, the janitor thinks of taking the kid and leaving. Fleeing. There are other fat babies at home. She already ran away from Central America. Look where that got her. She squeezes her daughter's shoulders. Restrained. Very British. From what I've seen. *This caning will build character, son. You'll grow up to hate me, but the Empire will be yours.* The janitor closes the door behind her. Softly. Demonstrating to the kid that a tantrum is not the play here.

So. Anyway. Me and the kid. In Bobbie's office. Stain on the Persian rug. Kid in a daze. Swaying. Face throbbing. Fat bull frog. Scared to death. I could lie. Say I am trying to teach her a lesson. For her own good. Not even. I want her to pay. Send her down a path where we won't ever meet again. One less hopeful to ride my ass.

The phone is ringing. Of course. Has been this whole time. Strident. Accusing. Endless false alarms. I let voicemail. Could be Bobbie. Screaming in the BMW SUV: "Lazy little cunt! Pick up the phone! Shit for brains! I get voicemail one more time I'll bite you a new asshole! FUCKING SOMEONE ANSWER MY FUCKING PHONE! No Cal cunt!" L.A. geography. I'm not from No Cal. It's somewhere else that has farms. I'm an immigrant. I'll always be hungrier than Bobbie and Schulman & Pals. Can't get lazy. I'm hungry, but this fat kid is starving.

"Fat. Little. Cow," I say each word slowly. Talking my stolen cell phone back from a crystal meth addict. Explaining that I am keeping the ring to a violent ex-boyfriend with a clenched fist. I am proud of the way I conduct myself. Never been a hothead like the rest of them. This will pay off for me in the end.

"Eat. These." I thrust the jar of Italian candies under her chin. Blown glass. Prague. Places the kid will never see. I unwrap a candy. The kid rears her head back. Stands her ground. A fighter. More steel than Schulman. Could arm wrestle him to the ground. I jam the candy into her mouth. Should be wearing latex gloves. If she bites me, I'll knock the teeth out of her head. And still die of a blood disease. That's the way it goes in this town.

I get at least six pieces down her throat. She falls to her knees. Gasping. Quiet. Efficient. No drama. She's not faking. I follow her mouth with the bowl. A fireman with a trampoline. I catch all the candies she hacks up. Save the rug. She sits back on her circus tent butt. Glad to be breathing again. Forgetting me. She will never look me in the eye again. Good. Now she knows.

I open the door. Call for Schulman. He lopes in. Eyebrows raised. Script in hand. Automatic tan. Gold dust from summer, fall, winter, spring in Malibu. The ride could stop, but Schulman's never seen the end of anything. Doesn't suspect. Smirking. Sniffling.

Decide to test him out. Experiment. Give myself a little treat. I got time. Got to admit, I'm curious. Shift gears. Talk sweet. Open my throat for once. Coo. Picture mermaids. Hear sirens. "Don't you just love kids?" I say.

Schulman relaxes into the door frame. Enviably idle. Looks down at the kid and me. Sees twins. Misses my warning. Yawns. Waits for me to entertain him. His crown tilts.

I smile at the kid. Make sure Schulman is watching. Seeing what he wants to see. I take the kid's wet chin in my hand. Gently. No need for force. She gets it. Supporting role. Background. Non-speaking. "Do you want another candy, sweetie?"

***

SAINT AUGUSTINE'S WIFE

They have been here three days, waiting for the lesions. The window faces an air shaft. She can't see the skyline of poorly fixed teeth, studded with gold cupids and neon stains. The sky is furious pink, like the sound of a high heeled shoe stamping. The air conditioner thumps, seems to be pronouncing the word *deadbeat*.

She lives three hundred miles to the west, in another city, sick with ambition, where everybody is on their way to becoming something. This place is where they come to give up, gamble it all, double or nothing, be seen with people they can't be seen with, sell things that shouldn't be priced. The last stretch of interstate is slick with desert oil. All the arrivals are headfirst, hurtling toward flat busted, a permanent limp, mysterious circumstances, all the odd ingenious uses of a leather belt, shocked every morning to roll over and find out exactly what NEVER CLOSED means.

She has not seen much of this city, just this stark room with its two of everything and its smirking tidiness. She knows it is the type of place you take someone you would not mind leaving behind. She wraps a balding towel around her waist. She can't stand panties, not even cotton, the Old Testament itch has gotten so bad.

He is staring up at the TV, newly brimstonic in the face of his troubles, transfixed by the broadcast of a clean shaven Rasputin peddling the bereaved Jesus. Jesus, like her, is in urgent need of his money. When they walked in the room, he threw his bag on the other bed and announced that he was giving up drinking forever. After three minutes of lying on the brown bedspread picking his nails and watching the Christ Channel, he tore into the mini-bar and has been steadily sucking on delicate little bottles ever since. She watches his mouth bob against the tiny glass lip and realizes that That Girl must have been underage. A detail he has kept clenched in his fist, hiding the last piece of the jigsaw puzzle, puckered and damp, a tiresome practical joke. He hasn't checked himself—she hasn't seen him—he says he has three days. It isn't helping her cope, him sprawled out, not moving, growing a beard and dedicating the rest of his diseased life to God. He proclaims over and over that he is going non-profit, that from here on out, it's all for the widows and orphans and juvenile delinquents, all the proceeds will go to the museum. Like most lifelong secularists, he has the museum and the Church confused.

She has taken six showers, he has taken none. The rash could merely be the result of not bathing. So the literature says. He is the one with the doctor. He gets office visits, sit down consultations and man-to-man discretion. The emergency room swabbed her, sucked her blood, pronounced her possibly-incurable, handed her a pamphlet, told her she'd know in three days, and went back to re-animating helmetless motorcyclists. She would have to wait and see what developed.

"We're lucky," he mumbles to his shiny satellite friend in the white suit. "Could be dead. Amen-amen. Amen."

She examines each of her teeth in the bathroom mirror, grateful for their permanence. She should have been born with moles on her face, a clubbed foot, a lisp, something marginal and persistent to prepare her for how she was going to end up. She screws her brick red lipstick up tall as a crayon and writes flowery script on the mirror, mocking the 200 wedding invitations she will never order from the engraver.

The reckless middle brother
invites no one
to watch him tie the knot.

Why should she marry him? Fifteen percent of the country is afflicted to some degree, the pamphlet says. She doesn't have to stick with him. DISEASED DARLING SEEKS LIKE-LESIONED. It is the doctor she wants.

A lifelong commitment. Prescriptions and check-ups and a courtesy call when the cure finally comes. He has corporate health insurance. She will surrender her surname to get it. This is a city of weddings. That's why they have come. He will pay for a witness.

He is repeating the 1-800 number from the bottom of the screen out loud, committing it to memory in case a phone moves near him. She has not spoken since they got here. She had raged at him for a week, seven days of shrill variations on the dull clarinet of *How could you?* A ferocious demand for information on That Girl, details, verbatims, glances, pauses, positions, until she became more sordid than the event, an interrogator beginning to find the bare bulb erotic, beginning to dream of its heated pear shape, to imagine its place in her bed. She stands naked in the fluorescent bathroom, the limelight rotting. She doesn't want to check herself. She doesn't want to see her bride's bed soaked in red splotches, failing the alchemist's chastity test. If it is true, then she is sterile. The end of the line. He doesn't want kids, anyway, but it had been nice to think that there might be an accident. Something lucky.

Now he is snorting lines off a slick tourist magazine, indifferent to the indifferent showgirl on its cover. She knows he will count three days as precisely 72 hours. There are no clocks in this city. Time is distributed too evenly. The unanointed might catch on that they are never going to get ahead. His watch has malfunctioned and has been beeping steadily since last night, a digital call to arms. The revolution will not be televised, but the Apocalypse will. The coke is burning new holes in his brain, pinprick constellations of charisma. "Praise Jesus!" he shouts, throwing the magazine at the television, leaving it splayed and bent on the floor, like something he never had any use for, never used. "Praise Jesus!" And he sounds like he means it, passionate and stout-hearted and ready for battle.

She traces the three coordinates on the chilled window pane:

1) Home (where they live)

2) Here (where they will get married)

3)That other city south of the border
(where he fucked That Girl and brought home a disease)

She connects the dots, a tortured triangle, the trick question on a geometry test. Vegas and Tijuana are the real suburbs of L.A. She imagines him in that foreign city with That Girl, the one who traded her childhood so he could have affordable sweat shirts and a good squalid fuck for the price of a couple of lunches downtown. Twinkle and rot and whining English that could only seduce a masochist. A collision of have-nots and looky-loos and do-gooders gone bad. Everyone there is rusted through, scraping along the burning streets. Opening doors and children's ragged mouths emit the same excruciating squawk. Nineteenth century diseases hide out under the cantinas, straining their florid, bug-eyed faces, building musculature, gaining confidence, *cajones*, still walking the streets at night, trilling their tongues, trotting to the fevered castanetas, feeding on sailors and cowboys and other devourers, winsome Californians like him. Senora Diseasa getting stronger, more transparent, rushing the border, perfecting her high pitched laugh. Down there, the Virgin Mary is everyone's favorite hometown girl, and She shakes Her gentle blue glowing head at birth control pills, at condoms, She frowns softly at disease. To Her it is only one more nail.

She hopes that That Girl had hissed, "Fuck you, gringo," as she eased his wallet out of his spent volcano pants and left him with his tequila snores. Left him pregnant with a red skinned virus which would cause a scandal when born, since his long term companion was not red.

"Pre-marital sex is a sin!" he explodes. "There's no justification for it. Look at the Pope. Look at—Fuck. I've been lost. I've been sleepwalking. The Pope refuses to be a moral relativist. I promise! Great men were celibate. All the—Jesus Christ. Nietzsche. St. Augustine...." St. Augustine had a wife and child before he devoted himself to fanatic Christianity. She wonders what became of them, the draped woman and her stern little boy fending for themselves at the mouth of the Nile, everything coming to them in scraps, all so the saint could hear the glorious trumpets of deprivation, could make a name for himself among the monks, project action movies starring God on the dank monastery walls, imagining himself in the leading role.

"... Andy Warhol. The Dali Lama. Nietzsche. I'm through with it. I'm— This is it. This is now. I'm changed. It's like my eyes are opened. No more sex til we're married!" He shakes his fist at the hard icing ceiling. It's the wrong gesture. Despite his good intentions, he has not yet mastered humility. "Christ!" he yelps, swiping at his crotch, but refusing to actually scratch. He keeps his eyes on the ceiling, as if it is the embedded sparkles that are causing his discomfort. He won't look.

She doesn't have to look. She is ill. It has curled up in her abdomen, a lippy smile of like-it-is where she used to store her swirling tail of lust. She knows that when the 72 hours are up, he will examine himself and find a spilled snow cone, lumps and red syrup, and he will take her to a wedding chapel as he is: hair matted, glasses splattered, half zipped, distracted. People forgive him almost everything because he is on intimate terms with money. She is in the sorry mob, begging, making promises, trying to impress, and the Bitch Goddess Lucre grows bored, grinds her spiked heel into the desperate foreheads and gallops off. He has the Bitch whipped into a frenzy. He sighs and the Bitch screams. The Bitch often beats down his door in the middle of the night. She's heard it. He treats his Bitch very very well, like gold, gloves on. Always clear headed and safe.

It's strange that they called her gold-digger, all those sour, determined girls who got trapped in their cubicles and waitressing uniforms and retail name tags. She thinks of these girls as victims pinned down in a mining accident, staring up through chinks of light with their doomed, accusing eyes. She escaped the mine. She never digs. The whole point is not to work. She didn't get any gold out of it, no real assets. She was a real girlfriend to all of them, one at a time, faithful and believing in a joint future. She was lazy, though. She can see that now. It shouldn't be called gold-digger. It should be called catnapper. Lazing around, incapable of surviving in any part of the world not covered by his plush carpeting. She called herself a freelancer and took lots of naps. She stayed young and agreeable. She trusted him. She purred and believed she was precious.

She has $1400 of her own. An apartment, the move, security deposit, phone—it will cost more. She could borrow. And then what? Wait in line at County General, analyze her saliva every morning, depend upon the kindness of capitalists. Degenerate from virus red to leprous yellow and soon the anonymous steel blue of a morgue drawer.

He never gambles when he is in this town. The Bitch wouldn't approve. It's the drinks and the shows and the girls that are a good bet. The casinos are for chumps. She decides to go to a casino.

"I have come to the desert!" he proclaims. He is standing on the bed now, testing the springs, scraping his hand across the ceiling, white flakes coming down like bleached oats. If he knew any of the stories, he would recognize that this is his manna, his bread from Heaven, and he would be forced to confront the fact that it tastes like plaster. She makes sure he notices her leaving, even though his eyes are closed. "You should see it," he says without turning around. "It's so beautiful I can't even tell you."

Fuck you, gringo. She does not say it. She cannot afford to.

Outside, the wind wails and scorches, angry that the sand has been paved over. She considers the rows of colored lights and it's hard to distinguish one place from the next. This town has a taste for twins and triplets. She decides on a place that is primarily orange.

The casino is empty, tables sleek and bare, spotted with slender chips, lights flashing in imbecilic cheer, wasting color. She is relieved not to have to watch money changing hands, an act that should be either intimate or digital, not thrust out in the open, wetted fingers, sagging bills worn down to a pale green gasp. Then the panic hits her, a cruel tickle in the same place she itches. She had made up her mind to do something rash, bet it all on the roulette wheel, find out once and for all if luck could continue to hold her. The red and black checkered wheel wags slightly, in the path of the overbearing air conditioning. Her itching rears up, a flare gun bursting. She has no Plan B, no certificates for employment, no safety deposit boxes to pry open, absolutely nothing to cash in. Where is the Bitch Goddess Lucre now that she's greased down and flexing and ready to arm wrestle? It is the ultimate dishonor, the Bitch's failure to show up for the duel. The Bitch doesn't find her a worthy opponent. She doesn't even make an amusing target. She is outraged. She stands utterly still, not even allowed to shake or the itching will get the better of her. She permits herself the indulgence of biting her upper lip. Sweat blooms in strange places, places she didn't realize she could bend. A man, rigid and straining for unctuousness, scurries toward her.

"It's a private party. It's a private party. You'll have to leave."

"I. Am. Ill." She is surprised at how gentle she sounds, how resigned, how like a person who knits. And it's all over, she gives up, sucking her stomach inward, sliding her hand between waistband and concave flesh, a malevolent tug at the simpering panties and she scratches for a full minute, staring straight at him, her features elongating with relief, growing wooden and handsome, a female totem pole. He stares back, horrified but looking.

"They're in the Silver Room." He marches and she sees that he expects her to follow. He glances back, a professional mixture of encouragement and disdain, and she wonders if her youth has ended, if good luck and bad luck will stop swinging wildly at each other, if the mundane laws of the universe will start applying to her, if she will get traffic tickets and discuss hair cuts and have unremarkable sleeps. Then the itching, back again, never left, and she remembers the sickness, the high stakes. The employee tugs open half of a double door and quickly steps aside, giving her a wide berth. His eyes are averted. This is the gingerbread house and he will not cross its threshold. It's dark inside with an orange glow, uninviting but she enters, more stubborn than curious.

People sit in padded chairs, about two hundred of them, arranged in haphazard clumps. This city of unconventional conventions packs them in, disparate humans of every income bracket and dialect and odd obsession conferring for days, heads together, performing their esoteric solvings in rooms named Silver, Tin Pan Alley, Coliseum, Eiffel, Cactus. It looks like a gypsy camp, like there should be fires and mangy dogs and thieving monkeys battering tin cups, shrieking for oily fish. There is a presentation underway, a slide show, narrated by a recording of a male voice, resonant with smugness, a voice that would be photographed head tilted, hair curly, tuxedo at the throat. The slides blink slowly, pictures of brilliant lights glazed in chem lab colors: violet, lime, magenta, many oranges. No one is paying attention. The mood is not boredom, but the same jittery communal complacency found in upscale nursing homes, immobility and polite mirthless chuckles. She tries to listen to the lecture, but it sounds intentionally obscured, too many household nouns, a code hatched by a ten year old for a secret club. "Apple beeswax pan tickertape."

A ruckus starts in the back corner. She moves closer and sees that five of them are playing cards. An old lady is the dealer, the ringmaster. She has the laugh of a blue jay, ruddy skin, wrinkles deep as tribal scars. "You're betting like a bunch of old biddies," the old lady kaws, and she decides she likes this woman, even though she has always despised plain talk before. "Who's gonna make this worth my while?"

She steps up, presents her wad of cash, a radish in time of famine. She has a habit of doing things with a flourish. This is how they behave in the hyperbolic city she came from.

"Go ahead," the old lady sneers. "I'll take ya." There are piles and piles of money behind this old woman, an absurd amount, unsorted, heaped halfway to the ceiling, like a child's vision of a bank. This woman is luck incarnate, patting the green mounds with unabashed greed. And it dawns on her: *this* is the Bitch Goddess Lucre. It was never a succulent mesh-legged rival. It was always this sunburnt hag, crouching canine, body a neglected anthill while her eyes gleam slick with numbers. The other one with her kitty tongue and joyous throat and newly minted nipples was just one of his floosies, never serious money. This is the big game, and she found it while he stayed in and guzzled Jesus. She laughs.

"Ain't nothing funny. Put up."

She bets it all, no hesitation, her life savings, her satin parachute. It is blackjack, the only game she knows, vaguely, and she loses it all in one hand. The Bitch Goddess Lucre swipes away the money with one claw and holds out the other to shake. "No hard feelings. Fair and square." She notices the extra appendage. A third hand, tiny and vital, five purplish fingers grasping and clutching, twirling in the eyeless pleasure of being alive. It juts out to the left of the Bitch's armpit, poking through a thready tear in her sweatshirt. She offers her finger tentatively, expecting a raccoon bite. The little hand grabs her and squeezes, waving in excitement, the infant's triumph: *We are the same and I have found you.* The Bitch is annoyed. "Damn accident," she spits. "Git. Git off." She raps the little knuckles and the fist dissolves, retreats into five wriggling fingers, dispersed and scared.

There's been a mistake. That little fist should be hers, a blossom born of the damp terrain of her young, supple, self-scorned body before the infection. A full baby would probably be overwhelming for a sick person like her. She would be distracted by itching and constant sexual rejection and the jeering threat of an early death. Nature was cruel, but admittedly wise, to make her sterile now. This little hand was an infant scaled down to a manageable portion for an incurably ill single mother, like a door knob placed several feet lower for the wheelchair-bound, or a fruit salad pureed to beige gunk for toothless elderly people. Even in her chronic scarlet condition, she could mother this little hand.

But who is going to believe that the little hand is meant for her, that despite her haphazard, all-or-nothing, freeloading, hand-to-mouth life, she is worthy of this little piece of motherhood? The only plan she can formulate is not to let the little hand out of her sight, ever again. She sticks close to the Bitch.

A bell sounds. Not a mechanical buzz, but a real iron clanging. Chairs scrape and reconfigure. An army of men in white bee-keeper suits jogs in, passes out dinner plates, a precision drill. Then they vanish. They plop a plate in front of her, too, no questions asked. It is fine banquet china, sturdy and diplomatic, abundant with kingly crab legs, vibrant greens, and a slab of steak. She is suddenly ravenous. As she eats, she looks closely at the other people in the room, squinting through the dim light, playing a reverse game of What's Missing. Extras sprout from their bodies, too many noses, eyes, ears, a spare chin affixed to a shoulder blade, an ankle growing out of a neck. Red marbled skin, intricate scabbings, carbonated pools of pus. "Whose party is this?" she asks.

The Bitch Goddess aggressively knifes at her teeth with a cinnamon soaked toothpick. "They bring us all up here once a year for vacation. As if that makes up for it."

"Up here from where?"

"From the site. If you're feebleminded, don't bother me. Go sit over with the rest of them. And don't ask for your money back neither. I won that off you in good faith."

"What are you going to do with that money?"

The Bitch Goddess freezes, a hound picking up a new scent. Only her extra hand is moving, a soft octopus fluttering. "HAW!" she finally pops. "HAW! That's a good point you make. What do I got to spend it on? HAW!" The Bitch Goddess slaps her on the back, but she is yearning for the touch of that smooth little hand, with its oyster stomach palm, already scheming the things she will do to it later on, manicures and Morse Code lessons, fondlings under table cloths, patty cake with wild abandon. "They give us everything. All the best. Is that gonna bring my husband back?" The Bitch's face darkens. The little hand balls up, assuming tornado drill position, a futile attempt to tuck up away from the storm.

"Did he die in the accident? I'm so sorry." A pleasant voice, pleasantries, she's looking out for the defenseless little fist, her cuticled treasure, trying to coax forth a wholesome environment, the TV off during homework hours, sack lunches, enormous-headed drawings magnetted to the fridge, calcium, rope climbing, she will grow it to her specifications, a real prize, sensitive but able to box, a quoter, a yearner, trilingual, stunning in a necktie.

"Die? Don't I wish. He ended up so bug ugly I can't stand to look at him. What is there to do with him now? Go ahead, call me shallow hearted. I never was much of a one for talking. Sure, he got old, but he had a headful of snow white hair and the same eyes as a jackrabbit. He could still go at it, old as he was. Now, his head's…. You've seen a watering pail? He's over there somewheres." The Bitch waves half-heartedly toward nothing, just away from herself. "Goddam this itching! My whole entire leg got it." The Bitch whips out a magnificent instrument, and when she sees it, this tool makes her proud of the human race, exultant over opposable thumbs. A blue backscratcher, a long thin stick with a curved hand at the end of it, a flattened icon of her tiny five fingered object of desire, both devotional and functional, the ingenuity! For the first time in her adulthood, she's glad to be breathing, swollen with optimistic predictions.

The Bitch shifts her weight and sticks the backscratcher down her pants and relieves her scaly thigh. The little hand goes limp with pleasure, and she is sprawling with hope. She has escaped. Here, among the accident victims, she will be only slightly ill and well cared for. The upward thrust of her home city courses through her, she is steeped in drive once more. That little hand will be hers. She will win it, steal it, study scalpels and grafting, she will seduce it over to her body as surely and persistently as she used to dazzle the rent money out of offhand executives like him. She does not have time to say goodbye to him, to go back for her luggage, to trample over his fake-dyed false Bitch Goddess

Lucre the tramp, to gloat. She has fallen in love.

The men in the radioactivity suits reappear, stacking plates and delivering striped pudding, vanilla chocolate vanilla chocolate vanilla chocolate, and clear plastic cups full of pills, strong stuff, not yet on the market, the elaborate offerings of a government swatting away its guilt, playing the stiff, tactful butlers, admitting nothing, catering to everything. She swallows the pills earnestly, eats only the chocolate stripes, dreaming of the day the little hand will grasp the spoon and feed her, tenderly wiping the excess off her lower lip. She dabs at her mouth with the maroon linen napkin, smiles at the little hand, slightly shy, unable to hold it in her gaze for long, she's that smitten, but ready. She straightens up. She turns the more symmetrical side of her face toward it, in case it is watching. She prays for restraint. She gets to work.

"Ma'am? See this ring? I'll bet this ring against your backscratcher."

"My backscratcher? What game?"

But it doesn't matter what game. She doesn't know any of them, and fortune is blooming upward from her itching crotch as the medicinal haze descends and she is going to win. She smiles. It will be a series of victories. She will avenge every game of strip poker she's ever played, adorning herself piece by piece. She will build her dynasty. She folds her trembling hands together in the shape of a church.

***

DISCOVERED

The only thing worse than an aging actor was an aged one. Tilda knew the restaurant was too loud. The entire lunch would be reduced to Millie pretending she could hear, and forging a headstrong monologue to disguise the fact that she couldn't catch a word Tilda was saying. Millie must have chosen this place because it used to be The Place to see and be seen back in the '70s, the decade when Millie's legendary looks began to fade and the plastic surgery started to show in daylight. Millie's style of dress and slang were lodged firmly in the '70s, as if she refused to budge another day distant from the famous beauty she once was. She expected even time to yield to her tantrums.

And there she was, making her late entrance, a stick of a woman in a leopard print pantsuit, flesh colored lipstick coating her sunken little cave of a mouth, heavy Jackie O sunspecs that overwhelmed her petite face like a knight's visor. And that dreadful hairpiece, a platinum blonde fall straight out of one of those old spaceship programs.

Girls from Millie's day would never think of leaving the house without over-dressing. There was a superstitious belief in those days that you could be discovered, that Los Angeles was overrun with ethereal talent agents who would notice you and pluck you from obscurity right on the spot and make you famous. The girls today were more savvy. They knew all the pumps they had to prime before dumb luck would find them. Tilda saw all the gorgeous young hopefuls today, brunching behind sunglasses, looking absolutely shocking, with their undernourished hair unstyled and their shirts unlaundered and their slack blue jeans broadcasting all the rumples of last night's coarse sex. Today it was chic to look like you were already famous and hiding from the media. Everybody now realized that Lana Turner wasn't actually discovered at Schwab's Drug Store. Millie must've known this all along, but her life as a studio star had made her an excellent co-conspirator. She promoted all the official legends, not caring if they were true.

Now Millie stood shaking by the restaurant entrance, cocking her head to and fro, probably blind as well as deaf, but beautiful women from their era never wore glasses. At 78 years old (plus the standard five shaved off her bio), Millie still managed to turn heads when she walked into a room, but now people shook their heads as well, exclaiming inside over the sad eccentric fate of women who stick around Hollywood too long. Nobody recognized her. They couldn't really be blamed. This clownish old lady bore little resemblance to the dewy black and white creature, luminous in her Max Factor fairy dust and close-up filters. Tilda sighed and forced her arthritic knees to stand so she could go meet Millie and escort her back to the table. Millie had been so brainwashed by the old studio that she still couldn't make a move in public without direction.

"You're looking well," Tilda lied.

"Let me tell you, baby, this is a can't-lose deal. The people are starved for glamour. Starved."

"Speaking of starved, why don't we order first?"

"It's all human hair. Yur-oh-pee-in." Millie clearly couldn't hear her at all. She would talk the whole time and Tilda would be expected to listen. Millie had some harebrained scheme for releasing a line of wigs. Tilda thought she meant grey numbers for the geriatric set, who may remember her, but Millie wanted to do high fashion for the young people. Tilda was ostensibly supposed to give Millie business advice, but Millie really only wanted someone to tell her what a good idea she had. Again. Nothing counted for Millie unless it was publicly lauded. Tilda was certain that when Millie was alone in a room, she couldn't even see her own reflection. Millie was so brash and difficult because she constantly felt she was in danger of disappearing. She needed many staring eyeballs—adoring or censorious, it didn't matter—to pin her in place.

Tilda watched Millie's shrunken little head yapping, and she wondered if Millie ever looked in the mirror anymore. They had both been small women in their prime. Now it seemed to Tilda that they had turned rodent-like, tiny and skittish as mice, with never-still jaws. Tilda interrupted Millie, speaking loudly but careful to keep her voice even. Only Millie was allowed to yell.

"It's very difficult to sell to young people. They're incredibly fickle."

Millie pursed her lifeless lips. Folds of excess skin sagged where the surgical plumpness had worn off, forming an obscene Georgia O'Keefe flower where her mouth should have been. She made several futile attempts to spoon her soup, the utensil clanging unnervingly against the deep ceramic bowl again and again, a warning bell on a buoy. Tilda thought Millie was gathering strength for the rest of her soliloquy. But she abandoned the spoon in its watery grave and said, "You think I'm old, don't you?"

"Well, we've both gotten old. There's no cheating time."

"You know what The Agent Boy told me the other day? The funniest thing," Millie paused right on time. She had learned her comic timing from the likes of Billy Wilder, and it was as sharp as ever. The Agent Boy was a kid that William Morris had assigned to Millie as a sort of courtesy. He was what they called a film geek, and he actually knew who Millie was. He always seemed to be hovering like a vulture who'd lost his necktie, showing up at birthday parties on a mission to collect anecdotes. He had an annoying habit of opening conversations with questions like, "So, is it true that Gary Cooper was a lousy lay?"

Millie's real agent, Pesky, had died years ago. Everybody turned out for his funeral, and they all stood around Forest Lawn trying to come up with the most spiteful barb. But Millie had cried like it was her father they were burying, her David O. Selznik black ostrich feather hat trembling with genuine emotion. She must've known it was the beginning of the end for her. Pesky had been Big Bob's agent, too, and Big Bob had wrapped his big bear arm around Millie's little distressed damsel frame, which of course ended up in all the papers the next day. This was just one of the many indignities Millie had managed to heap upon Tilda's marriage to Big Bob.

"The Agent Boy told me," Millie went on, "'It's not so bad getting older, Millie. Now you can actually be Jewish again.'" Millie tittered, which is how girls used to be taught to laugh. Tilda wondered if this were an intentional jab. Tilda had lost her faith after they refused to bar mitzvah Little Big Bob just because he couldn't memorize all that crap. She could vouch for the fact that he had tried his damnedest. He and Big Bob were locked in his bedroom for weeks, drilling the stuff, even though Big Bob wasn't even Jewish. "Hell, it's just running lines," he'd said. But Little Big Bob hadn't been able to master it. Maybe she was being paranoid. Maybe Millie was actually developing a sense of humor about herself after all these years. Her real name was, after all, Mildred Stumstein, from some anti-Semitic little pig farm town in Illinois where her intellectual longbeard father had been the rag picker. They changed her to Millicent Mumford, but Big Bob still called her Mildred to this day. So did Tilda. Every time she said "Mildred," she pictured mildew, hoping Millie would see the accusatory rot in her eyes.

"How is Little Big Bob?" Millie asked, confirming that the Jewish comment had indeed been an underhanded tactic to wound her.

He's 44 years old and they're still calling him Little Big Bob, that's how he is, Tilda wanted to snap. But she restrained herself, even took a bite of her grilled cheese to show Millie that she wasn't gritting her teeth.

Little Big Bob was their battle ground. After Big Bob left Millie for Tilda the mousey (but younger) script girl, Millie made their lives a living hell. Millie was gorgeous when she was enraged, radiant with purpose. Tilda got the feeling she was crossing a Greek goddess and would end up under a cruel, peculiar curse, like growing spider legs or becoming transfixed by her own reflection.

Big Bob was sanguine in the face of Millie's tantrums. He had been married to her for three years and was used to it. "Hell, it's just her way," he'd say. "She's afraid if she quiets down, the people will all go away." Millie once threw a glass of ice water in Tilda's face at a Bing Crosby cabaret show. Big Bob's reaction had been to get up from the table and amble after Millie and spend the next two hours in the kitchen comforting her while Tilda blotted her ill-fitting Edith Head gown with a napkin and everyone's necks went stiff from not daring to look at her.

Things only changed once Tilda gave birth. Millie had tormented her all through her pregnancy, but the minute Little Big Bob let rip his first outraged scream at Cedars Sinai, Millie disappeared. Tilda reasoned that she must've grown bored with the whole thing, or have fallen for one of her gigolos.

But it turned out Millie hadn't retreated. She had recoiled and set up her most vicious strike. One night Big Bob sat Tilda down and announced, "She wants part custody."

"But he isn't her son!"

"The thing is, she's gonna claim that I didn't let her have a kid when we was married, and she's aiming to stir up all sorts of trouble as far as an annulment and like that, and Pesky says it'll be bad press and going to court and airing my dirty laundry and all."

"I can't let that woman near my baby!"

"Hell, it won't really be her. She'll hire some people. A French nanny and all that. He'll be fine. It'll be a little vacation for you."

Tilda had railed mightily against this ludicrous plan, her post-partum hormones caterwauling with a brave new ferocity. She swore she'd kill anyone who laid a finger on her son. She padded around the house pressing Little Big Bob's floppy, soft-boiled infant head to her quilted robe with one hand while the other brandished a butcher knife.

Big Bob didn't try to argue with her. He just made some phone calls.

When the suits filed into her living room, Tilda immediately dropped the knife. She wanted to rush across the room and hide Little Big Bob in the liquor cabinet, but instead she handed the baby over to Big Bob and meekly heeded his suggestion that she rustle up a round of coffee. She would not offer them cream or sugar, a pathetic rebellion lost on monsters like the suits, who had rasped the taste buds off their tongues speaking generations of lies. These were the real sharks of Hollywood, shimmering with an anonymity so perfect it hurt the eyes. Few people were important enough to ever see them. They had the nondescript suits of accountants and the cold tenacity of great whites. They practiced a diabolical form of law, paid for by people rich enough to climb above the judicial system.

They had plenty of practice in family law. The suits had obliterated all traces of the Mexican birth certificates of the missing twins born to Marion Davies and William Randolph Hearst. They arranged for the publicly devout Loretta Lynn to secretly give birth to an illegitimate child fathered by Clark Gable, then adopt her own baby, milking the fanfare for saving an unfortunate orphan. When Cary Grant was finally to be awarded his only Oscar, for Lifetime Achievement, in defiance of the studio he had crossed years before, the suits dug up a call girl to scream paternity suit, driving Grant out of the country so that he missed the awards ceremony. Then they ensured that she vanished when the judge ordered a blood test. The suits orchestrated the change of a baby girl's name from Brando to Blake just before her mother was murdered. The right client could try to flee the country after his ex-wife was fatally stabbed, be found liable for wrongful death and battery, and the suits would still arrange for him to keep custody of his children.

Tilda sat silently as the suits passed around the documents with Millie's name on them. Not one of them brought his coffee cup to his lips. Tilda signed. She was married to a movie star. Her child would never be her own.

The world loved to see their favorites procreate, but Tilda knew that Hollywood offspring were as endangered as newborn guppies. Every time she saw the magazine spreads of a star cavorting with their well-swaddled baby, she shuddered. The occasional columnist grumbled that these people treated their babies like accessories. Tilda knew the truth was far worse. They treated their children like bargaining chips, held them for ransom, got them appraised and re-appraised, gladly traded them when it was advantageous. These people lacked parental instincts because they saw no value in one-to-one relationships. Why cultivate such a puny audience?

"What are you talking—*these people?*" Tilda's mother used to scold. "You're going to be one of them. You think you can join in with people like that and not start acting like them?"

Her father, the failed rabbinical student, would glance up from his Talmudic reading and concur. "How is it possible to be *in* something and not *of* it?"

Tilda wouldn't answer. She just looked at them, at their strained, senseless pride and ingrained smallness. Their surrender to an ancient code of conduct. How could she explain the appeal of Big Bob to two people who were content to disintegrate into dust, leaving no noticeable legacy, as if they had never walked the face of the Earth? They were the only ones who didn't understand.

Despite Tilda's annoyance at her parents, she was troubled by their predictions of her dancing with a herd of satyrs and growing goat's feet. Tilda intended to be different. She would enjoy Big Bob's lavish lifestyle, without surrendering herself entirely to its seductive wash. She would hold tight to her own thorny little stickler personality, her sense of right and wrong. She vowed to remain unswayed by Big Bob's crowd, which was just that: a noisy, jostling crowd, not a circle of friends.

She went in with her good intentions and discovered that these people were impossible to resist. The insular gaiety of their madcap social lives was more convincing than any of their on-screen performances. They were famous because they were captivating. They could capture anything, flay your defenses right off your hide and plunder whatever they wanted from you. They could envelop a person they'd known for five minutes with an understanding so intense it was transformative. You would never be so attractive, so clever, so close to what you were meant to be as when these people fixed you in their shining eyes. She fell in love with them, and they didn't even like her. They would kiss her on both cheeks, then tell Big Bob behind her back that she was a cold fish and he should chuck her. She knew all about these betrayals, yet every time they met face-to-face, these people would easily charm her back. They would squeeze her hand and brush her hair away from her ear and spread out the bright checkered picnic blanket of their enormous confessions, patting the seat beside them. They would lower their voices to the ticklish hush of pillow talk, nestling her with black sheep bleats, until she was sure they were only frightened misfits, crying out for a very specific acceptance, a rare balm that they could somehow sense buried deep inside of level-headed

Tilda, something she had never known about herself, but that she could now feel kindling, inflating, filling her with the roaring, gas-mirage power of a hot air balloon.

The moment they felt her expand, she was doomed. They would break into mean-spirited impressions of her nasal whine. "Biiiig Bahb!" they'd shriek. "Biiiig Bahb! They're ahhhl making fun of me again! Biiiig Bahb! Staaahhp them!" Calling back and forth to each other with the beady eyes of myna birds, getting louder and louder because they were afraid to stop.

Tilda could see that instead of relationships, they had elaborate coercions. She could see this in the same way an opium addict could see that the stuff would kill her eventually. It was always worth taking another hit. These people spent money like it had no value and doled out their approval as if it were the world's most valuable asset. They were cunning withholders, social blueballers. They bounced Tilda up and down like a rubber ball. To them, she was child's play.

Few of these people had played as children, except on vaudeville stages where child labor laws were non-existent, stuffing their outgrown soft-shoes with cotton wool to absorb the bleeding while they croaked through the week's nineteenth performance. Those were the luckier ones. Most of them had been put to work swabbing hotel rooms or scrubbing dishes or swilling hogs as soon as they could stand, all of them so pretty and so poor that any entitled adult could help themselves to a handful.

These people made up for all of this now, seeking fun as if it were vengeance. They folded $100 bills into paper airplanes and sailed them off roof gardens. There was always some kind of bet going, and dirty sabotage was an expected and much-relished element. They bet they could make the next five room service girls cry. The rules had to be amended to disallow pinching. They kidnapped each other's pets. They passed the banquet plates around musical-chairs style until the bawdy jazz tune stopped and someone had to eat poached tilapia with a side of snot. They spent a lot of time on boats, like gangsters seeking the sanctuary of international waters. They ran a 130 foot pleasure cruiser onto the rocks, evacuating the sinking ship with all the splashing brio of a pool party. Millie stripped down to her gossamer slip, the same sheen as the moonlight, and balanced on the deck rail, swaying like a priestess with her ivory arms outstretched, connected to this world only by her curled toes. She dove into the ocean with the eternal vitality of a mermaid.

Tilda scurried around searching high and low for a life preserver, her little crab-apple cheeks huffing with fear as the icy water stung her ankles. She found the ship's sole floatation device and yanked it off the wall, whinnying Big

Bob's name into the cold gales. Big Bob staggered toward her, six bourbons past gallantry. He grabbed the life preserver out of her hands and flung it after Millie, the O of the skidding tube impersonating the O of Tilda's mouth. Millie spit water through her teeth and tinkled a laugh that belonged in a tropical lagoon. The water was 56 degrees. Anyone else would have drowned.

These people kicked and cartwheeled through the freezing torrents cascading onto the deck, crooning the same blue limericks they recited when dipping merrily into a fountain in front of a grand hotel. They pried the grounded prow apart and dragged the wooden planks across the rocks and onto the shore, where they built a bonfire. When the fire rescue showed up, they bossed the captain into letting them all climb aboard and racing them to the nearest beach bar shanty with lights flashing and sirens wailing. The boat had been borrowed from some producer. No one offered to pay for it.

Two of the party were left behind when the overloaded fire engine shilly-shallied off with Big Bob, Millie, and their crowd hanging from every surface like train passengers bound for Calcutta. The two leftovers hadn't moved fast enough, hadn't dared muscle their way onto the sardined vehicle. Tilda and Joe Schmo. Tilda sat on a wet boulder and watched Joe Schmo dig in the sand, desperate to find his wedding ring. Everyone had been playing treasure hunt on the ship, slipping strands of diamonds into flower vases, hanging black pearl rings on toilet roll rods. Tilda had cheated, tucking one sapphire earring into her shoe, where it ripped her stockings and pierced her heel. Joe Schmo had only his 8 karat gold wedding ring, which he was still paying for on installments to Sears Roebuck. He had gotten swept up in the bacchanalia and risked more than all the others combined. These people got their jewels for free, on loan from Harry Winston. If they lost them during their drunken antics, the gossip columns picked up the story and Harry got a million's worth of publicity.

The reward for the treasure hunt was that you got locked in a cabin with the person whose jewels you found, a high-roller version of spin-the-bottle. Joe Schmo had been so hopelessly ensorceled by Millie that his wedding ring had popped off as if catapulted by his very visible erection. Joe Schmo's wedding ring had gone down with the ship, but he was still burrowing in the sand, as if looking hard enough could rewind time to the point before he'd taken it off his finger.

Joe Schmo had been sent by the publicity department. They were constantly sponsoring contests then shipping some yokel to Los Angeles to live with his favorite star for a week. Everyone in Grand Chute, Wisconsin, told Joseph Schmidt that he looked like Big Bob, and discovering what a pale imitation he was when standing side-by-side had knocked the wind out of his sails. This always happened. The contest winners were an imposition. The star would lash unspoken vitriol upon the studio bosses by refusing to charm their houseguest. They would be coldly polite while making it clear that the fan had absolutely nothing—*nothing*, as in not even the same species—in common with them and should never have come. The contest winners moped around the star's house with downmouth, whispering "Yessir" and "No'm" and not looking anyone in the eye. Joe Schmo had had a fearsome sweet tooth, and had preferred to take his meals with Little Big Bob, who was only three years old and would cackle as Joe Schmo clowned around with his bowl of mush and syrup, rubbering his comely features into the grotesque neediness of Harpo Marx.

Joe Schmo collapsed over his sand holes. The ocean spit salty foam in his face, belittling his tears. He lifted his anguished eyes up toward Tilda, the other odd one out, a whipping girl in the cold wind, stung by the violent flapping of her wet silks and fallen hair. "How do you take it?" he asked.

Tilda could take it because she knew Big Bob was different from the rest of them. He had fallen into acting when he was on leave from the Navy and a mincing Viennese exile director had seen him striding out of an Olympic Boulevard tattoo parlor, bare-chested, fanning himself with his shirt. The director read Big Bob's freshly-inked heart, beaded with droplets of blood: THROB. He fell topsy-turvy in love. Big Bob thought it was all a tremendous joke, and he glided to greatness on the vibrations of his inner belly laugh.

It was the soaring aspiration that twisted the rest of them. Big Bob didn't have this. He never participated much in his crowd's exploits. He just hung around, at ease but unmoved, as if he had gone to great lengths to purchase box seats to an opera but the music wasn't to his taste. He was a normal indifferent father, laconic and tolerant, never raising a fuss when Tilda asked him to watch Little Big Bob. He didn't play with his son, nor did he teach him any bad habits. He would study his scripts while Little Big Bob crawled quietly at his feet, gnawing on his own fists. Big Bob treated his son as he would a footstool that needed to be presented with a warmed-up dinner plate at six.

Tilda was sure that Millie, on the other hand, was a corrupting influence. After the suits named her a third legal guardian, Little Big Bob spent his summers with Millie, skiing in Switzerland or laking in Maine. Tilda suspected that her son was exposed to every sort of debauchery. Millie and Big Bob's crowd was majestically bisexual and unapologetically perverse. This was not because they were particularly exploratory or tormented by fetishes. They were merely practicing the special privilege of those who go from rags to riches: They would never again have to choose one thing over the other. They did it all, every which way.

Tilda had never been tempted by such hedonism. Her father's shabby little Judaica shop had been forever on the verge of bankruptcy. She grew up to be a hoarder, not an indulger. Once they were married, she thought of Big Bob's money and status as a security, not something to be enjoyed. When she and Big Bob returned from their honeymoon (a disappointing, low-budget quickie trip to Puerto Vallarta, arranged by Pesky to evade the hostile press. It had been brain-boilingly hot, the beaches bleached as teeth, so she napped the days away while Big Bob wandered the streets)—and when they returned to take up residence together at Big Bob's fortressed Bel Air estate, she set the table with her sturdy old chipped dishes.

"Let's have them fancy plates they sent for our weddin," Big Bob demanded.

"Oh, those are too good to use every day."

"Too good to use?" he snorted, incredulous. "Hell, *nothin's* too good to use."

When Millie had been Big Bob's wife, she had encouraged his insatiable appetite for comfort. Tilda reeled when she took over the household accounts. Millie had tried to spend every last penny in pursuit of sensory pleasures. Tilda tabulated the list of imported champagnes and rare-spice mud baths and costume balls that cost more than college tuition. Nothing Millie bought remained. She had consumed it all.

Tilda fretted over every minute Little Big Bob was in Millie's so-called care. When Little Big Bob would return in the fall, Tilda would strip him down and examine every inch of him under an intense floor lamp, searching for signs of abuse. He would be a bit fatter, but there was never any evidence of foul play. Tilda kept up these examinations until he was fourteen years old, when he had taken off his clothes as ordered, then yelled at her, "You'd be happy if there was something wrong with me!"

"Little Big Bob, I'm trying to protect you."

"You don't even know what you're looking for." And he had walked naked to his bedroom and slammed the door. Big Bob stood in the living room with his arms crossed and didn't cock an eye as his son passed by *en flagrante* and steaming like a bulbous cauliflower. Tilda thought she saw a look of collusion pass between them, but she knew she had imagined this. Big Bob was far too intellectually lazy to form any collusions. Like most actors, he went ahead and put his bad behavior on public display and received adoration for being misunderstood.

"Little Big Bob is doing quite well," Tilda finally answered Millie, after reviewing her flip book of past injuries in a silence that carried no weight for her self-absorbed companion. Tilda speared her dill pickle, imagining that the spurt of green cucumber seeds was a nasty plague she could cast upon Millie. "He's still working with the Indian children in North Dakota."

"I spoke to him on the horn last week," Millie revealed, all undertones and subtext. Tilda's first thought, even before: *She's plotting with Little Big Bob!*, was: *She's only pretending to be deaf. She can hear me fine. She just wants to get out of pretending to listen.* Tilda and Millie had buried the hatchet somewhere along the way, but Tilda had never truly ended her quest to find some definite offense that Millie could be punished for.

"Oh?" Tilda asked carefully. "What did he say?"

"I'm bringing him on as Executive in Charge of Production."

"For what?"

"For the wig deal."

"But... Little Big Bob isn't a businessman. He's out in North Dakota—"

"He's agreed to come back. In fact, he should be in town by now."

The bitch. Tilda had been begging Little Big Bob to come home for years. She had single-handedly built up Big Bob's production company into a force to be reckoned with. At one point, in the early '60s, they were producing five television programs, mostly variety shows that don't get syndicated, but now that cable television needed to fill all that time, the money was rolling in again, and there were all kinds of things to do. She was old and tired, and Big Bob himself had never been interested in the business side of things. Tilda had always planned to turn the reigns over to Little Big Bob, but he had fled to his Indians and wanted nothing to do with Hollywood. She had visited him at that bleak reservation with its tarpaper and alcoholic bloat and had cried for weeks afterward at the sheer waste of it all. Now Millie picks up the phone and he comes trotting back to help her scalp some Eastern Europeans, probably war refugees selling their hair for food.

"Little Big Bob can't run a business, Mildred."

"Why can't he? He's got a tremendous head for figures. I remember how he used to fool with that chemistry set."

Tilda remembered it, too. She remembered waking up at two in the morning and finding Little Big Bob in the kitchen bare-chested and pyjama-bottomed, holding a beaker up to the light with a dazed expression on his face. She had to clear her throat and even then he moved slowly, as if his mother and her kitchen and the entire house were inconsequential and not yet proven.

Big Bob had the same affectation of staring off into the middle distance, but for him it was a method. His unseeing gaze added an expansiveness to the cramped sets and inane scripts that were always straining to contain his brawny frame. Once Lolly Parsons had asked Big Bob what he was thinking of when he gave the camera his trademark faraway look, and he had answered, "Canada."

Little Big Bob, on the other hand, didn't have the edge of his father's accidental wit. He was clutching that chemistry beaker the same way a baby grabs something to orient itself in the overwhelming flow of stimuli that is everyday life. He hadn't the first idea about chemistry. He was just daydreaming. Her son was the type who got out of bed in the middle of the night to daydream.

"He's never done anything like run a company. He isn't… astute." There. Millie had tricked her into insulting her own son. A wolven smile flickered across Millie's collapsed pumpkin mouth as she acknowledged the kill.

"You don't even know your own son."

It was worse than the ice water. Tilda stood abruptly and would liked to have stormed out of the restaurant, but her limp made her exit pitiable, and she felt Millie's gummy smile on her sloping back, revelling in her retreat.

At home, Big Bob was stretched out in his recliner as always. Tilda paced around him and he could tell she was angry, but he didn't ask. She wondered if he had ever asked her anything. He hadn't even proposed interrogatively. He had said, "It's about time we was married." Tilda was still looking forward to the day when the urgency would leave her relationship with Big Bob. They should be settled and complacent by now, or bored and split up. It was always like they had just met and were testing the waters, deeply enamored but afraid of each other, vulnerable to outside forces. Tilda was sure this was because of Millie and her constant meddling, the way she had turned that whole crowd against Tilda and tried to usurp her son. There was always something dangerous between Tilda and Big Bob. It was ridiculous at their age. She decided she would not mention Millie. It only gave Millie the upper hand, and Big Bob would be patently noncommittal and she would end up seething and blowing her blood pressure through the roof. She sat down and counted to ten. When she opened her eyes, she noticed a lumpy garment bag heaped by the flagstone fireplace.

"Little Big Bob is home?"

"In the kitchen."

It was just like Big Bob not to tell her their son had arrived, and just like the two of them to sit in separate rooms.

She found Little Big Bob slumped over the kitchen counter, shuffling a stack of saltine crackers into different arrangements. He looked chubby as ever, but his eye sockets were deep and ringed. She blurted out, "Are you sick?" without meaning to.

"Hello, Mom." He straightened up to his full height and Tilda stood on tiptoes to peck his cheek. His skin was still baby soft.

"How long have you been here? Are you hungry?"

Little Big Bob shrugged, equally unsure about both questions.

"I could set up a few meetings for you if you'll be staying long. We could really be placing more syndication rights, negotiating better deals, if there was someone to do it full time."

"I'm here about the hair thing."

"Right, but as long as you're here—"

"My poetry class made you this." He nodded toward a childish watercolor painting of mountains and a sun magnetted to the refrigerator.

"Oh," she said. "Oh, my. How vibrant. And did they make one for Daddy, too?"

Little Big Bob grimaced. "It's kind of for both of you," he said. Then he wandered out of the room, leaving his crackers behind. She nervously ate them up, picturing herself as a neurotic little mouse who might be discovered at any moment and swatted out of the kitchen. Though who would do this she didn't know. Big Bob and Little Big Bob took no interest in anything.

That night she leaned over Little Big Bob's twin bed with the blue ship sheets and kissed his forehead. He suddenly grabbed her hand. "Stay?" he asked. She sat beside his bed and stroked his fleshy hands until he fell into a restless sleep. She was happier than she'd been in years.

The next day, Millie came over and she and Little Big Bob locked themselves in the den for over an hour. Tilda tried to interrupt their powwow by bringing them a tray of lemonade, but Big Bob saw her coming from his recliner and said, "For God's sake, woman, let them be."

"They might be thirsty."

"Hell, Tilda, what is it you think they're up to in there?" She blinked and breathed, embarrassed by her suspicious mind. Big Bob kindly saved her. "The guy who needs some of that lemonade is me."

She poured two glasses of lemonade and sat with him for a time. He slurped but didn't speak. Tilda looked at him with the frank eye of a merchant's daughter. He was still handsome in a crumbling way. His pendulous earlobes and cheeks and chin appeared weighted down by a life spent in public service or high treason or hardscrabble ranching—a life he had not lead, but had imitated on film. He was just a big casual lug who had fallen into a rabbit hole of good luck. She couldn't keep blaming him for her disappointments. The production company had never been put in her name, for example. It just wasn't done at the time. The fact that their son had inherited all of his vagueness and none of her shrewdness. And Millie. Why had he married such a scorpion? What kind of fool would fail to see how she would poison his life? There was no use asking him. He had no capacity for self-reflection.

"What are you always contemplating in this chair?" she asked. "Canada?"

"What?"

"Never mind. At least you're not out running around behind my back."

"I don't get it," he said. "Canada? Who do we know in Canada?"

Millie flounced over and kissed Big Bob on the lips before she left, but he didn't even bother to get out of his chair. Tilda was sure she saw a tug of embarrassment cross his face. Millie looked so ghoulish these days that even Big Bob was no longer enchanted.

Millie, of course, couldn't leave it at that. "He's the only boy I ever loved," she sighed, her apricot colored fingernails digging into Big Bob's plaid shoulders. "Though I don't know if he ever truly loved either of us best, Tilda." Big Bob shifted uncomfortably in his chair and cleared his throat. "But who needs old King Frog here when I have my prince?" and she pinschered at Little Big Bob's shirt front. Then Little Big Bob solemnly escorted her out to her car.

"She's still got a big mouth," mumbled Big Bob. It was the first time Tilda had ever heard him insult Millie.

"What?" she asked, for confirmation. But Big Bob just stared silently at the ceiling. There was no tension in the air. Just absence.

"Well, I'm glad to see you're finally developing some powers of observation." Tilda didn't care if he heard her or not. She was in the best mood of her entire married life. She launched a serious house-cleaning project, spurred on by the marvellous old songs humming through her brain, ballroom numbers from when she first met Big Bob and he passed her from friend to friend, Tilda spinning from one handsome silver screen idol to the next, their beautiful faces arched in curiosity as they sized her up, their feet politely compensating for her starstruck stumbles. The music swelled and she swooned into their customized flattery. With every beat, she ticked off one of the millions of jealous girls she had bested. She hadn't started from much, but there must have been something special about her. She must have been pretty once, though she hadn't believed it at the time.

That night, she went to Little Big Bob's room to tuck him in again. He jumped when she entered, and she saw him scoot a box under the bed.

"What've you got there?"

"Stuff. From when I was a kid."

She bent down to read the box. Her inflamed knees screamed. "Your old erector set? I don't remember you playing with that one much."

"I hated it."

"It's not your cup of tea." She straightened, swallowing a groan, and kissed his forehead. "I thought maybe I'd read to you tonight. *The Wind in the Willows*. You always loved Mr. Toad."

"I'm not tired yet," he said. Then he sat Indian style on his bed and closed his eyes.

"You're turning into an Indian yourself," she said.

"Native American," he murmured, without opening his eyes.

Tilda watched him for a minute then left the room. She wanted to ask Big Bob if he thought their son was strange. With all the mental diseases they had nowadays, maybe he had one of those. Surely there was a pill. But Big Bob was already asleep. He exhaled a long mournful moan that sounded like a shack leaning. Making noise in bed wasn't like him at all.

Little Big Bob floated on an inner tube in the pool and Big Bob lounged in his chair, two poles of inertia around which Tilda was a whirling dervish of activity. She sent the maid out grocery shopping and continued cleaning the house top to bottom herself. She was sure her two boys weren't offering to help because they just didn't notice, both of them staring off at his own personal horizon.

Little Big Bob's ship sheets were soaking wet, and for an instant she was afraid he was back to wetting the bed. He had developed this habit when he was inappropriately old, around eleven. Tilda blamed it on some gin-soaked trauma he must've witnessed at Millie's, but she could never prove anything. To her relief, the dampness on the sheets was just excessive perspiration. She *tsk*-ed and stripped the bed.

She ran her broom underneath for dustballs, and banged into the erector set. She flung it down on the bare mattress ticking and was about to balance it on top of the Monopoly in the closet, when she opened the box and peeked inside, to make sure Little Big Bob had replaced all the pieces. The little metal thingies were all jumbled up, of course. Tilda dumped them out on the bed so she could arrange them by size. The cardboard lining of the box fell out, too, along with the photos that had been hidden underneath.

The photos were so grainy and dim that none of the subjects looked familiar. She held one up to the light. It was mostly of someone's skin. Terrible composition. Whoever had taken these shots must've been three sheets to the wind. She flipped through the stack. Sometimes you could tell it was a little boy. Then the little boy was holding an erect penis.

The photos dropped to the floor and waited for her with sinister patience. She could either put these photos back in the box and close the lid, or she could examine them until she had some explanation for why her son would have these pictures. She looked out the window at Little Big Bob floating lazily in the water, suspended in time. She said a quick prayer over him, offering an atheist's bargain, and locked the bedroom door.

There were really only two pictures that told what was going on, one with the penis in hand, and an extreme close-up of the little boy's mouth wrapped around the tip. Was it a little Indian boy? No, he was pale and chubby. The pictures were in color but had an old fashioned white border around the edges, a spiffy touch that seemed intentionally mocking. Then she noticed the boy's pyjama bottoms. Blue ships. She looked over at the anxiety-soaked ship sheets piled beside the bed. She leaned forward and vomited all over the fleet, retching so hard her stomach turned into a strongman game at a county fair, someone was pounding her with a hammer and a heavy disk was rising slowly up her esophagus over and over. She dabbed the sour saliva from her mouth and looked out the window. Little Big Bob was still floating in the pool, unchanged. She slammed the photos back into the erector set box and carried it with her as she ran out of the house, limping every third step.

Tilda banged on Millie's door so hard her bony palm split open. The door was opened by one of the small dark Spaniards they had all been reduced to, no loyalty or discretion, no intention of remaining servants for long. Tilda grabbed the maid's caramel arm and flung her out of the house. She darted inside and locked the door.

Tilda stood panting in Millie's dim entry hall, clutching her stomach cramp with her bleeding hand. Her overtaxed knees popped, threatening to collapse. She was disoriented by the bespoiled state of the place. The '70s glamour was now cobwebbed and spit-shined. Millie's days of grand entrances, slithering down the mirrored spiral staircase onto the silver and gold tiles, were over. Millie had closed the top floors of her fake castle and moved her boudoir— where she watched TV and ate her meals and made her dwindling phone calls, but never slept, never made romance—to the ground floor. Now she emerged from the shadows, testy and ridiculous in a purple silk kimono with matching turban that only accentuated the fact that she was bald underneath. Tilda hurled the erector set at Millie. The hard edges of the box struck Millie in the chest, and she toppled backward, but didn't scream. "For fuck's sake—" she protested.

Tilda stepped over her and glared into her ruined face, the skin sliding every which way, no longer part of the act. She had a systematic plan to torture Millie with cleaning supplies and noxious food mixtures. It would take her days to die. She tried to drag Millie to her feet, but slipped and fell down beside her.

"What? What?" sputtered Millie.

Tilda grabbed one of the photos, a hopelessly blurry one, and thrust it at Millie's washed-out eyeball. But Millie must've seen these photos, or something like them, before. She instantly recognized it.

"Oh God. Oh dear God. You found out."

"You ruined him," sobbed Tilda. "My beautiful boy. You will die for this, Mildred."

"I will—? No, baby, no, no. He was like that before me."

"Shut up!" screamed Tilda. The force of her voice ripping through her lungs knocked her back again. "Stop talking!"

Millie's gnarled, shaky hands rooted around in the photos, bringing each one to her face before summarily tossing it aside. *The same way she disposes of people,* Tilda thought. She clamped down on Millie's hand, marsupial and curled as a chipmunk's paw, and wrested a photo away from her.

"These were taken—" Millie began.

"SHUT UP!"

"I wasn't there. Look at the ring, baby. Look at the ring. It was all on your watch." Then Millie shut up, for the first time ever. Tilda listened to Millie's crowded breathing, too much life forcing its way through her passages, and wondered if she were being tricked again. She got on her hands and knees and found the photo she had pulled out of Millie's grasp. The man's hand on the boy's bare back. So what? She peered at the man's gold ring. It had a big marquis diamond flanked by a cluster of rubies. It matched her wedding ring.

Tilda sat quietly, holding the photo tightly while the world stirred around her and all the atoms in everything solid dispersed into a swarm of charged specks, dates and times and people zinging around with no rhyme or reason, lighting up in some triumphantly random sequence. She watched Little Big Bob clutch his chemistry beaker late at night, and she felt so endlessly sorry for thinking he had been born slow and dim. He was only hoping the little glass tube could be his carousel pole as he desperately tried to catch his balance.

"He always liked boys," pronounced Millie, enunciating sharply.

This isn't a Chekov play, you bitch, thought Tilda, though she shouldn't have blamed Chekov when the whole thing had the tawdry shock of dinner theatre murder mystery performed in the round. This was her son, her poor custody-shuffled son, his life ruined. She wanted tragedy in a grand proscenium. Instead she had these haphazard photos of her husband abusing her son inside neat little white frames, like TV sets, as if it were all as immaterial as something fleeting across the airwaves.

"Who knew?" Tilda asked softly.

"What do you mean, who knew? Everybody knew. Everybody that had anything to do with his career. Except for you, and I suppose he needed someone simple on his arm. I mean, he likes women, too—the small, skinny ones, that is." She flicked her cobra eyes over Tilda's spare, boyish frame, as if she herself had not always had the same unfeminine physique, all of her curves added by the camera and its light tricks, by the audience and its need to add contours to a flat projection. Millie's allure had always depended upon collaborators. "It's just that he has that little deviance."

All those years. People laughing behind her back. Cringing. Procuring teenage hustlers off Santa Monica Boulevard. All of this parading under her nose while she made the breakfast and counted the money. And her son....

She had believed that Big Bob was different.

Her father looked up from his sacred recitations, looked across the years and into her eyes. His humble devoutness had crystallized into something substantial and lasting, something shining. Something she had missed. "How is it possible to fall into stardom?" Tilda's father posed, peering over his steepled fingers. "Falling would be the wrong direction."

She heard Big Bob's bass whisper, tilted with mischief: "*Sssshhhh.... Don't let her find out.*" But he wasn't saying this *about* Tilda. He was saying it to her, back when he was still married to Millie and romancing Tilda in secret.

In the master bedroom of the mansion that was not yet Tilda's, the young Millie collapsed on the bed, losing her shape as naturally as a jellyfish, crying her eyes out over her stolen husband and unborn children; over all the smiles she would have to manufacture for the public out of sheer will and bald mimicry because she had never, not for one minute, experienced happiness; over her terrifying foreknowledge that her looks would fade and she would end up more alone than any unnoticed person had ever been. Tilda had never given Millie's feelings a moment's thought. She had convinced herself that Millie didn't have any feelings. She had wanted what Millie had and had seized it. She had eagerly lain down with a scorpion. What did that make her?

The ocean roared its cold dark wake-up call into Joe Schmo's face. He looked up at Tilda, who was sitting on a wet boulder, forgotten by her husband. "How do you take it?" he asked.

Tilda's father tutted at her, disapproving. She had changed the words, flubbed the line. Presumed to alter the text.

That night when the boat sank, burying all those precious jewels and one cheap wedding ring on the ocean floor, Joe Schmo hadn't asked Tilda, "How do you take it?" He had asked, "Why did you take it?"

While those people monkeyed all over the ship, cramming their treasures into hidey holes, Tilda leaned close to Joe Schmo, who was looking glumly out over the deck rail, hoping to spot land, trying to see clear back to Wisconsin. She squeezed his hand, brushed his hair away from his ear, lowered her voice to the ticklish hush of pillow talk. She convinced him that if he gave her his wedding ring, she would guarantee that Millie would find it. He would win an episode of hanky-panky in a locked cabin with one of the world's most lusted-after women. He, Joe Schmo, of Grand Chute.

Still, he had hesitated. He said no. He said no again. And again. His voice was high and tight in that curdled back-home buttermilk accent and he kept repeating the word as if he were picking a single sharp banjo string. Tilda stood there with her hand out, offering him a trade she knew she couldn't fulfill. The moist night air rang with squeals and slams while the wine-spill of a sultry torch song flowed from the phonograph. The wind Februaried over their skins in cold gusts. The waves lapped. The boat rocked hypnotically. Tilda brushed her bow mouth against Joe Schmo's sunburnt earlobe. *"This doesn't count,"* she whispered. She shrugged her bare elfin shoulders and awarded him a goofy smile, the same soothing clown face she had seen him give her little son, a smile she had stolen from him. Joe Schmo gently placed his ring on her palm, as if he were resting it on a pillow at the starting end of a wedding aisle.

Tilda closed her fist over Joe Schmo's wedding ring. She walked off. When she rounded the corner of the deck, out of his sight, she tossed the ring into the sea. It hit the water with a *plish* too tiny for Tilda to hear.

This was the type of joke they played on that boat. He should learn to take it. Tilda plucked up the words she would use to tell the story later. She would make those people laugh. She would make them admire her.

But the whole boat sank, turning Tilda's story into a drowned rat. She never told anyone. It was a total loss.

The next day, Joe Schmo abruptly packed up and left. Big Bob was off on one of his long golf rounds with his favorite caddy. Joe Schmo took Little Big Bob's fat little hand and gave him a manly shake. Then he squeezed his own nose, mouthed, "Honk honk," and planted a swat on Little Big Bob's fanny. Tilda yanked her son firmly out of his grasp.

He reached for Tilda and she jumped back with a squawk. He only grabbed her hand, intending to kiss it. He had never tried this move before, one of the gestures he had admired and studied at the pictures. He misjudged, clobbering his nose with Tilda's knuckles, knocking off his sweat-stained hat. Tilda thought she felt him bite her wedding ring, the fat almond diamond and caviar nest of rubies that cost so much and promised so little. She felt his slobber murking her shine. She drew back her hand and gripped herself in a little fist. She was afraid of Joe Schmo. Afraid he had gotten wise to her, that his bumpkin frost had melted and he was brewing his red hot revenge. She was afraid he would be back.

Joe Schmo left with his cardboard suitcase, a carry-all too small to fit a pair of men's shoes. Little Big Bob scampered to the big front window and waved and waved, slapping the glass with his palms. Tilda grabbed her son by his shoulders and spun him around to face her. "What did that man do to you?" she asked. She grilled Little Big Bob, asking if Joe Schmo had touched him or looked at him funny. She insisted that they re-enact the horsey rides Joe Schmo had given the boy on his back, pressing Little Big Bob to show her exactly where Joe Schmo had put his hands. *There? Or there? What about here?* Little Big Bob ground his fists into his eyes and burst into tears.

Tilda called the police, who had a special fast-track procedure for high-profile citizens like Big Bob. They nodded gravely as she squeaked out her vague suspicions and appealed to them to bring in Joe Schmo for questioning.

The police returned in three days, craning their necks past Tilda, hoping to catch a glimpse of Big Bob, who had made himself scarce. They had bad news. They were unable to locate Joe Schmo. He hadn't returned to Grand Chute, Wisconsin. They assured Tilda they would keep an eye out for him, taking the alleged assault on Big Bob's assets as seriously as they would the national defense.

This outcome satisfied Tilda. She already felt silly for having feared that country mouse. Joe Schmo had committed the only Hollywood sin: he failed to make a lasting impression. The emotions he had stoked in her quickly vanished. She couldn't even picture his face.

Tilda knew what happened to Joe Schmo. He had been too ashamed to return home without his wedding ring. He had checked into a transient hotel downtown, determined to use his pretty face to earn a new ring and enough pride to return to his hometown and childhood sweetheart. The city opened its maw and absorbed him. He became one of the innumerable pretty people who flock to Los Angeles only to find out that for some reason, they just aren't pretty enough to earn money with their pants on.

Joe Schmo would slink along the baking sidewalks in front of the big hotels, slip into rented cars with meaty business travellers, take what they paid him and spend it on cheap wine to blot out what he'd done. He would eventually grow old, faster than the rest of them. His hand would become too shaky to use his shaving razor. His boyish mouth would bristle, and his Hollywood career would be over. He would droop on benches, his brain cacophonied by traffic, breathing in exhaust fumes, spurting shaving foam into his palm and licking it up, intaking enough alcohol to keep himself alive so he could get up and weave to the corner store for more shaving foam.

Tilda knew what had happened to Joe Schmo, and she knew where to find him. She could have tracked him down easily, or paid the suits to do it. She could have bought him five wedding rings and a first class ticket home. She could have gotten him a bit part on one of Big Bob's shows. Or she could have had him killed. She never considered doing any of these things. Joe Schmo simply didn't count.

Only now, at the age of 68, did Tilda discover who she really was. She was as arrogant as the worst famous person, hell-bent on pleasing herself, blind to the suffering of everyone else. She was restricted to a smaller scale than those people, that was all. In her own little realm, she was a star. The famous were empty vessels. Whatever it was they shined forth, they had stolen it from us. They were only imitating us. Look at them and you are looking into a magnified mirror. We distract ourselves by loving or hating them while our own houses fall, assailed from within.

The problem with getting old could be summed up in two words: TOO LATE. Tilda couldn't save her son. Or Joe Schmo. She couldn't stop her husband. She couldn't apologize to her parents. The one person to whom she could possibly make amends was Millie. Millie, whose life-sustaining pool of adoration had shrunk to people dying in oxygen tents in Palm Springs and adjustable beds on the Upper East Side and electroshock nursing homes in St. Louis. Millie, who noticed how everyone scattered when her hair thinned, who took this as confirmation that the sheet of ice rinking her insides would always remain uncarved by any blade, would always be slick and numb. Millie, who prolonged her ravenous existence by feeding on the devotion of her very last genuine admirer, a manchild who she pretended had not been abused into a half-wit waster. Millie was connected to this world only by the curled toe of

Little Big Bob.

The 83 year old Millie sensed the evaporation of Tilda's rage. She stretched out her vein-engraved body, as if she were still an unattainable coquette in a white negligee balancing on the deck rail of a yacht. She held up one of the awful photographs. "Who's the kid?" she asked casually. "Do you know him?"

Tilda sat silently, thinking carefully about her answer, tossing her son's name up and down in her head like a poker chip.

***

ONCE REMOVED

Chiefton's dad won an Oscar and his mom is an enduring Billboard chart-topper with her own posters and calendar who stared down from the bedroom wall with hazel I-dare-you-to eyes at an entire generation of boys as they had their first wank. He is celebrity once removed. None of us have to work, but the rest of us are working too hard anyway, trying to wear the right colors and find the newest diet and to always sleep with someone more impressive than the one before, and most of all to come across like we don't care about any of it, like we could go someplace where nobody knows our family names and be just as bored.

Chiefton actually doesn't care. We all tried to look rugged for this trip into the desert, but Chiefton's the only one who actually didn't shower. There's some kind of pillow fuzz trapped in his overgrown black hair, and on him it looks like proof of time travel, like he lives in an age when he rides stallions and sleeps in the forest and carries an iron sword so heavy it takes both hands to hold it. He stretches. His muscular limbs and careless blue t-shirt expand past the black rectangle of his hard school bus seat, and it seems like he's going to keep unfolding and unfolding until his body floods the entire bus. He catches me staring at him—well, actually, he *chooses* to catch me, because everyone is always staring at him, and he could look back at anyone he wants. He gazes into my eyes and yawns and I panic that he can see through me, that he knows one of the networks is developing a morning talk show with my mom and me, just because I'm related to her. I sit in the meetings and won't say a word. They keep bringing me different combinations of drinks, asking my mom, "She doesn't like bubbles? Get her some ice. Does she like ice? Ice and flat water. What about tea? What flavors we got?" I chew my gum then stick it on the side of the glass, a hardening brain, ridgey and pink. Later, on the phone, they tell my mom that I obviously have a Zen thing going on, besides being gorgeous with the family genes. I'll be counter-programming to the chirpy type of teenage girls on the other stations. I'll be alt-alt. "Does she do the tarot or the feng shui?" they ask my mom. She assures them that I'll learn.

Chiefton can't stand strivers, he won't have anything to do with anybody who wants to be industry in any way, shape, or form. Paprika reaches around and pulls Chiefton down below the seat back, where I know she'll feed him tabs of X off her tongue. I stare at the scuffed seat with sober hatred that seems to turn into a pounding sound. Then I notice that there *is* a pounding sound, but I didn't think of it first. Somersault has been crunched up right behind them and kicking Chiefton's seat with a viciousness so deep it's turned rhythmic, so it will be easier to make it go on forever.

Is Somersault my ally? All I can see of her is one skinny sunkissed leg, folding then bringing the bare foot *SPLAT* on the seat back, over and over. It's the sort of shot you'd start a movie with, and have every person in the audience dying to pry back the seat and get a look at the bewitching creature with the pendulum leg. I immediately feel guilty for thinking about stupid movies. I read a lot to try to block out all the mass media garbage I grew up with. I look around the bus, and they're all thinking of something, smiling at whirling hallucinations, not one person looking out the window at the craggy brown landscape. We're mostly beach creatures. Joshua Tree is too prickly for me. Dried-up places seem angry, like people who think too hard about sex. It's Chiefton who insists that we go to the desert. He says it's clean.

I try to look out the window, but it's blinding white, and my eyes eagerly wait for each yellow diamond-shaped road sign with the twisting arrow, so what's the point? I'll never appreciate nature. We all hate the desert. We're just waiting for our chance. The old school bus lurches and makes a clattering racket with every bounce. The epicenter feels like it's right below my bony ass. My hard seat assaults me over and over again. This bus is not so much a vehicle as a machine for producing headaches. If any of the rest of us had planned this trip, we'd have gotten a plush charter bus with adjustable airplane seats and a keg. Chiefton is into unadornment. If you live a simple life, he tells us, you can only gain, never lose.

I look around at the other supposed non-strivers. There are about twelve of us not counting Somer, all spread out on the bus, preferring to sit beside gaping backpacks overflowing with distracting stuff instead of sitting with each other. Towels around heads, iPods plugged in, washing pills down with Gatorade, smiling at blank seat backs, nobody is over 20, but I get the feeling that we're all waiting to die. We've been traveling in a pack for a long time, ever since we started going out at night and found out that people do not react to us in the same enchanted, prostrate way they had always thrown themselves at our parents, but that we could never quite be part of a crowd, either. If it weren't for Chiefton and his natural leadership abilities and his anti-industry message, I would be shooting up in some obvious club while songs from the '80s whose lyrics I'd messed up as a child synthed through the speakers and slides of my mom and all my friends' parents in their prime flashed on the wall with their big hair and obvious jewelry, wearing grins that taunted us with the fact that we'll never get laid as much as they did back in those days. I look at all the kids on the bus, the uneven sprinkling of famous body parts, the unmistakable eyes, the million-dollar nose, the world-renowned legs, the dimple that charmed the universe, all wasted on these slumped-over humans, specimens from the second or third generation, who are missing charisma or talent or ambition. I wonder what we have ever talked about, and can't think of a single conversation worth remembering. What did we even have in common outside of the accident of our births into industry families? We all have strange names, but our parents were self-conscious about it and looking over their shoulders and missed the target somehow and we all sound like things that can be ordered out of a catalogue: Gem, Florette, Basque, Snipper, Lolly, Spats, Cane, Pike, Lariat, Chapel, Paprika, Chantilly. Only Chiefton and Somersault's parents got it right, as usual, because they could give a fuck what anyone would think of the names they chose. When Somer was born, the L.A. news interrupted a college sports report to go live to the hospital. Maybe it was listening to her dad bellow at the paparazzi with the voice of a warrior when she was just an infant leaving the hospital that made Somer so mean.

In my backpack is a rolled-up magazine with a page folded back to mark a fashion spread featuring Paprika with her torso wrapped in a sheet, wearing thigh-high lacies. She is arching her back as if someone's telling her to be either a cat or a coat hanger. You can see the big round photo lights reflected in her eyes, which make her seem obvious and desperate, the same as if she left the price tags on her clothes. If I show the ad to Chiefton, he'll be so disgusted that he'll never touch her again, which doesn't mean he will finally notice me. Chiefton thinks of everybody else the way dogs think of humans: we're a different species, some of us are nice, and the physical markings we use to rate each other and tell each other apart are completely indistinguishable to him. He likes me exactly the same as he did when I was 30 pounds fatter and had to wear a one piece. It sounds like this would be the sign of true friendship, but actually it's eerie the way we are all so interchangeable to him. He reached over and patted my knee one night by the campfire at Angeles National Forest and the denim in my jeans seared to my flesh and I could tell why his father has been with over 2,000 women.

If I show Somersault the magazine, will she help me? Or will she tell her brother that I'm a striver and a backstabber and obvious and that I read fashion mags? It's stupid to trust a 13-year-old girl with a broken heart. Somersault has been troubled since birth, and she gets off on turning on people, but she's not truly mean because she's not interested enough in anyone to get to know them and do any real damage. We all just leave her alone. At my eighth birthday party, when Somer was still a toddler, my mom went into the kitchen to yell at the caterers, and found Somer pointing a plastic knife at our dog, which was either the Yorkie or the poodle. My mom only told that story once, and then it was out of shock, without thinking, because the last thing my mother can afford is enemies. "They're different," mom would hiss at me when Somer tore apart my plastic beach pail and threw clods of wet sand into my eyes. She stood there panting, fingernails bloody, sand glazing her chin and coating her bikini, streaked across her belly like molting reptile scales. She always managed to look like she was the one who had been attacked. The Pacific behind her was so calm that it seemed to be baiting her. Even as a little kid, I could see that it was not the kind of wildness anyone would want to discipline out of her. It was the thing that made us all watch her.

"Somer," my mom would proclaim in her TV lawyer voice, "what an adorable suit. Tell your dad I said hello." And Mom would tug me back to her deck chair and make me read her soft-core romance novels out loud while she sunned under elaborate coats of sunblock, to reduce the damage.

They are different and everybody knows it. The mega-famous have a genuine liking for farm fields and nakedness and when they get fed up enough, they're going to leave Malibu for good and never be sorry. This is what makes them so irresistible, that they are always on the verge of leaving. They don't need us. If only we could say the same about them. We have to have proof that there are stunningly beautiful people in the world who aren't even trying. I told this theory to my mom and she said I was crazy. A star needs her fans. I said that's not the type of person I'm talking about, there are too many so-called "stars" these days, and she threw her crystal pyramids at me and screamed that if I was so goddamn smart, how come I never finished high school. I told her it was because I never learned to organize my thoughts, then turned and walked through the crystal shards in my bare feet, with my mother mumbling, "Those stupid glass things cost $5,000. Who gave them to me? Shit." I bled in my room while my mom memorized an excuse for where the crystals were for the next time the producer who gave them to her came over.

Somer is bad news but you can't take your eyes off her. Chiefton always brings his little sister along, and always pays her the respect of not trying to hide any of his bad behavior from her. When they sit side by side, him sticking wild daisies in her hair, her face relaxed into a non-expression that we project happiness onto, a hush falls over us. It is almost too much magnetism, and I can feel myself turning inside out, being dragged to some pole where I will see something strange and gorgeous that almost no one will ever get to see, a white carnivore that can't be photographed through the blizzard, then I will die there.

Chiefton reaches his hand back behind his bus seat and grabs Somer's foot. At last, she stays still, toes stretching. He massages her foot, probably with his other hand down Paprika's halter top and his tongue on her thigh. I can tell by how passive Somer keeps her foot that she's in that confusing phase when people are doing things to her, but she hasn't learned how to give back. My mom sat me down when I was Somer's age, after she found the weird European condom wrappers and the Cigarillo butts in our boat house. She told me that all exceptionally pretty girls go through this phase, but that it was very important that I don't keep lying on my back and getting serviced, but that I figure out how I can go on the offensive and get what I really want out of them. Otherwise, I could look forward to sexual boredom at a very young age. She gave a few graphic examples and I got embarrassed. I wonder if anyone has thought to warn Somer about the dangers of being ravished without giving back, and if she would like me if I explained it to her. They're so hard to talk to.

Somer is stone silent, doesn't sigh or anything, just flexes her toes. They make it so obvious, but no one gets creeped out. We make exceptions for royalty. Chiefton and Somer are cooped up together on a ranch in Montana for months at a time, and if any of us were left alone with either of them for even a few hours, the same thing would happen. I can't remember Chiefton ever even trying to spend time alone with one of us. Even when he's fucking, he's never more than a few yards away from the group, and usually only covered by a beach blanket or a Tijuana poncho. None of us wants to let him out of our sight. Somersault often pelts the heaving blanket with stones or AAA batteries, a steady stream, counting off all the time he's wasting away from her. You can tell she takes it personally.

My brother was sacrificed to the Ivy League. First he was sent away to a boarding school back East, then Harvard and some other schools wrote my mom letters inviting him to join the freshman class, and even though he never caught on to the academics, he discovered social causes and stopped shaving and moved to New York. My mom never invites him home because he's too confrontational and picks apart our recycling habits, but she wears a Harvard baseball cap with her shades when she's half-trying not to be spotted.

The bus careens to the side of the road and the brakes sound ridiculously overdone, sound effects from an airplane disaster movie. Everyone rubs their faces and rolls their heads around, stalling like amphibians that would prefer to stay in the water. Only Chiefton stands. He slaps the metal roof of the bus and shoots outside. Somer is right on his tail. Paprika the obvious striver bitch kneels on her seat and makes a big show of slowly re-tying her halter top around her stupid giraffe neck. That neck only looks good on Paprika's mom because she has one of those thick Polish accents, jam slathered on a hunk of brown bread, the kind of voice that gets everybody hot because you can imagine that you're a spy and about to be caught at something very high-stakes. On Paprika the bitch, that neck is wasted. I notice that everybody is staring at her with silent hatred, a pack of sluggish hyenas that would rather go hungry than do the actual killing for themselves.

Outside, it is dangerously hot and Chiefton and Somer are already standing on a tall boulder that looks like a plaster cast of acne scars, so tall that they have to have levitated to have gotten up there so quickly. They are facing away from us as we stumble off the bus and gather at their feet, our skin pissed off and spitting out blisters in this broiling sun. Someone sees a scorpion and half-heartedly kicks sand at it. It gets mad and scrambles straight for us until someone else beats it to death with a plastic 2 liter of Mountain Dew.

Paprika is trying to get a foothold in the crevices on the boulder, so she can join Chiefton on the mount. Somer scowls down at her, but Chiefton pays no attention. He slips his arm around Somer's tiny waist and holds some binoculars up to her face. Eleven people down below imagine what they would see through the binocular lenses if Chiefton were holding their waist like that. Mine is a swimming pool filled with pink feathers, but I shouldn't be so tacky and show-girly. I should have it filled with natural goose down. And no one allowed in but Chiefton and me.

We realize there is no place to sit, so we prop ourselves up against various things—large rocks, stunted splintery palm trees, even the flaming sides of the bus. The driver, an obese black man, is drowning in sweat, but he's stoic about it. He reads one issue of *Sports Illustrated* and fans himself with another one. Chiefton has contracted him for a certain number of hours, and he has no intention of getting off the bus. He's no fool, he's seen our drugs, but he doesn't want to know. He looks at stop-action photos of boxing and plans his next meal.

I am biracial. I used to peek at older black men, stealing glimpses of their features, wondering if there was any match. I wondered about every dark man I saw, even the lowlies like this bus driver. I used to do that, but Chiefton enlightened us that *could-be* is for strivers. We should live in the here and now and accept the gifts of the real earth instead of dreaming for something different. I have pieces of black men in my brain, like a slide show, but I don't watch it anymore. I've accepted the fact that my mom swears he wasn't anybody famous, or even known, so that side of the family doesn't affect me.

This bus driver has one of the best noses I've ever seen, wide as a ski ramp, a nose with history and grandness. A nose with so much weight it makes his face seem monumental. That nose would take one whiff of my mother and tell her to shoo. I got a nose job when I was thirteen. My mother sent me to her surgeon with one of her headshots for him to copy. The bus driver looks back at me with empty eyes. He wants no part of me.

Paprika starts screaming that she sees a rattler. "Oh my God! It's right at my foot! Chiefton! Fuck! Chiefton!" Chiefton looks down with detached interest, his head cocked. Somer kicks a shower of rocks and baked brown dust down onto Paprika, making her shriek and leap away. "You little bitch! You made me move! I could have got bit!"

"Hey!" Chiefton's voice echoes, even though Paprika's did not. "Don't be abusive."

Paprika loudly chokes back a sob, then spits muddy saliva onto the ground. When it's clear that Chiefton's not going to watch her fit, she turns tail and walks away from all of us, heading for a mountainous cliff formation in the distance. We hear her flimsy shoes smack the back of her heels as she marches through the low-growing scrub brush. I reach into my backpack and grab onto the rolled-up fashion mag, without taking it out, as if it is my partner in crime and I must slap my hand over its mouth to keep it from speaking up too soon.

Chiefton sits on the boulder and faces us, his legs dangling over the edge. Somer stands behind him, hands firmly grasping his shoulders. The sun has dropped lower all at once, an airplane losing altitude, and the beam of orange light is coming at Chiefton and Somer horizontally, illuminating their outlines in strands of fire so they look like they are temple ornaments being forged.

There is nothing we can do but swallow X and acid and gaze up at them and listen to Chiefton talk. It's a Socratic dialogue, but we're all too blissed-out and in awe of him to answer any of his questions. He tells us how important it is not to harm dolphins, that the LAPD is just another gang, that the public schools are actually training minorities to be future prison inmates, that the cylinder is the strongest shape, stronger than the triangle, how love of the body is the purest form of love because it involves being stripped down and unadorned and making love can make anyone anonymous for a few minutes. The sun sinks lower until only the lowest part of the horizon holds a strip of light, and a few unseen coyotes give single yips from somewhere much too close and Chiefton is beautiful and I want to experience that purest form of love more than I have ever wanted anything, but so do all the rest of them. Snipper is rocking back and forth on his backpack, masturbating in his usual obvious way, his rock star father's famous lips reduced to groaning over a mound of canvas stuffed with comic books and packets of sunflower seeds. The rest of them are staring up at Chiefton, their sweaty faces wrapping him in a rapture that none of us could have created alone. When my mom was my age, the President saw her crying on a TV Christmas special, and she got an invitation to dinner at the White House. All of that is crass and obvious and makes me sick, but still I have to wonder, who will ever look up from what he or she is doing and see *me* and notice that there is something different inside me? I'm 19 already. I have no plans. If I'm not careful, I'll be co-hosting a talk show in the fall, covered in moss and tarnish, standing next to my luminous mother, who will always make sure she weighs at least three pounds less than me.

It strikes me that Chiefton doesn't register that Paprika is gone, and now that it is getting dark, she will be coming back, wearing a pout as the dot on the *i* of her long neck, loosening her halter top ties while complaining on and on about sunburn, one sandal inevitably broken and held in her hand so she can hop dramatically across the expanse of shrubs and coyotes, waving her shoe at us every step of the way. I grab the magazine out of my backpack. I know what I'm going to do, but still I spread Paprika's photo shoot across my lap and stare at it for several minutes, until I worry that it's getting too dim to see that it's her in the picture.

I get up and hobble toward Chiefton on sleep-paralyzed legs. Everyone shoots daggers into my back when Chiefton's sonorous voice stops flowing and I hand the magazine up to him. Somer's eyes flash down at me and seem to expand to all pupil, a hungry cockatoo perched on his shoulder.

"Ah, fuck, Christ. Oh, Christ. Have you seen this?" Chiefton waves the magazine toward the rest of them, but they can't possibly see it in the dying light. "Fucking pathetic. Vanity! Vanity is such an adornment. Don't wallow in the mud. We're all better than that. Remember. Please remember what I'm about to tell you: *We have nothing to sell.*" He pauses. They flutter beneath his eye contact. "I'm hungry. Let's get back to L.A."

He scrambles off the boulder in a flash. Somer leaps down with the intention of breaking my foot, but I jump out of the way. She stands in front of me, gorgeous, enraged, her lips curled back, ready to tear into my throat. But she's losing sight of Chiefton, who ducks into the dark square of the bus door. She runs off to follow him.

Everyone files into the bus, disoriented from sunstroke and drugs and a whole evening of looking directly at Chiefton and Somer. Nobody scans the cliffs for signs of Paprika. What's one less fashion model? At the last minute, I turn and look for her, standing on the steep entrance steps to the bus, exhaust already gunning out of its rear. Her obvious baby pink backpack with the toy monkey pull tab sits on the ground, rocking a little in the Santa Ana wind. We're not going to actually leave her here. Chiefton has strong convictions, but he's not cruel. He must realize that he needs us as much as we need him.

"Everybody on board?" The bus driver wants me to climb in and sit down. His veiny eyes seek out Chiefton in the rearview mirror.

Chiefton makes a go-forward sign with his hands. "Let's roll, *brah.*"

Even when the bus starts forward and throws me several feet up the aisle, I can't believe this is happening. I steady myself by gripping the chair backs as I pass. It's pitch black outside, no landscape in motion, so maybe we're not actually moving, maybe the bus is just jerking and bouncing in place, a fat, out-of-practice drunk screwing on an old couch. As I reach out for the next seat back, a warm hand grabs me. It's Chiefton. The one time my eyes weren't glued to him, he reached out and chose me.

As he tugs me into the seat next to him and begins licking my neck and running his hands over my hip bones, I know that I would have traded anything for this, that I'll tell Paprika's mom that we saw her get into a black Trans Am with Texas plates, that we yelled at her to come back, but she just gave us the finger and got into that strange car, with people she didn't even know.

Chiefton pauses and cups my face in his hands and whispers, "You're so unblemished," and I spring on top of him the way my mom advised me to and for once I intend to get exactly what I want. We are still going at it hours later when I finally notice that Somer has been kicking the seat back, and one of his hands leaves me and creeps back toward her, and when you're this close to her, Somer isn't just kicking, she's hissing, "Bitch, bitch, bitch, bitch, bitch," her voice never dying out, on and on forever, to remind me that I'm still only a mortal, that this won't last.

***

REAL ESTATE

SLVRLK

Silver Lake is not the next place people are going to move to. People already live there. White people. First it was Mexican, then it was gay and the Boys stubbornly built aviaries and hanging hibiscus gardens and cafés roofed with preening and longing. It used to be a place you drove through with your doors locked to get to Dodger Stadium. Now it is the Hollywood Hills for people who can't afford Hollywood Hills. Jeanette has never wanted to live there until now. The realtor was reluctant to show them this house because she's seen real money and isn't fooled by Jeanette and Jack's buffed faces, the way they match in a way you can't put your finger on, the way their equal good looks make them appear almost brother-and-sisterly. If they were dogs, you'd breed them.

PRICED TO SELL

Jeanette gave up acting and got a real job at a travel agency six years ago. It's one of those things that before you do it, you believe that it's going to kill you, then afterwards you see that in ordinary lives, nothing so dramatic as death by boredom is going to happen ever. Giving up acting hasn't made her stronger or clever or able to not notice passing a mirror. It makes her money. If you work steadily at a real job, you can save up money and get a car the valets won't sneer at. Acting isn't everything. There are other ways of being the center of attention, but it's hard. When you show off at a travel agency, everyone starts telling you that you should be an actress. Jeanette feels the mush of temptation every time they say it. There's something addictive about making people watch you, even if it's only for 90 seconds, and even if they almost never cast you. Jeanette has to make up reasons why she can't be an actress anymore. A clinical inventory has been taken. Jeanette can list her faults:

1)   Toes of irregular length
2)   Splotchy skin on legs
3)   Collar bone not pronounced enough
4)   Eyes too small; disappear when smiling
5)   Breasts too small (This is a general comment for all women in The Business, unless they are in the minority group of Breasts Too Large.)

Still, she gets propositioned in the milk aisle. She is more photogenic than beautiful. In birthday party pictures, she looks anointed compared to everybody else. She has learned to relax her smile, and can nail the camera with that intense, creationist look that makes many people rich, but not everybody. It used to be that if you looked this way, a prince would find you, or an oil tycoon, or the man who owned the town car dealership, and you would be taken care of. Nowadays, if you were born luminous, you have to get out and work it.

Jeanette was featured in several cigarette ads, surrounded by a group of men and women who also know how to gleam. She doesn't smoke, but that's okay because they weren't allowed to put the cigarettes in their mouths for the ads.

Jack is staring at the realtor, jittering his toes. Jeanette can sense the tremor through his Italian shoes. He's constantly restless, and when he's bored, it's fatal because it's like he's starving—he loses all compassion and becomes sportily cruel. He thinks this house is overpriced. Jeanette finally convinced him to give up acting and enroll in paralegal school. He will start next week. He auditioned for one last feature role, and he got a callback, but it's been five days and his agent hasn't called. The role is a ski instructor who tries to save the lead, but gets killed by an avalanche. The casting director asked Jack to tone it down and play it straight and Jack keeps saying he knows that was a mistake, he should've gone for it, it's an avalanche for chrissakes, it's fucking cold. Jeanette can tell that he thinks that giving up on The Industry will kill him. It won't. He'll learn to start measuring time in increments other than how long it's been since someone called. When Jack has a steady income, too, they can afford a mortgage. They'll have something permanent. The posters for the cable TV movies they've been in will hang in the entry way—blue and green artists' renderings like political cartoons without any opinions. Jeanette isn't happy that Jack has to give up acting. She's just relieved not to have to be jealous anymore.

VUS

Jeanette knows that this house is not overpriced because it has stunning views. The downtown skyline, partial hills, and the grey reservoir, protected by chain links, spiked with invincibility, surely hiding mechanical sea monsters. From up here, L.A. looks primary and benevolent, a grid of self-assured streets with nursery rhyme crookedness, elegant palm trees, shiny little cars zipping up and down, it all has the sheen of excellent customer service. It's an old show biz adage that the people you audition for *want* to love you, they're always hoping that you'll stun them with your talents and end their search, they're really on your side. From up here, the entire city seems to have that welcoming, bated-breath attitude. The people don't look like ants. There are no tiny people down there. The people are all inside cars, which look as jaunty as golf carts. You know that almost all the cars contain only one person, but you imagine that they're all packed with people who are wearing just the right jeans, cracking jokes, rushing to parties where even more of their friends will join them and someone will not fail to bring a volleyball.

Jeanette leans against the patio railing and imagines that living above this view will make her European. She'll smoke out here and wear silk scarves and indulge in the melancholy thoughts brought on by wine. Will she take a lover? Out of the corner of her eye, she sees Jack in the empty living room which is not painted in the color eggshell, but which has the heat lamp and ovaries feeling of the inside of an egg, with its rounded ceiling and arched doorways. Jack is standing very close to the realtor, a girl with a severe black bob and aquiline nose who would look good as a graphic design, but lacks the human subtleties of beauty. This is the type of girl who has spent her entire adulthood earning money. When people tell her she has a look, she should do commercials, she sneers into her gin and shakes her head and she actually means it. Everybody in Los Angeles wants to go to bed with her, to taste a creature so maddeningly devoid of the usual wants. It would be like fucking Ghandi, and you're certain that between her legs is a glowing lake instead of the pornographic usuals, liquefied light rays lapping gently at your petty desires, slowing your rush toward everything you believe to be essential and hard-won. She must sell a lot of houses. Jeanette flirts with her business clients, and it helps, but it's obvious that she's not the least bit interested in what she's saying and doing. Her warm telephone voice (from voiceover class) paints a homemade vacancy sign.

Sometimes she has lunch with her gay friend Andy (women aren't bitchy enough for her), who is an ex-heroin addict, and they'll swap shocking anecdotes about humiliating things they did in their old lives—stripping at a casting director's Cinco de Mayo party, for free; sucking off old vagrants for the change they made begging. She and Andy both miss their messed-up selves, and wish out loud that they had known each other back then. Andy could have turned her on to smack and she could have gotten him into industrials. They both could have stayed extraordinary a while longer, or died before it came to this responsibility, tipping a perfect 20%. Andy will love this house, which is important. She doesn't exactly trust Andy, but he's the one person she is sure will come to her funeral. She's told him what songs to play and what to read. Andy doesn't think that far ahead. "Just put me out with the trash, girl," he says, white teeth and gnarled grey gums from his years of secret needle bites. Andy will sing "They Can't Take That Away from Me" when she dies. She knows plenty of better singers, but Andy will sound sincere.

Jack leans in and brushes the realtor's jet hair away from her ear. He glances at Jeanette, then goes ahead and whispers very close to the diamond stud puncturing the realtor's earlobe. Jeanette turns away. She swings open the patio gate and starts down the steep concrete steps.

1 OF A KIND

Like most actors, Jack is short and boyish. He still looks like a 16 year old who just discovered the weight room last summer. He's cocky as all get-out, but you're confident that you're more experienced than he is and you could make him do anything. He carries his limbs loosely, jangling like a puppet, copying men with the height and sedateness he'll never have. On screen, surrounded by other short people, he comes across as the tall one, though he isn't any taller. His best trick is that he can look at a thing as if it is brand new, unheard of, unabashedly fascinating. He can look at both a tape dispenser and his wife this way. And the camera of course. The tape dispenser and his wife have grown spoiled and impervious. The camera still shivers and feels singled out for greatness.

Jeanette turns her face upward and looks through the glass patio door. She can tell that Jack is giving the realtor his look right now, even though the realtor is standing rigidly and Jeanette can't see Jack's face because he's moved in almost nose-to-nose with the realtor.

POOL

The pool is tiny and amoeba-shaped, which makes it impossible to swim laps, but perfect for floating and hanging on the sides with a vodka tonic in one hand. Jeanette imagines that drifting in the colorless water on an inflatable raft, she will look from above like an exquisite garnish on a gourmet plate—a fringed celery stalk or a stripe of cherry sauce, slurring across the pool with a tangy, devil-may-care elegance. She and Jack have both been unfaithful. When she first came to L.A., it surprised her how traditional-minded most actors are. They all want a marriage, a house, children. They want to be awarded these things, and expect their average-joe set pieces to be markedly better than average: broad-shouldered husband, wife with eye-popping tits, a pool, a violin prodigy who will support them in their old age if they never make it. It is their sensualism that gets in the way of their picket fence yearnings. When Jeanette catches another photogenic person staring at her from across the room, she can already feel their tongue on the nape of her neck. There may be some wires crossed in her brain. Sight, sound, taste, are all just the pale heralds of touch, and it always crescendos into a coupling, at minimum. So many actors were raised in nests of chaos that Home would be their greatest act. Jack's diabetic grandmother raised him, with frequent stays on moldy Navy Surplus cots in a Pentecostal church basement whenever she felt moved by the Holy Ghost to donate the month's electricity and grocery money.

Jeanette studied acting in college. She believes that it is a craft, like making cabinets or casting spells. Jack is self-taught. He acts from his gut. He is cast more often than Jeanette ever was, but he gives unreliable performances and is often replaced before shooting is over. He reacts like a boy who can't run or hit, but who has developed the talent of loudly blaming the umpire. Jeanette hopes that having a mortgage will make them both feel grown up, beyond certain disappointments. They have agreed not to have children because they would prefer to travel.

"*BLAAH!*" A single piercing squawk from the realtor. Jeanette looks back at the house and watches the sound streak out of the patio doors, unfurling like a party horn, then immediately retract back inside, where Jack has made the queenly realtor laugh.

Jeanette slips out of her sandals, in a perfect movement of grace and dishevelment. She's an accomplished disrober—another skill she thought she could live off of. She sits on the edge of the pool, dangling her feet in the water. She's not sure why she doesn't scramble back up the hillside steps and stop Jack. She isn't ignoring the problem, she's just tired of the way they're always reigning each other in. She kicks her feet languidly, inspecting her pedicure through the ripples. Refracted through the water, her feet look malformed and overburdened. She gazes at her jumbled piano key toes with hatred.

"... THINK SO?" The end of one of Jack's sentences gets away from him and darts out the door, followed by a self-conscious hush and an accidental *THUMP* on the wall. They seem to be in the bedroom now. Even though there isn't a stick of furniture in the house, they are both creatures of habit, though Jeanette imagines that the realtor's habits are in every way different from Jack's, who sleeps until 11:00 in a silk eye mask, sips green tea in bed while inspecting every inch of his body for new flaws, reads the front page headlines of the trades but never opens them, then takes the day from there.

Jeanette slides into the water. Her short cotton dress isn't much of a hindrance, and she's one of those people who look healthy and calculated when wet instead of overzealous and plastered-down. She scrapes her hand along the pool's rough baby blue cement floor. She opens her eyes and can't feel any chlorine at all. She bobs to the surface and absently treads water. "Jack?" All of the neighbors can hear, but there's no answer, no one named Jack will claim her as she keeps afloat in this misshapen swimming pool that she converts into dollars and tries so hard to make herself want. She hates herself for calling out, wants the word back.

She dives under again, where the water refuses all sound. She notices a flickering speck near the drain, and checks for her wedding ring, but it's still firmly in place on her finger. The speck spins around and expands rapidly, until it is the size of a spotlight, shimmering on the bottom of the pool. Jeanette is transfixed. In the midst of all the dancing sparkles, she catches sight of Jack's unmistakable head. Then he recedes into the background, as if he is camouflaged by a planetarium ceiling. She should come up for air, but something is about to happen here. The flickering congeals into the moving images of a film projection. It is color film, but blurred by the water, wavy and cubist. It is footage of Jack, peeling off the realtor's black jacket, caressing her skin while she makes a mental note about the light fixture, bored.

The film slow fades to a new scene. Jack and the realtor months later, miles away, on the Santa Monica Pier, the realtor cold and haughty, Jack tugging haplessly at her sleeve. She answers her cell phone and he politely holds her snow cone for her. After a few minutes of staring out at the infected Pacific, he grows bored and agitated and flings the snow cone into the water, but does not leave. He paces up and down with his hands on his hips, occasionally bending over to exhale loudly and grab his ankles. If he had been there with Jeanette, he would have kicked at the dock railing and started a shouting match with one of the weekend fishermen. The realtor doesn't have to ignore his antics because she has genuinely forgotten about him, engrossed in her phone conversation.

Jeanette's head is pounding, and her chest feels as if she is caught between the palms of a fanatic at prayer, but she doesn't want to miss the rest. She opens her mouth and gulps. Water floods up her nostrils to her brain, the same bubbly assault as one more round of bad champagne before failing at sex. She sinks closer to the picture.

The next scene is months later. Jack is stubbled and pudgy, the starched collar of his paralegal's dress shirt cutting into his neck like an ox yoke. Jack and Jeanette are in the living room of their new house in Silver Lake. Their old furniture has stopped looking kitschy and started to look tawdry. Jeanette is dressed for work, arguing heatedly with Jack. Jack leaps up on the couch with his old agility and rips off his shirt and tie. He is obviously quitting something, possibly many things, possibly everything. At the end of the driveway, the realtor *beep-beeps* her red Alpha Romero, and Jack tears out of the house, taking the stairs two at a time, his new Saturday belly jiggling. This must be the climactic scene, and Jeanette is relieved because she's starting to see black patches and ceasing to imagine how refreshing the oxygen will feel when she goes back to it. But there's more.

The realtor pounds a SOLD sign onto the top of an existing sign in somebody's front lawn. Jeanette angrily confronts her. The realtor rolls her eyes and continues pounding the sign. Jack lopes up from behind and shoves Jeanette hard in the back. The realtor glides out of frame without a backward glance. Jack stands over Jeanette with his fist clenched. She reaches out her hand and strokes his cheek, which is by now bloated and rosy with amateur alcoholism. He lets her, but his rotund little body does not relax. He abruptly turns and waddles off.

Jeanette is so near the bottom now that all she can discern of the movie is large splotches of color. Still, she gets the gist of the last scene. An overhead shot of her floating on a raft in the pool, not looking like a garnish but like an aimless skeleton. Jack hopping up and down at the edge of the pool, waving around the mortgage statement, cursing her for trapping him, enumerating the ways in which she's ruined his life. Jeanette has apparently heard it all before, because she doesn't stir, just floats with grand indifference. Jack cannonballs into the pool. The enormous splash stings Jeanette, knocking off her sunglasses. She sits up in time to see Jack lumbering toward her, slow-motioned by the water, leaping at her with all his heft. The raft bends and squeezes out from under her, making a clean, unpunctured escape. Jeanette is not so fortunate. Jack's plump fingers crush her windpipe and he forces her down to the bottom of the pool near the drain—the same spot she's in now—and holds her there, drowning her, forcing her to watch his distended face grin like an old man who once played Puck.

The blackness spreads through Jeanette's oxygen-starved brain, eating away at the picture, a soft charcoal black with the consistency and busyness of an early morning drizzle. The picture surrenders easily. The circle gets smaller and smaller until all that's left is Jack's eye glowing on the bottom of the pool. Before she loses consciousness for good, Jeanette notices that Jack's eye is staring at her with his old famous look, as if she is never-before-seen, never-to-be-repeated, utterly new, inarguably his favorite of all time. It is the eye of a man who will applaud until his hands hurt.

WON'T LAST

Jeanette imagines she will wake up floating on the surface of the pool, sputtering and choking, and there will be a delicious bit of drama as she calls Jack repeatedly in her urgent-message voice and he comes flying down the terrace half-naked to fish her out, diving into the pool slim and treasurely and on the verge of earning some real money. A good actor is one who has learned to inhabit the present moment. Jeanette cheats a little and thinks of the future, so inevitable and so unspoiled.

Ambition ripples through her, spiky as quills and sensate as antennae. It seizes her drowning body with a mighty thrash that propels her to the surface. Her lungs inflate, squeeze her diminishing heart to one side. Her center is an expanding bellows of air. The sun wraps her wet face with the therapeutic pat of a facialist applying a steaming towel. The air is tinged with orange blossoms and Jeanette heightens this to the tart tickle of sherbet as she tenses her throat to shout the gagging consonant that launches Jack's name.

"Jack?" She is already forgetting what she saw on the bottom of the pool. The thrilling sensory assault of the world above water is so overpowering that it blots out all unpleasantries, banishes all caution. Her imagination is limited to three-reel tropes that rapidly lose their ghostliness, rendered invisible in the light of day. She is a slip of a person who can easily slide into and out of any part. She has memorized her reflection, but she doesn't recognize this fluid quality, no more than a mollusk would take note of its lack of vertebrae. She hoists herself onto the lip of the pool. The breeze nevers her mind.

"JACK!" She really means it this time. Playtime is over. She has had her dip in the pool and Jack has had his dip in the realtor and sometimes they will trade roles and it's only baby-splashes, nothing to goad anyone's ire, nothing like facial scars or one nominated for an award when the other is not. They will buy this house. Things will be good. *Will be* is a foreign phrase. She puckers her lips, whispering the word *will*, smiling out the *be*. Kiss, grin. Her tongue trips.

Jeanette swipes the water out of her eyes and watches Jack step out onto the patio. He surveys the surroundings with the calm, attentive expression of an instant forgetter, clothes already arranged, already embodying this new scene. Jeanette takes a dripping step forward to join him, coaxing herself back to RIGHT NOW, the only place in all of L.A. where an actor can live.

$$***$$

AUTO-EROTICA

Unruffled wouldn't be the word for him since there is nothing on him that could get ruffled. Nothing to stand on end and need smoothing down. Entirely streamlined: dark hair shorn close to the skull, placid un-sunned skin lacking identifying marks, expensive clothing in neutral colors and crisp lines, the intentionally indifferent mode of dress that only men of innate style can carry off. A gaze so direct that if he dozes off, his pupils are in the same place when he wakes up later, focused with the same intensity, no split second of messy grogginess. He only dozed off once. He always smokes a single cigarette afterwards, taking his time in such an un-self-conscious way that he has to be European. I secretly hope he's German, as I have a thing for Germans, based upon one pathetic fling in college, which even now I re-evaluate in my head from time to time, trying to find the correct equation of open-heartedness and catty feminine wiles that would have held his interest. I admire the German belief in right answers. It's very like math, which is my forte. Statistically, there aren't enough Germans here to make it worth my time to look for one.

I can't tell if he's German because we've agreed not to speak. If I could speak to him, I'd have told him that I don't let people smoke inside my house. Frankly, it's nicer this way, with him lingering. He never showers after, and I let myself think wishfully that his acceptance of stickiness and bedroom stench on his otherwise impeccable form is somehow a compliment to me.

Following a non-uniform interval of time, he gently stubs out the cigarette on the sole of his Italian oxblood loafers. He gets dressed in the same languid manner, and pecks me on the lips in a gesture he manages to make far more frigid than a handshake. His car is small and sporty and aerodynamic to a fault and grey of course, the least needy and most curve-conscious color. He tears out of my drive in a conspicuous show of acceleration which makes me believe that he, too, works for himself. I worry about the neighbors' impressions of his lunch hour visits, until I remember that I am in L.A. and the neighbors are busy manipulating their own affairs, stacking toxic combinations of people in outrageous circus pyramids. I can almost hear the hurdy-gurdy urging us all on.

I spend a week scouring antique shops for the perfect modernist ash tray to put beside my bed, rectangular and orange and would be miffed if you told it that it was utilitarian as well as handsome. It is the sturdiest thing in my house. I stare into its blank base, willing the week to subtract some of its days so he will return sooner. The yawning receptacle makes me yearn. I'm not used to wishing for uncertainties. The ash tray is a set-up. My first act of betrayal.

* *

Iris is one of the smart ones. More friend than client at this point, I think, but it's always some nebulous combination of the two, never a neatly balanced six of one, half dozen of the other. You never hear that expression in my crowd. It's not Yiddish. Iris is paper doll petite and dusky and sparkling and delightfully pushy. She produces studio movies, but her family's been rich on the East Coast for a long time, so she understands money. I copy her clothes without ever asking her where she got them or which designer. I don't replicate her look well enough for her to notice, but that is due only to my fashion incompetence and much larger frame. We must be friends, because when we talk, we end up complaining about men.

"Honey, you're BRILL-yant. What do you want with a boyfriend? They're trouble. They eat your energy."

"Yeah, well, at this point, I've got plenty of excess energy, if you know what I mean."

"That's why they call L.A. the auto capital of the world." She toasts me with her third cappuccino. Even the dark bags under her eyes seem to twinkle, seem to be part of a perfectly-conceived costume. It's the same quality that makes dapper middle aged men attractive. Unheard of on a female. She dazzles me.

"Auto capital? You mean choose a man by his car?"

"Car, schmar." She takes me straight to Drake's on Melrose, conducting a script meeting over her cell phone while holding up samples from the vast array of vibrators and dildos hanging on the wall. The display of members looks clinical yet disorderly, with the plastic bags and not-quite-matching groups, like finds from a dig that are catalogued as well as can be, but still puzzle the archeologist.

I settle on something largish and sleek and metallic called The Silver Bullet. Iris "*uh huh*"s sagely into the phone, then covers the mouthpiece and whispers to me, "Auto-erotica."

* *

Unflappable isn't the right word, either. He's incapable of flapping. It was never a possibility. He would never do anything even vaguely frantic. The ash tray was not a good set-up because he balanced it on his hairless chest as if he were aware of its weight but not its shape or color and tapped his ashes into it without comment. It's very odd fucking someone whose name I can't use. It's supposed to make me feel uninhibited, but instead of thinking of my own pleasure, I'm calculating ways to drive him mad enough to speak. He gasps a little. I feel as if I have roommates, or we are in the back seat of a borrowed car back in Indiana and the other couple has gone for a walk by some male pre-arrangement. Two people who don't exactly like each other but who are complicit in not wanting to waste a rare opportunity. That's my problem. He's become rare. Special. Valuable. Good looking men with nice cars and lengthy lunch hours are a dime a dozen in this town. I am convinced that he has an accent, that there is a luscious umlaut perched naturally on his tongue. I put him down in my plus column. He is a prize.

* *

My job is getting more intolerable every year, even though I own the company. I have only six employees, but we handle almost everyone who's anyone. So many big names in Hollywood are really shabby little three person operations with irregular cash flow. We manage people's money. Or more precisely, we micro-manage. I am an expensive nanny who lives in their bank vaults. I think of Reagan describing a trillion dollars as a stack of money climbing up to the cosmos, and I know there will never be a measuring tool that will give entertainment people an accurate idea of how much they have to spend. All they know is they have a lot and they want a lot and everyone around them always seems to have more. Things are worse now because every merchant and shyster in town has started telling entertainment people that whatever they are buying is a tax write-off. Drugs, cases of Oregon jelly, call girl masseuses, drunkenly scrawled contribution checks to French Canadian separatist groups, the charges come across my desk and my clients won't even take a breezy scolding anymore. They insist that so-and-so told them it was a tax write-off. These are people who have more money than they ever thought possible, more than they know what to do with, and they seem hell-bent on making their financial success as meteoric as possible. I'm convinced that the Hollywood pawn shop brokers and I share the same client list, just at different stages of their careers. I borrow these people from the pawn brokers for their better-to-burn-out-than-fade-away years, then return them to the desperate midnight trips selling and buying back their electric guitars. I return them worse for the wear, but it's not my fault. I try to be the voice of reason. I tell them the sycophants are going to scatter the moment the money runs out. "My *friends*," they say, "are *not* sick-o's." I'd quit today if I could. And I could. But I'm spooked by all the crash landings I've witnessed. I'm determined never to have a bright past. I have a mortgage now, too. A three bedroom bungalow in WeHo. It was overpriced but it's important to own something tangible. Not just for the financial benefits. As motivation to get out of bed in the morning.

Iris christened the house with an 1884 bottle of red Chablis from the private stock of a Marin County winery, a beverage more expensive than anything my parents ever tasted, splashing over my concrete veranda. Porch, we would have called it. My mother would have clucked at the glass shards and announced that someone was bound to get hurt. Iris had brought not only the wine, but a pack of expensive friends. I work constantly and I only have work-related friends. Iris's gem-like friends would make anyone feel like no price was too high. She raised her glass to the crowd, women thin and shiny as dimes. "To Janie's castle!" roared Iris. "Now she can bring home lots of strange men and bury them in the back yard if they aren't ladies-first fucks!" We all laughed. My smile was not that much different from theirs. I finally felt good about buying the house.

* *

I put a stack of books under the ash tray, literary stuff I read in undergrad but don't quite remember. It will be disastrous if he actually flips through one, because of my clumsy underlining and highlight job, the once-vibrant yellow faded to an acidic trail of dried-up urine, now defacing the words instead of spotlighting them. I felt compelled to underline practically everything in those days. Everything seemed important and noteworthy. This has to be the definition of naive.

* *

The Lead Singer is screaming at me on the speakerphone. Yes, he has two pool tables already, but this one has a purple felt top instead of green and he has to entertain people, doesn't he, "And it's a tax write-off anyway, so what the fuck's your problem, bitch?" In respectable businesses, you can file some sort of grievance or lawsuit if someone calls you "bitch." Here in Hollywood, verbal abuse is a normal recurrence, as unnatural but necessary to endure as all the dieting, stretching for normalcy through blunt repetition, but never quite losing its deviance. The word *fuck* still stings me every time, the prideful consonants at the end striking like the surprise venom of a scorpion's tail. To Iris and her crowd, it's just a dollop of hot Dijon mustard, something with a little kick that they're proud of acquiring a taste for.

The Lead Singer is not on drugs, but he has a constant entourage of at least fifty people and he compulsively buys to make them happy. The trades say he's six months late delivering his next disk, which means he must have royally pissed off his publicist. I'd love to stick these peoples' account spreadsheets into a plain, impartial manila envelope and deliver it anonymously to the trades. It would start a panic blacker than black Monday if everyone in town realized that everyone else was also in serious debt.

Later Iris calls. "Janie, I've got a really silly idea. Promise me you'll say no."

"What is it?"

"My ex—"

"Joshua? The tax forms?"

"No, no. The other one. Frank. Frank knows this guy who's selling a racehorse."

It takes a moment for me to realize that the purchase is going to be a horse. Always the least practical thing. But Iris is usually different.

"I know, it's preposterous. What do I want with a racehorse? It's just that I grew up in the horsey set, stables still feel like the bubka's house I never had, and Janie, this horse is drop dead gorgeous. Arabian. You like horses?"

"I'm not sure."

"Well, for God's sake, tell me no. That's what I'm paying you for."
"Buy it," I say. "What the hell. You've got the money."

* *

He doesn't notice the books, and I hardly notice the sex because I'm dying for this man to show some speck of interest in me. Maybe he's secretly wishing the same thing. He tells himself, "I zhall haf one zigarette. Ef zhe talk, gut. Ef not, zo. I leaf." I make a show of pulling the denim-colored washed silk comforter up around my shoulders. I try to sound off-hand, but it comes out like an over-rehearsed line, which is what it is. "Aren't you cold?"

He sniffs and jerks his head in a half-shake, swinging it away from me but not swinging it back. He does not hurry his cigarette, but he remains fixated on the far corner of the room. I have embarrassed us both.

* *

"That damn nag does nothing but lose," complains Iris. "I should sell her and get my money back, right?"

"If she's losing, you'll sell at a loss," I counsel. "It's just a pleasure buy anyway. It's like a trip to a casino. You have to walk in knowing you're going to lose. It's all statistics. You're paying for an evening's worth of entertainment. Does watching the horse run make you happy?"

"I never go to casinos," says Iris. "I loathe Vegas. The lighting is cruel."

* *

Iris takes me to Hollywood Park to see her horse run. On the way down, she's as jittery as a prom-bound teenager, prone to loud radio music and sudden outbursts exclaiming our destination. "We're going to watch my pony race!" Horses scare me. They're tall and massive with the necks of sea monsters and the eyes of something that understands every word you're saying but for some reason will not speak back.

I expect Hollywood Park to be utterly derelict, full of flab and desperation. But the Owners' Box is different. And Iris's assistant boy, Greg, is articulate and witty in the book way rather than the sitcom way, and he touches my arm several times. Iris keeps sending him off with whispered instructions.

"Iris, how much are you betting?"

"Just a hundred bucks. Just for sport. You know I'm too much of a tightwad to throw away more than that."

"A hundred dollars exactly? How many times?"

"And sweetheart," she is helming this conversation, "Greg is gay."

"Yeah, I got that."

"No, you didn't."

I sulk through the rest of the races. Iris's horse, Third Reel, almost places, but doesn't. Iris and I are both in black moods. Greg fetches us lemonades and goes home with a sprightly jockey wearing a green diamond jersey and a weighty moustache. I kick at the piles of ripped-up tickets on the ground and am reminded of Hollywood snow, how it looks fake because it's too clingy, trying too hard to stick. Real snowfall is transient, barely there, something you're more likely to miss.

"I should send her to the glue factory," mutters Iris on the way home. Then she blasts the stereo and sings along to syrupy Barbara Streisand. What's the point of asking her how much she lost? She's a survivor. Money falls from the sky and sticks to her.

* *

Iris is the one who showed me the website, a service for discerning people of a certain income. "You've got to quit brooding over men. All you need is someone delicious and discreet to fuck you one day a week. It's like getting your nails done." It sounded sleazy to me. "Dear heart, everyone does it this way now. Do you think those beautiful couples are actually fucking each other? Please. They haven't eaten in a month. They don't have the energy. They get someone in to service them. What're you going to do? Go to the bars and take your chances? We're too busy."

"It's like ordering a hooker."

"What hooker? No money changes hands. The guys are in the same position you're in. Everyone's looking for the same arrangement. Consenting adults. No fuss, all fuck. My friend Nedra found a lovely stud who hasn't given her a moment's trouble." Nedra is tall and slender and inviting as a birthday candle. I imagined myself surrounded by the same grateful men as Nedra. Iris felt me wavering. "If you hate it, cancel him. You're not investing your feelings."

She wrote my ad for me, and headlined it "VOW OF SILENCE."

* *

I call Iris to see if we can do lunch this week. I need her to tell me how I can rouse my Possible German. Greg sounds annoyed on the phone, and he acts like he doesn't remember me even though it is his job to remember everyone. He tells me Iris is booked solid.

"For how long?" I ask.

Greg sputters as if I have just read him a word problem involving two trains and a block of ice. "For the foreseeable future," he finally whines. "Her schedule is impossible."

I tell myself I'll call Iris at home that night. But calling Iris is like calling a man. It involves a lot of preparation and second-guessing, and in the end you just eat a pint of ice cream and don't call. The reason I don't have many friends is because one millimeter under the surface, I am desperate to be liked. It's exhausting.

* *

Following a volley of tersely charming e-mails, I arranged to meet him in the bar at Sunset Tower. Getting myself gussied up to meet a man whom I was interviewing to be my stud felt like an exercise in inadequacy. The strategically lit art deco curves and helpful tinkle of the barside piano made me feel like a charlatan piece of abstract art on the auction slab, reliant upon an unseasoned eye to buy me.

You don't notice him when he's a stranger, but once he's fixed you in that unwavering gaze, you will be checking doorways and airport gates and under café table umbrellas for him forever. I should have called it off right then. I was already in the red, pre-negotiation.

"Hi," I chirped in the nervous false brightness that possesses me when I'm trying to pretend to be Californian and self-satisfied.

He regarded me thoroughly, and I couldn't tell if his detachment was polite or icy. He handed me an unmarked envelope. I half-expected it to be an essay on romantic philosophy, explaining why an arrangement of anonymous weekly sex was degrading to both of us, extolling the value of emotional risk and time-honored courtship. Inside the envelope was a medical checklist of lab results proving him to be free of HIV, chlamydia, herpes, genital warts, etc. etc., signed by a convincingly illegible doctor. He had blacked out his name with thick, decisive marker lines.

"I'll get tested before next week," I offered. It was like saying, "I'm fine, too, thanks." Obligatory and ritualistic. I wasn't worried about the test. I'd never slept with anyone I wasn't dating exclusively. Even when I slept with boyfriends, I always used a condom as a baby-guard. People think I live in L.A. because of the excess money here, but it's actually the excess romance. This is probably the only place where a person too awkward to make friends can still be guaranteed a series of boyfriends, of varying quality. In recent years, my job has made me too discerning for my own good. When you deal with gorgeous, charismatic people all day long, it's hard to come home to anything less.

"The address." He tapped the envelope with a ceremonial-looking fountain pen, then handed it to me. I can't for the life of me remember if he spoke with a German accent. It's hard to tell from just two words, especially when you aren't familiar with the person's voice, and you're concentrating hard on blanking your expression so you won't look rapt. It was interesting that he assumed we would meet at my house. I was glad to have a real asset to bring to the deal.

* *

Iris shows up unexpectedly at my office. Her face is sweaty and her suit is rumpled. She looks like one of her action heroes, wrongly accused and on the lam and nourished only by swiped donuts and spilled coffee. "I have a slush fund, right? Extra money?"

"What's going on?"

"It's unexpected."

"Tell me."

"I have to take a trip. You remember my friend Bette? She's suicidal. She's tearing the place apart. She's convinced that she needs a sex change. I'm flying her down to Acapulco."

"For a sex change operation?"

"No, no. Just to distract her. Dry her out. It's an intervention."

"How much do you need?"

"Twenty thousand."

"Can you get by on ten?"

"It might take awhile."

"Don't make a habit of it."

I'm insanely jealous of her insane friend Bette. My problem is that I've never been the squeaky wheel.

* *

He is as unaffected as glass. Someone must rub him down every so often, someone with a painfully delicate touch who can keep him so devoid and transparent for the rest of us. I can't stand his indifference. I am not sophisticated. I am not cosmopolitan. I don't belong in this whirlwind city where the people change instead of the seasons. I am singleminded and plodding and devoted and I am incapable of sleeping with someone without becoming seriously attached, against my own will and better judgment. How dare he come into my house week after week and fail to acknowledge me. Then I remember that I set the sterile parameters. Or Iris did, manager of my social life. Is it so terribly violating to change midstream? Ride it out. That's the only way anything ever pays off. Stay in it for the long haul. Only invest what you can afford to lose. Goddammit, I'm out of Indiana and I'm fucking rich, but I cannot afford him. It's equally hard to fail at false intimacy.

I cannot sleep so I wander my house, not seeing the rooms, just sensing their value in the intuitive way I always notice money. I resolve to take up smoking. Maybe the physical act of sucking on a cigarette will signal to him a solidarity that the sex never did. I pull a sweatshirt over my pj's and drive to the 24 hour market. I can't find the odd, gold leaf embossed brand that he smokes, which gives me hope that he is actually German. I may be grasping at straws.

* *

Iris has been betting large sums at the track. Men with thick Asian accents and no return phone numbers call regarding a surprise second mortgage on her house in Holmby Hills. The strokes of complex calligraphy characters seem to be swan-diving through these men's English sentences, deliberately adding ballroom dance steps to something that should be purely numeric, still and resolute. I don't know how she thought she could hide this from me. It's so out of character, impetuous and disrespectful of her money.

I lock my office door and practice what I will say to her. I try to sound sisterly, then motherly, then like a machine whose function is pristine objectivity. When I call her office, Greg tells me she hasn't been in all day. He sounds beleaguered and snaps, "Somebody else better damn well start covering for her ass because I am over and out." Iris is a workaholic. Workaholics only replace work with some other addiction.

* *

"Talk to me," I whisper in his ear just before I come. But it's just me and The Silver Bullet, a hand-held man whirring dependably but stupidly, full of sound but devoid of fury or any other passion. Big cautious me adding up my accounts, going with the indivisible one. Auto-erotica.

* *

Iris calls, claiming to be in Florida scouting locations. She asks for $55,000. I tell her I know about the gambling debts and I've lined up a buyer for the horse. There is a stunned silence on the line, the same darkening vacuum as before a tornado, expanding as slowly and implacably as an overnight bruise.

"I need that money. I'm coming for that money, bitch." She hangs up.

I feel jilted, altar-left, sodomized and laughed at over cocktails. Nobody is who they're supposed to be. It's equally hard to lose a false friend.

* *

"*Merde*," he exhales, in an accent that doesn't sound quite Paris, but maybe there is a constriction of his airways in the face of the gun. He doesn't betray any panic, swooping the cigarette away from his lips with the usual loving grace, as if it is just another in a series of pleasures instead of his last. So I narrow him down to the French-speaking world. This is as much as I will ever know about him. Who will inherit his zippy little sports car, assuming it's paid off? Possibly a niece or a little sister who he's warned not to trust boys.

Iris's hands are shaking badly, all her fingers wrapped around the midget gun, TV cop style. She takes a giant step toward us to compensate. She knows the art of checks and balances. If she were one of my musicians or actors or writers, it would be a prop gun or she'd have forgotten to load it or she'd shoot up the walls first in a kaleidoscopic show of rage so that someone would hear and call for help. But this is Iris, old money, deliberate, the woman I admired most. She is glistening with dollar signs and ever-ascending decimal points, a suit of armor that will allow her to escape even this unscathed.

I wonder if the range will be described as point blank. He is lying next to me buck naked and as I decide I will close my eyes, I desperately wish I had someone's hand to hold. Iris's every breath comes skidding in and out of her. She sounds like something that is being hunted. I hear him take another drag off his cigarette, no more shallow or deep than usual. I picture the view outside my bedroom window. A rosy sky, a patient pool, palm trees without shadows. I am out of Indiana. I am rich. I live somewhere famous. Statistically, this is a dangerous city, teeming with violence. I know the numbers, but it doesn't seem real. Iris isn't going to speak to me. No last words. The finality is all image: glinting metal and bodies strangely arranged, recoiling desires twisted past the breaking point, weary, losing their snap. Everything is larger than life and the end is met with strangers and shrugs.

***

LITTLE MISS MIGHT-HAVE-BEEN

I have to take the Morning After Pill at night because on my days off we keep a rock star schedule.

"Excuse me," I blare. "Do you also give out questionnaires to men who get Viagra?"

"Hey, it ain't me. It's the State." His hair is greasy with clearance rack gel and his white coat looks more barber than pharmacist. I slide the form right back at him. "Just give me the meds," I demand, sand graveling up my voice, the only impact of a two pack a day habit I originally picked up as an appetite suppressant. Sand running down through my hourglass figure, a body which will suffice as long as my breasts can be propped up high enough to distract from my wide load ass.

He tells me the price. I repeat the number, softening it, turning it into a lacy dropped handkerchief. He just raises his eyebrows in an impertinent, I've-been-through-this-before expression. I can't really hold it against him. He's on the clock and there are cameras and my political statement with the questionnaire has put me into Category Two: Women Who Will Require a Time Commitment and no amount of smiling and forward-leaning and fabulously-cute remarks are going to put me back into Category One: Women He Will Imagine Fucking Later. Only Category Ones get favors and discounts.

I pay with leftover money, hard-livin' bills, thin and leather soft. I toss down the money with the same haughty contempt with which I tip cocktail waitresses who disappear with my boyfriend after his sets, wringing him out in some storage closet built for two, emerging with better posture and a surreptitious smile. I always leave a perfect 15% to keep them in their place.

I glance around the drug store for a patron, but this is the outer Valley and the only reason to be here is cheap rent. The men have retained their bushy hair and over-tans, but have been cruelly conditioned to look away when they feel the urge to buy a luxury item, such as an intimate smile from a well-packaged woman. The men out here walk heavily, drag themselves along with the dire concentration of electroshock patients, their foreheads beading with perspiration over the task of moving around among fantastic siren-nippled creatures without admitting that they see anyone there.

I swallow the first pill at the drinking fountain, city water tasting stagnant and black. I imagine rain pooling on top of the La Brea Tar Pits, see my stunted primordial ancestor shaking herself dry after a cool dip in the pitch. They could be poisoning us.

I indulge in a split second story as the pill squeezes down my throat and vanishes into the outer space of my digestive system, a rocket leaving the earth's atmosphere, something I just have to believe in based on charts and written proofs because it has escaped all my senses. The little pellet pill is a bullet speeding toward the lazy embrace of egg and sperm, interrupting the little creature they are tentatively melding into, a trembling, furry thing as cuddly and ultimately annoying as a gerbil. The pill drives a wedge through this maybe-miracle. It's only a fairy tale. There's probably nothing there.

When I woke up, a half hour ago, I gathered all the condom wrappers littering the bedroom, tried to piece together their ripped foil and popsicle-colored coding. I had no idea how many there were supposed to be, but I was suspicious about last night. Gus lay there asleep in his extravagant nakedness, his jeans wadded around his knees, looking like a fiberglass sculpture anchored by a denim pedestal.

I drove to the drug store by myself, caked with dehydration and doom. It was street cleaning day in front of our apartment, and only three foolish cars remained, wearing the dunce caps of pink parking tickets on their windshields. I had to wonder what the story was, what caused these three motorists to miss the deadline: the who-cares sleep after a glorious fuck, general alcoholism, new in town and friendless and so overwhelmed by seeing all the places they've seen so many times before in the movies that they didn't notice the street signs? Three cars is a lot of negligence for one short street. I can't help but think that there may be an apartment full of festering dead bodies that the cops won't find until the boot goes on those cars and the paint starts to blister and peel in the dependable sun.

I tried to detect emptiness in my womb as I drove down the farthest end of Ventura Boulevard. There are many streets like this in L.A., extending for an improbably long distance, going on and on with increasing existentialism, fingernails still growing on a buried corpse. Way out here, Ventura is oppressively flat and bright, rejecting twilight every night like a failed organ donation. It seems to be panting, a fugitive pressing himself flush with the earth, praying for his life and cursing his pursuers. The buildings are low and begrudging. There is an air of lawless colonialism, a conspiratorial hush which suggests that Mexico may ambush at any minute.

Ah, fuck. You're supposed to eat with these pills. I don't have any money. I stride past the shelves of meal replacement bars and feebly congratulate myself on never resorting to shoplifting. I get back in my car and follow decrepit old Ventura Boulevard into Encino then Sherman Oaks, where it is live bait again, wiggling with bare-armed Valley folk all out searching for something. Not the same thing. But they all have their eyes peeled and when they stop moving forward, they bounce on the balls of their feet. Back East, crowds are soaked with impatience. Here, it's anticipation. It's a strong musk, and even after all these years, I have to admit it still turns me on.

I have maybe 20 minutes before the medicine will make me seriously nauseous. I scan the bright little shops, strip mall cousins, looking for a quick score. Last time, Gus had stroked my tummy and described ripples on a blue pool in a still forest. Gus is a master at the sincere embrace of the cliché. This is why he would have made a brilliant pop star. I am a little angry all the time now since it's become clear that he will never make it, that for some reason the fate he was equipped for will never come along. He's had a lifetime of preparation. He was born with it, the peculiar talent that made him sing in a barbershop quartet at age 4, delivering high pitched jokes between songs from under an enormous straw boater hat; that slapped tight jeans on his adolescent behind and had him staring out from behind a thicket of long hair while exploring the multiple stages of virginity with strangely willing girls behind the skating rink (all the women seemed bewitched and it was natural for him to love them intensely then confuse their identities, how could he keep them all straight? They all trotted to him with an animal gait, their faces powdered by want); the thing that made him fail high school by three credits and pack up and move to L.A. at age 18 and step off the bus and take a picture of the first palm tree he saw and buy a waterbed and easily meet boys with gear and vans and vague label connections, and play out everywhere, The Troub, The Whisky, The Roxy, all up and down the Strip, with the laughably cliché facts of his life shining like a bald boomer head from the stage so that someone should have recognized him from an album cover they'd mentally composed out of all the other album covers and plucked him up and made him a star.

But for some reason, he got passed by. And I was still paying his rent and we kept moving farther and farther from Hollywood as I lost every job from the congenial partying and consequent tardiness and abuse of sick days. I learned to gloss over the holes in my resumé, sitting across from frosty daycare center owners, pretending to love children, to be such a simpleton that I wasn't offended by minimum wage and no insurance and the many tones of yellow secreted by other peoples' kids. My real life, I wanted to announce, took place in the holes in that resume. You know Stephen Stills? I've ridden in the back of a limo with him. Brian Fairy? Don't kid yourself—he's not gay. Dede Ramone? He never slept. Never. Gus knows a lot of dead people now and he won't even listen to the radio anymore. I have to work more hours to pay for all my medicine. We are becoming isolated.

I could go home and be conspicuously sick for Gus, but I'm trying to show him that I'm mad, and this will take several days. I'm mad because he's been hanging out with The Freak, the skinhead down the hall, who is the building serial killer. Since the attacks, there's been a nationwide panic over terrorists among us, sleeper cells ready to strike. Here in So Cal we say, no shit, we've been living cheek to jowl with psychotics all along, like The Freak, whose Allah is a putrid iguana that he lets roam his apartment, that he brags about getting blow jobs from, The Freak waiting just two floors below us, a stumpy carefully non-descript dresser who has an obsession with a very minor porn star who uses our neighborhood grocery store, his walls papered with over-lit glossy mag shots of her looking needy and big haired and overburdened by her heavy tits, her pubes shorn down to a fussy French beard, little triplet rips where the iguana's claws have scuttled up the wall. She and the iguana share the same name, and I have to feel sorry for the iguana, having a stage name that is such pure exploitation: Tabitha Tikkle. And The Freak has equal control of the entry buzzer for our building. I have to share a dumpster with him and leave notes on his windowless van when he parks too close. He claims he saw Gus play way back at the old Gazzari's, but when did a skinhead ever show up at Gazzari's? And now Gus takes his guitar over to The Freak's lair every afternoon like a gung-ho Boy Scout drawn to the basement of a pedophilic denmaster who has promised to show him how to work a microscope. He returns home spent, flushed and full of secrets. I worry that he's being brainwashed. I used to worry

138   *Stacia Saint Owens*

because he seemed depressed. I wonder if I should make him get a job, but he's just not cut out for it. I sent him out into the workforce once, when he stopped getting gigs and got sloppy about his trysts with USC sorority girls. A foreign stud earring poked me in our bed, and I held it up between thumb and index finger like a ripe grape in the time of Egypt when the land was unyielding and treasures came small. "Babe…" Gus started, but this was one cliché I could not bear to watch him perform with his soothing varnish and friendly vaudeville face paint that stopped just short of clownish. I popped the stud earring into my mouth and swallowed it, then smiled at him, knowing I would look like all the slow, bed-ridden blockbuster movie villains before computer animation made them spry, knowing I could telegraph danger to him by mimicking his beloved clichés. The earring was not small and I swear it had to be real diamond with the way it tore up my throat going down. But the gesture worked. Gus cried in two or three manly heaves then wrote a song about it, changing my name to facilitate a rhyme. I was not satisfied and batter-rammed him with cold vengeance into getting a job at Guitar Center, where he spent a Tuesday and a Thursday standing with a stunned expression, name tag slanting, assaulted by a hellish stream of teenage boys playing "Little Feet" and Hendrix's "Star Spangled Banner" on no-money-down amps. I will never make him work again. I have no talent for casting curses.

I walk into a used CD store on Ventura where the competition is fierce, but the game is quick. I don't get these young girls with their shapeless t-shirts and refusal to accentuate anything, these post-grunge beauties who always look as if they are only a few minutes from having woken up or from crashing again. But readers of men's magazines have by now been trained to see something consumable in these laundry basket girls, who are undeniably small and uncrushed.

I don't have much time to raise my lunch money, so I have to go for second string. The clientele is almost exclusively male, though they don't notice this and fail to register the chess board advances of the few women. Luckily there is an entertainment law type, full of bluster and inadequacy, too fat and lazy to expect one of the young girls. I spend an eternity trailing him in the Classical section. It's dull, dull, dull, clacking through all those cloudy disks. Impatience is deadly in this game. A large part of the pick up artist's appeal is the impression that she exists in an alternate time zone, that her moons rotate at a glacial pace, that the sunrise and sunset are just trick photography to her, that she may be dead broke but she is holding a bankbook labeled All the Time in the World, that she will stay young forever, frozen in an upturned pose of adoration. I try not to convert Law Man's horizon-huge back into minutes wasted. I can kill some time along with some maybe-cells. I concentrate on Little Miss Might-Have-Been, swimming algae-like in my contaminated fluids. I tell her Little Red Riding Hood, Snow White, Puss in Boots. You've probably noticed, I conclude, that the prettiest always wins. The girl gets three choices and it's a one shot deal. When the Prince comes along, she has to be prepared to drop everything and be carried off with no prior warning. There will only be one chance, and most people don't even get that. It's all about being ready, night and day, for years on end. Believe me, honey, I'm sparing you a lot of idiocy, a lot of brutal waiting. If you exist at all, you won't remember this little run you made at my birth canal. You chose the wrong path in the wood. That's why you're being devoured.

It's like talking to a carrot I am peeling: stupid, but I don't even want to consider that it might have feelings and blood-curdling screams beyond my register. I think of my college degree in Dramatic Arts, which might also be imaginary, one of my fictional resumé enhancers. And I could have dreamed Gus, to give myself a mission and an excuse for lack of personal ambition. If I were going to invent a boyfriend, wouldn't I make him monogamous? Why would I kill him off without giving him a record deal first, at least a one hit wonder? *Once upon a time,* I tell the crinkled little thing, who is dying. She releases noxious fumes, bloating my belly. Someone has to buy me some food.

I finally resort to grabbing at Law Man's pudgy hand as he grabs for Bartok. Then I blink and exclaim, "Oh," but do not release my hand until he gets it and amidst talk about the L.A. Symphony, which I can guarantee you we have attended exactly twice between us, I lure him into the RECENT ARRIVALS/ POP section and choose rare British import double disks and ask naïve questions so he can feel like the founding father of *Rolling Stone,* dredging up the same esoterica that he hoped would get him laid in college, but didn't. It's a new era for him, lucky day, I am agreeable, pliable, he's shorter than I am but I look at the floor then raise my eyes to his level, giving the impression of looking up to him.

Where did I learn this chicanery? It's all part of getting by while waiting for fame, for my boyfriend's blessedly cliché rise to pop stardom. Gus could even have dropped me the minute he got a request call on MTV. I wouldn't have cared. It would have been one of those legendary prolonged break ups with drunken house burglaries on both sides, restraining orders and desperate fucks in the tiny bathrooms of majestic hotel suites, keeping everybody waiting, keeping them all *ahem*-ing and watch-glancing, ignoring the squeals. It would have gone on and on and I would have been mentioned in the liner notes fondly then bitterly then with cult-like Yoko pussywhipped politeness. I would have published a book of early photos documenting various stages of facial hair and in the end shacked up with him again somewhere like Taos. I suppose I have my own clichés and I resent their abortion.

Law Man informs me that Lou Reed actually recorded *Berlin* in London and I nod with a half smile like a docile panther, something slinky that will wrap itself around his leg if he succeeds in scratching it behind the ears before it can bite off his hand. He drifts toward the register and I follow, daring to turn my head back to acknowledge the respectful stare of an unmade sheet girl tracking a well-heeled cheap bastard mired in the Classical section, where the disks sell for a mere $3 a pop. I allow my ample tail a little wag, a *you'll get better at this as time goes by, kid* to the girl.

Law Man notices this and thinks I'm getting frisky. He lunges for my CD's and stacks them on the counter next to his. "We're together," he tells the saleskid, too loudly. My take is valued at $63. Not bad. But I'm starting to feel the sickening lunar pull of Morning After Pill nausea. The part where the Evil Queen exercises her powers of Meanwhile.

I rush Law Man a little, whisking him out to his car, not hemming and hawing enough to seem genuinely interested. He earns his Crashing Bore stripes by bringing up 9/11. I don't have time. I light a cigarette and set him straight. "Look," I say. "We both know the truth. When we woke up on the West Coast and saw the replays of those planes crashing into the skyscrapers, we all thought: 'But why aren't *we* a part of that? It looks exactly like the stuff we're good at, we love disasters, we cream over mudslides and wildfires and typhoons and earthquakes and riots and traffic pile-ups. We would have put on a show—run amuck in the streets, clogged all the freeways, shot each other up, hired private helicopter rescue lifts then overloaded them with electronic appliances and trophy wives. We have been waiting all this time for Armageddon. Why didn't they choose *us*?'"

"I think that's a totally irresponsible attitude," he proclaims. "But you seem like the irreverent type." To which I am supposed to flirt back, but I am seriously out of time. Little Red Riding Hood is kicking at the bedclothes with her hobnailed boots. I scrawl my standard fake number on the back of the receipt and stuff it in his pocket with an efficient milk money pat. My blatant hurry is a mistake. I've robbed him of his submissive fantasy, in which a low cut woman picked him out of all the world because she noticed the same hidden qualities his mother used to talk about. He sees that I am semi-pro, and he does have the receipt, so he pounces and tongues me with all the venom of a man who's bought a Corvette but still can't get chicks. Dark forests spring up, thorns in my eyes and poisoned leaves and wolves thick with bloodlust, which forms a paste in their mouths and makes them sound deceptively Southern and drunk.

I should never have let him kiss me. It's such a slippery slope. Everything about this town is a waterslide chute toward prostitution, and I've always resisted, even when I was young and stupid. I had all the typical obsessions, dime-a-dance halls, phone sex, internet jack-off sites, just look at the hourly wages! But Gus always forbade it. He said that stuff made people into hookers, that money can't be my prime motivation. It would be really horrible if he got famous and I was regarded as more groupie than girlfriend, some open-legged Nancy Spungen that everyone was laughing at. So I trade exclusively in the batted eyelash, the ripe suggestion of something I am never obligated to fulfill. I keep my profits low.

Law Man seems to have delusions of grandeur regarding the street value of $63. I want him to just try putting his hands on me, I will him to so much as brush my shoulder. I'll knock him flat on his ass. I can picture the line so vividly, a red velvet rope, and if he crosses it I will prove how wrong he is about me. It's been said that the two truths about women in Los Angeles are 1) we are the prettiest creatures in the world and 2) we hide our balls very well. There is a randy snake slithering up our inner thighs, an indigenous reptile from some long lost City of Angels coat of arms. He coils up in our crotches, flicking us with his insistent tongue, hissing up our cunts: "*Sssssell sssssomething.*" To be female in L.A. is to be a whore. It's all a matter of degrees. We measure those degrees down to nano-units, as precisely as scientists measure light waves, assigning colors that no one else can see. We sniff at the dumb cows in the back of *LA Weekly*, sunglassed faces and boob jobs and desperate, dizzy descriptions of their massage techniques. Then we buy the boutique dress with enough cleavage to insure that we never have to buy our own drinks or cigarettes. Correction. Someone buys us the dress. It's circular, but it doesn't have to be vicious. I've never sold anything more than a smile. Just try to touch me, pal.

But he suffers from an attorney's caution. He disengages and takes a long wolfish stare at my tits then folds himself into his little sports car without a word of parting. Transaction complete. I spit on the oily concrete of the parking garage. I feel hopeless. Not exactly violated, but tired of it, with many years ahead of me, getting older and more susceptible to bartering.

Saleskid laconically picks up each of my CD's and offers me $27 for the same titles that he just sold for $63. God, I want that kiss back. I try to argue about the Lou Reed disk, but saleskid is a So Cal native, nothing unpleasant gets through to him, he just yawns and stretches and prospers. By this point, I am sweating and have to cling to the edge of the counter to keep from succumbing to the beautiful horizontal floor with all its possibilities for reclining and rest. I buy an overpriced candy bar from the check out display and gnaw off the wrapper, the darkly dyed paper tasting sweet and treacherous. The Evil Queen again, spying through her mirror. They might have to call Gus to come pick me up. But he would be over at The Freak's by now, happily strumming his acoustic and absorbing lunatic one-man plots as spewed by his host.

I sit on the floor and prop myself up against the counter. Saleskid doesn't mind. Lounging is a birthright as far as he's concerned. When he sees furniture-rejecting postures, he doesn't think of monkeys, he thinks of home, of bong-hitting mom and magic brownie dad and all those great desert camping trips they talked about but never actually took. I look up at saleskid and he is eating candy, too, not bothering to hide it, radiating an unusual hue that could be the new star quality, the type the young ungroomed girls would lap up. I worry that I have chosen badly.

The little possible-pipsqueak inside me is fighting tooth and nail against the chemicals. We are sisters, so similar that only one of us will be allowed to live. I feel so sick I want to swear allegiance to something inhumane, to utter "Heil Hitler!" or rub bloody palms with the Evil Queen, or lie back for one of the salivating wolves, just to demonstrate how far beyond reason or caring I have been swept by this pain. There is nothing to distract me from the sickness, no candied houses or kind birds or upright talking animals with royal aspirations. The only couple within earshot is unskilled. She keeps asking questions for which she doesn't already know the answers, and when he doesn't know, either, the conversation crashes against the rocks. "So, like, did Tom Petty ever record without The Heartbreakers?"

"Ummm… I don't—Yeah. I wonder. Huh."

They are irritants, so I put my head between my knees and concentrate on the beige linoleum. The scuff marks look like villages, touching in their attempts at communal defense, their careful recording of births and deaths and taxes paid to the Evil Queen. When I first met Gus, he had me drive way up into Hollywood Hills then led me through a wire fence for a view of the smog and sprawl of nighttime Los Angeles, lights twinkling like birthday candles fighting off a wishful breath.

"I look at those lights," said Gus, solemn and resplendent, an angular boy with no job who was obviously going to be a star, "and I think: Every one of those lights is one person's dream. This city is made of all those dreams." And I laughed in his face, and went on laughing even when he looked surprised and hurt, even when I caught on that clichés are the fiber of his existence, that his adroitness with the banal is what makes strangers love him, buy him drinks and let him crash on their hide-a-beds and fuck him in cramped hostile spaces without expecting him to learn their names. All those years of preserving and polishing him, of keeping him visible and available, of sharing him with hungry strangers, displaying him in a glass coffin, kissable and for hire, and the big lift-off never came. Gus has stayed young in that bug-in-formaldehyde way of adults who never had to work, but when he was asleep this morning, I paused from my condom wrapper puzzle and felt his bones for the fat of a delectable child, only to find that he had deceived me. His shoulders are slightly slumped and one day they will be stooped and there will be no devoted stylist or worshipful celeb photographer or magic toad to camouflage it. I kept him free of responsibilities all this time, and he has ended up with the spine of a bank clerk.

The Freak is going to consume my Gus somehow. Cook him and eat him, tie him up and torture him in a cabin in Angeles National Forest, drown him in the L.A. River by dunking him repeatedly while reciting Zeplin lyrics, iguana on his shoulder, a mash note to Tabitha Tikkle folded up bite-sized inside his Doc Martens, ready to be swallowed if he is caught. I something-like-love Gus, but I feel too sick and wasted to be his good fairy. The maybe-baby is doing trampoline flips in my stomach, hoping to be transformed into a pebble or an echo or a golden ring instead of slain and never mentioned again, the fate of all the weaker characters.

I may have made this whole thing up. I may have lost my grasp of the details that prove that each day is distinct, and therefore, so is each life, however pedestrian it may appear. I take these Morning After Pills all the time, three nights a week. I keep pointing at the same door, drinking from the same goblet, collapsing into the same near-coma. Gus has had more than one chance to be heroic, but he just hunches his shoulders and goes on lunching with a troll. There are legions of maybe-babies, organizing to crash into me when I am standing tall again.

Ventura Boulevard is so bright it's blinding. It's night but there are floodlights so an afternoon scene can be shot starring a 33-year-old woman playing a 16-year-old with god-given C-cups. I exchange a glance with this woman through the plate glass windows, and we recognize each other, not just our features, but we wear the same perfume and both broke our right arm at age 12 and have chosen the same favorite song, "Drive My Car" by The Beatles, all the uncanny matches of two people separated at birth. I might be that actress, driven to elaborate daydreaming by hunger hallucinations or residual X from last night's binge, or the questionable sense-memory techniques taught by a sadistic acting instructor in a smoke-choked Hollywood Hills guest bungalow. Or she might be my daughter, victorious over my deadly pills, but nursing an inborn neglect complex that makes her require roomfuls of applause. I look again but she's pretending to be busy, threatening to sever our DNA, withholding all forgiveness with the infinite righteousness that only a daughter could muster. She laughs with a hefty man in a headset, but she is really emitting a bird call to warn tonight's maybe-baby.

I arch my back against the counter as the maybe-baby unleashes birthing pains inside me. She recognizes her slain sisters' hair plaited snake-sure round the mass grave and she will not go gently. I have become the Evil Queen, but I don't remember choosing this. I was once the fairest in the land.

Kill it, I beg the universe. *Just kill it and I'll choose better next time.*

***

SHOW DON'T TELL

ACT I

An office. The 22nd floor over Sunset. Fluorescent lights. The room is very square.

"She has a face you just want to slap."

The Little Girl stands on a low plywood platform that someone has stapled turquoise blue carpet remnants over. Her bright purple dress clashes with the carpet.

The Casting Director shakes a rolled-up piece of lunch meat at her, pausing to chew or think. The Little Girl's Mother holds her breath. She doesn't see turkey bologna in the Casting Director's hand. She sees a magic wand. She makes impatient, exaggerated faces at the Little Girl, urging her to pipe up and say something adorable.

The Little Girl looks blank. She would be daydreaming, but she has spent all morning in an industrial hallway with no windows, looking at sides for a toy commercial, her Mother saying over and over: "And she even talks if you pull her hair!" until the Little Girl memorized the line and could say it for herself, although she couldn't sound as delighted as the Mother. She hasn't had enough sensory input to compose a daydream. She yawns. Her Mother devises a punishment for later.

Stacia Saint Owens

"Market her as a brat. Or a nerd. Glasses. Prop books. And thin her down or plump her up. She's too in-between. Lots of work for little fatties."

The Little Girl's Mother takes a deep breath and intends to gush her thanks for the professional advice. But the Casting Director speaks again.

"Is this my crouton day?"

The frizzy Assistant shuffles madly through the calendar, trying to determine whether the Casting Director's diet allows for any bread that day.

The Little Girl wonders what a crouton is. She repeats the word in a sing-song voice as the Assistant motions for her Mother to take her out of the room. Time is up.

The motel kitchenette. Everything wobbles.

"You can eat anything you want for dinner. Just no bread."

The Little Girl chooses a hunk of cheese and a peach. The colors match.

The Mother has gotten her fake glasses from the Salvation Army, but there's no money for clear lenses. Whoever owned the glasses had two different prescriptions for each eye. The Little Girl's right eye bulges out all fishy and her left eye appears squinty. She has a permanent wink through the owlish glasses.

The Little Girl opens one of the prop books as she grates at the cheese with her two front teeth, pretending to be a rat. The books are hard and dark with golden writing on the spines. They were chosen for their covers. Inside is a black and white drawing comprised of millions of thin, narrow lines, depicting some place in London. A fair-haired girl in a long dress looks pale and lost and very, very good.

"Get them books off the table," her Mother says. "You'll ruin 'em."

Tamara's Mom's apartment. Too much carpet.

The Little Girl's diet is not going well. She and her Mother are at Tamara's house. Tamara's Mom is divorced and a New Yorker and gets child support payments. Tamara is still in school. When she has an audition, her Mom just takes her out.

Tamara demonstrates Show and Tell to the Little Girl, who used to be in her class. Tamara presents a pack of bubble gum, speaking through her nostrils. Tamara is Ethnic. She has a memorable nose and angry eyebrows.

"No gum for you, sweetie," says the Little Girl's Mother. "Every calorie counts."

Tamara slowly unwraps the gum, pinches it between her fingers, tilts back her head and drops it into her big mouth. Her thick lips are glossy with mucus and flavored lip balm. They look like the pale rubber worm from a pack of fishing bait.

"You could have told me about the cattle call. Considering." Tamara's Mom is also nasal. She is stapling together pages for her Learning Annex seminar, "How to Make Everybody Love You." No one knows exactly why she is qualified to teach this topic. She typed up a packet of handouts and talked her way into the job.

"Phil's only seeing kids he already likes the look of. A select few. He's never laid eyes on little Tamara," *because you're too paranoid about over-exposure and it's your own fault*, the Little Girl's Mother wants to add.

"I'm not going to over-expose her," whines Tamara's Mom, reminding the Little Girl's Mother of a porch fridge straining in August. "Over-exposure cannot be undone." She uses both hands and hops all her weight onto the stapler.

A bar. More furniture than people.

After her How to Make Everybody Love You seminar, a few extra-lonely men hang around to ask Tamara's Mom for additional advice.

She takes them all to a bar on The Promenade in Santa Monica. It is only afternoon, so the men order juice and green tea and iced coffee. But Tamara's Mom likes to keep reminding everyone that she's from New York. She orders a scotch and soda. The men's pulses race.

Tamara's Mom lights up a cigarette without permission or apology. She re-iterates that the key to captivating anyone is to fulfill their fantasies. She asks the rotund Insurance Broker in the bulging khakis what his deepest fantasy is, matter-of-factly, as if she needs an example for the chalkboard.

"And be specific," she says, exhaling a smear of smoke. "Is it with a basset hound or a St. Bernard?"

The men burst forth with raucous laughter, relieving tension. They're not certain, but they think they've caught a live wire and one of them will get to take this woman home. They shift their eyes, darting looks at the others' hairlines and waistlines and estimated credit lines.

"Oh… alright," says Insurance Broker. "I've always wanted a woman to get dressed up in a little black French maid's thing then to take a feather duster, actually, a pink feather duster… and…"

When he finishes, he blushes into his drink. The others shift in discomfort, waiting for their teacher's pronouncement.

Tamara's Mom looks straight at him. "I have a friend who has that exact same fantasy. You should call her. No, really, you have to. I'll call for you. Remind me later."

Tamara's Mom has lots of friends who want to meet men from her How to Make Everybody Love You seminar. One of these friends is the Little Girl's Mother. She specializes in fantasies involving children, but only in a strictly peripheral way. Tamara's mom splits her take from her seminar with The Learning Annex 60/40. She splits her take with the Little Girl's Mother 50/50.

A hotel room. Much nicer than the motel where they live. Carefully unobtrusive décor so it won't invade the business travelers' dreams.

The Little Girl's Mother leans into the bureau mirror and scratches at her teeth, which are not as white as she would like them to be. They should be dazzling. But she spends all her money on lessons for the Little Girl so she can stay competitive.

She wasn't planning to work tonight, so her hose have a long run from foot to thigh and her second toe keeps catching in the hole. It feels like a trap to catch a mink or a lynx, a trap that won't make the animal bloody, will preserve its saleable skin, but it will have to wait for days with its neck caught, its legs scratching furiously, wasting the last hours of its life in terrible panic, never understanding that it can't possibly escape.

The Little Girl peeks out from a crack in the bathroom door, observing her Mother with her foot on the bed, picking her toe out of the hole in her hose.

The Mother whirls around and marches to the Little Girl. She grabs the Little Girl's hand and sits her down on the tiled bathroom floor so she is facing the wall. She shoves a spiral notebook and a pen into the Little Girl's lap.

"Don't you dare turn around. You get to work. I want five pages by Sunday."

The Little Girl is supposed to be writing a screenplay. This is Plan B, in case none of the Casting Directors ever recognize her talent. Even if it takes her one year to write it, her Mother knows that she will still be one of the youngest screenwriters ever. It's an angle.

A man enters. There is muffled talking outside the bathroom door. Then the door opens and the man leans inside. He sees the Little Girl's back and her high pony tail, a bramble of mousy ringlets with white blonde highlights. The Little Girl makes a straight line on the paper so she can do a capital letter *I*.

The Little Girl's Mother pulls the man back and swiftly closes the bathroom door. She is the babysitter and that was Little Sister doing her homework and Mommy and Daddy will be home from the benefit dinner for the blind any minute now. It is quick work and she gets paid the same night.

The motel. A different one where the Mother gets a discount for cleaning rooms three mornings a week.

The Little Girl sits on the sagging bed with the thin coral-colored bedspread. The Mother opens the spiral notebook. The Little Girl has made no progress on the screenplay. Instead, she has written: I WANT TO GO TO SCHOOL over and over again, so many times that the Mother takes it as backtalk, the same as if the Little Girl had thrown a fit.

The Mother uncaps a pen and scrawls into the notebook, mumbling, pressing very hard on the page. She thrusts it in front of the Little Girl's face.

It is a tally of expenditures. Some of the totals are monthly and others are annual, but the Mother has not made any distinction. She's never been good with money because she's never had any, and when the Little Girl starts working in movies, they'll have so much money they'll have to get somebody else to add it all up, a professional math wiz.

Almost all of the expenses are related to the Little Girl's career: jazz dance lessons, on-camera seminar, fake tan lotion, hair extensions, drug store home highlights kit, Abdominator device to tone stomach, etc. The total is a very big number. The Little Girl understands this.

"I want to do Show and Tell."

"That's for kids that got no speaking skills!" her Mother snaps. "You don't need that."

A community center auditorium in Midwilshire. The color aqua prevails. Also the scent of chlorine.

The Little Girl and her Mother have waited three hours to read for a UCLA student film. The Director loves the Little Girl's glasses. He commands the Cinematographer to zoom in for a close up.

"She's got a real screwball look, doesn't she?" says the Director.

The Cinematographer is engrossed in lining up the shot and doesn't answer.

The Little Girl's Mother feels proud. "She loves to dance," the Mother announces to the room. All the students just suck on their cups of coffee and peer at the Little Girl.

"Alright. What grade are you in, precious?" asks the Director.

The Little Girl purses her lips, tucks her head against her chest and shakes it. She begins to sway from side to side, watching how far she can make her skirt billow.

"Look up at the camera, sweetie. Up here."

The Little Girl keeps her head down. Her skirt is nearly circular now as she half-spins.

"Anthony? Anthony? How many more we got?" asks the Director, turning away from the Little Girl and toward one of the people with the clipboards.

The Little Girl's Mother advances toward the Director with her hand out for a thank you shake, but all the heaps of denim in the room immediately snap on alert and someone intercepts her and ushers her and the Little Girl out.

In the car. The car is always on the verge of exploding. It rattles and vibrates and upchucks smoke.

"Why didn't you talk? What are you trying to pull?" wails the Mother.

The Little Girl is running her nail down the skinny teeth of a plastic comb, playing it like a harp. "This is my blue comb," she says, making a wide sweep with her hands as if playing to a crowded classroom. "My aunt gave it to me for my birthday. It's very special to me because my aunt gave it to me. It's good for combing and boys can even use it too. It also plays music."

The Little Girl rips her fingers across the comb. One of the teeth snaps off. She retrieves the piece and fumbles with it, fitting it exactly along the break. "Can we get some, um, um, Superglue? Please? It works miracles. Please?"

"Where did you get that comb? Huh? Breeze Louise Simmons, answer me!"

"Found it." Really she stole it from a very little girl at the audition. The girl was about one. She came stomping and bobbing up to the Little Girl with a huge gummy grin on her face and hit the Little Girl with the comb. It didn't hurt, but the Little Girl grabbed her pudgy hand and bent the fingers back until the other one cried. When her Mama rushed over and scooped her up and jiggled her, the Little Girl reached down and picked up the comb off the floor and kept it.

The Mother is afraid that one of the How to Make Everybody Love You men has slipped the Little Girl a gift. She sometimes gets sure that one of them is taking liberties, even though she stays on them like a bulldog the whole time and only treats them to that one harmless glimpse of the Little Girl.

She pulls over to the shoulder of the freeway to get her grip. She thinks she smells something rotting, but the car always smells. She thinks of all the rotting and corrupting in the Bible. Even if you just go near a sin, you get tainted.

She stares at the Little Girl. She's not growing any taller, thank the Lord, but she is becoming different.

The Mother grabs the Little Girl's poodle head and strokes her hair. "Don't get any bigger, baby. Please don't get any bigger. People around town are starting to know you how you are. We've worked too hard on this. We can't blow our recognition."

The Little Girl likes the feel of her mother's acrylic nails on her scalp. She begins humming, "*Crouton, crouton, crouton...*" She sticks the comb in her mouth and runs it against her teeth. The little harp sound is louder that way.

The Mother snatches the comb, pinching the Little Girl's upper lip. "Are you crazy, putting that thing in your mouth? After all that tooth bleaching? You oughta be ashamed, little girl!"

The Little Girl looks straight ahead at all the cars crawling by, moving like sprinters forced into waltz time, shuddering with unused speed. She does not feel ashamed.

Her eyes hurt from the glasses with the wrong prescription. She takes them off and rubs her eyes then practices plucking her eyelids away from her eyeballs to look at the red underneath. It's like having a red umbrella.

The Little Girl's Mother starts to scream at the Little Girl not to damage her eyelashes, but a sudden Noah's flood of despair washes over her and she sobs and sobs, gripping the hot steering wheel tightly in both hands, as if it is the dial to a safe that either contains a million dollars or is about to blow up.

A warehouse soundstage in Van Nuys. Emptiness with clusters of clutter.

Phil, the Director, asks the Little Girl to skip across the stage. He tells her to play hop scotch, but she doesn't know that game.

"Fine, fine, don't worry, that's okay. Good job, honey. Willena will take care of you."

Willena takes the Little Girl's hand and leads her behind some stacked electrical equipment and gives her three pale, off-brand crayons to play with. Nobody's considered paper, so Willena says, "Shit," and goes to find some.

The Little Girl draws on the side of a black lighting kit, making a shaky, waxy green line. It isn't supposed to be anything. She can't think of anything to draw.

"We'll just have to see you topless, first of all." Phil is bent over looking through the camera lens. He uses himself for Cinematographer. The Little Girl's Mother isn't sure who he's talking to. "Okay. Whenever you're ready, Rhonda."

"I don't—" the Mother starts. Phil sees genuine perplexity on her face, magnified through the camera. That face makes him unspeakably weary. He has thought of putting a sign up above the door: ABSOLUTELY NO FEIGNED SURPRISE ALLOWED. But she wouldn't know *feigned*.

"It's a mother-daughter thing, Rhonda. I'm sure I told you that."

"But—I'm sorry—I don't—NAKED?"

"Not the kid. Just the moms. The kid's in it for like a split second. If even. Fully clothed. Doing kid things. Totally different location and everything."

"But—then I...?"

"Yeah, it's a jack-off picture, Rhonda. That's what I make. Don't act like you don't know that. Look around you, for chrissakes. Are you going to waste any more of my time or what?"

"But with CHILDREN?"

"No, not *with* children. *Including* children. As an artistic enhancement. I'm not crazy. I don't wanna do 15 to 20 for this shit. It's gonna be strictly soft core, absolutely no interaction with the kids. It can't be sold above board of course, but that just maximizes profits. Hot Mamas, Yummy Mummies, Bored Housewives. It's all very tame. I'm a businessman. I've checked it out with the lawyers. I've got a very good case if they try to fuck with me. Ground breaking, Larry Flynt type thing. Do children appear in R movies with some explicit scenes? I rest my case." Now Phil is really worked up. He no longer sees the Little Girl's Mother standing in front of him. He is practicing this speech for when he gets the chance to say it to important people. "I'm creating a new genre. I'm crossing cinema verite with erotica. If I was French, they'd give me an Oscar for this. What no one in this town realizes yet is that I'm a fucking genius."

"I don't know, really. I have to—"

"Nobody forced you to come here, Rhonda. The bottom line is, what are you willing to do for your kid's career? Do you know how many millions of people are gonna watch this?"

Rhonda takes off her top slowly, signaling to God that this wasn't in her original plans.

Phil adjusts the light reading. Then she takes off her bottoms. She starts to feel encouraged, thinking of all the exposure.

"Do you want her with or without the glasses for the shoot, Phil?" she asks. "She can do it either way."

Another motel. The type of place you live just before you go homeless.

The Little Girl's synthetic hair extensions are going gummy at the ends. She sits on a hard plastic chair molded all curly to look like a seat at a European street café.

Her Mother stabs at the Little Girl's roots with pointy bobbie pins. If a bobbie pin falls on the floor, she gets down and hunts around for it.

The Little Girl is slurping strawberry Slimfast through a straw. Wooden broom sticks are suspended from the ceiling on bicycle hooks to make extra clothing racks. The parameters of the room are filled with flouncy dresses for the Little Girl's auditions. The room is a thick jungle. The spangled rainbow of fabrics hangs down and snags on anyone who passes. The Little Girl doesn't have a favorite dress and she never feels like playing dress up.

"Can we go to Tamara's house?" she asks.

"You gotta practice for the shoot. Tamara didn't get cast."

"Why not?"

"Her Mom is too protective of her. Her career's going nowhere. I feel sorry for her. We should pray for her."

The motel parking lot. Bottles and butts.

The little girl skips and skips. When she disrupts the rhythm to leap over a painted white line, her Mother makes her go back and do it again.

The car, in the Van Nuys warehouse parking lot. Already hot at 7:30 a.m.

It is the morning of the shoot. The Little Girl does not want to go inside. Her Mother is livid. She flings open the car door and drags the Little Girl out.

The Little Girl screams, "No! No! No!" over and over, very shrill. She scratches at her Mother with stubby glitter nails. Her Mother scratches back with long curved talons, each with a white Egyptian eye on the tip. It symbolizes wisdom.

The AD comes running out of the warehouse and separates them, using the same amount of force he uses to pry apart coke-fueled frat boys at the club where he works weekends as a bouncer.

The Little Girl's glasses go flying. She hits her head hard on the rusty side mirror of the car. She stops screaming and touches her injured head with one hand.

"We can't have this," glares the AD. "I mean, are you nuts? Do you think what we're doing here needs extra attention? Do you want the cops all up in here?"

All her life, the Little Girl's Mother has responded to lectures the same way. She bites her lip and shakes her head and looks at her shoes. She can never concentrate on the words.

"Phil says we don't need you."

"What do you mean? Until when? Our call time's—"

"We don't need you. We can't have this."

"Let me talk—"

"Here. For your trouble. Now go. Now."

The AD hands the Little Girl's Mother a white envelope. Inside is a check for $40 from Phil's personal account. The PAY TO line is blank.

****

ACT II

"Let me just stop you there. It's way too long. You realize that, right? Half—no, a third is all you need. You're how old?"

"Thirteen."

"And this is your real life story? You're actually thirteen?"

"Next week."

"What?"

"NEXT. WEEK."

"And people know you're thirteen? It's common knowledge? You got ID or something?"

"It's in my school records."

"I thought she kept you out of school."

"After I ran away, I went back."

"So you ran away from your stage mother so you could go to school? That's an angle. Roberta! Come here! Is she thirteen?"

"Why? You want to fuck her?"

"Watch your mouth for chrissakes. How do you know she's not my niece or something?"

"Harold's on line two."

"I'll get back."

"She could be."

"Are you an emancipated minor? All legal, airtight? Because what I do not want is Mommie Dearest busting through that door and crapping all over the deal. You know a lawyer? I'll get you a lawyer."

"What for?"

"Come on. You're not really thirteen. Hey. Look at me. You're not thirteen."

"Can I have my script back?"

"Who else you shown this to? Anyone?"

"Can I have my script back?"

"No! You can't have your script back, you little dizzy Lizzy. We're gonna take this script and flash light at it and project it on a big fucking screen and make a million bucks. Gotta talk to the lawyer first. Who do you live with?"

"Myself."

"How—Okay, I won't ask. My interest in you is purely professional, you know."

"Uh, yeah."

"It's all wrong, this script. You know that, right? There's lots of stuff here that can't be shown on screen. Screenplays are all pictures. Show don't tell."

****

ACT III

A hotel room, but a nice one this time. A glass wall overlooking the Pacific.

He takes me here to help me re-write my screenplay. Then he fucks me on the big bed with so many linens piled on it that it seems to be a department store display, someone must be trying to sell them. My seduction consists of making it clear that I'm not a virgin and that no one is expecting me home at any particular time. He puts me on bottom, even though I am a scrawny bird compared to him, and his weight crushes me.

He comes quickly then pants and cries into my tiny neck. I pat his head, toying with the hair plugs.

He's right. There's a lot that can't be shown. I have lived 27 years and though my body has remained unwomanly, I have stopped going to auditions.

156   *Stacia Saint Owens*

There is a scheming in my eyes that no one can put their finger on, but in a room full of real children, I no longer make a convincing child.

He will either give me $10,000 option money for my screenplay, or my Mother and I will blackmail him for sleeping with a thirteen-year-old. Tucked under my pillow is a washcloth for dabbing up irrefutable evidence. It's never come to that. They'd rather pay for the script and fool themselves that it's all fictional, just entertainment. Just an idea they were toying with. Anybody in this town can tell you that ideas are cheap. Everybody has them.

In addition to the $10,000, they also have to give us a name, a colleague they can refer us to, tell him this friend-of-a-friend they've never met has a script he might be interested in, if I call he should take the meeting. They like this part. There's always someone they'd like to screw over. Hell, this makes it well worth the 10 grand.

They never ever tell on us, but I've heard that we are whispered about in certain circles. Some very big people have mentioned us. "We're really getting to be known!" my Mother crows. To be honest, this pleases my Mother more than it does me. She even wrote the screenplay. She doesn't mind painting herself as the villain. She'll do whatever it takes.

Sometimes my old childhood stubbornness takes hold of me. Sometimes, just before a crucial pitch meeting, after my Mother has circled the surrounding blocks countless times and finally found a parking space to hide our car from the valets, I simply refuse to get out.

"You've made me into a whore," I whisper in a voice designed to make her have to ask, "What did you say?" so I can answer, "Nothing." But she never follows my script.

"If I've made you into a whore," my Mother says, "You're a $10,000-a-night whore. Don't you forget that."

I sit there with my arms crossed against my prarieland chest. I think that I will either kill her or run off and never come back. These are my only two ideas, and neither of them are very good.

"Why don't *you* do it?" I demand.

The answer is simple. She can't. My Mother enters rooms and everyone clams up and steps back. Not once has anyone been happy to see her, not even me. My Mother is painful, high-wattage and thin-skinned. People look at my Mother and they sense that she is going to burn them down.

That's why it has always been so important that I make people like me, dance a jig, sing a tune, win everyone over, bridge the terrifying gap between my Mother and the rest of humanity. There's been a lot of rejection. When you go places with my Mother, people want to get rid of you quick. People have never taken a shine to me, either. I am the crazy lady's accessory, her crumpled plumed hat, part of the uniform of her insanity.

She still believes that I am going to succeed, but what else is she going to think? That she is going to die orange-skinned and unacknowledged, a woman who has spent many nights in the back seat but has never bought a new car? If I can make people applaud, she can stand just off-camera and watch their faces light up. It's the only way she'll ever get to see that.

I can't pretend that I figured this out on my own. My childhood friend Tamara wrote a book about it. She said that some people become stage mothers to God, or to their corporations, or to a sports team. If you're starved for affection and you can't figure out how to get any for yourself, you'll become a parasite in order to survive, and devote your life to plumping up your host. Hating her Mother has been very profitable for Tamara, though I strongly suspect that her Mom actually ghostwrote the book and Tamara just posed for the photo on the back. Tamara's Mom's Plan B for her daughter was a Ph.D. in Psychology. My Mother pointed out that she may have book smarts, but she isn't meeting the right people. Not like us.

In the end, I get out of the car. My Mother sticks her head out the window and yells, "Limber up! Limber up!" because I am walking off at a clipped and duty-bound pace that no thirteen year old could anticipate. To loosen up, I do not visualize a stadium full of people cheering for me, as my Mother has taught me. I think of Ignatio.

When I was nineteen, it became certain that all the early dieting had stunted my growth, stopped me at the stick-figure stage, left me with the sort of hands that fumble over shoelaces and will never host a wedding ring. I tried to run away at least once a week. I would never go any farther than the dingy burrito counter on the corner. I would sit there miserable, swinging my stumpy legs under the stool, sucking down a large limeade and calculating how I could get away with poisoning my Mother.

A Honduran boy called Ignatio worked behind the counter. He was short and compact and he tried to make me laugh, tossing the tortillas above his head like pizza dough and making lame jokes about the banda songs blaring through the mono radio in the back. I didn't know how to talk to people, and I'm sure I came across as mentally slow. But he persisted until I mumbled my name, then he repeated it back in an accent that made it sound gentle as cigar smoke.

I ended up losing my virginity with Ignatio, and this event, too, was short, accomplished during one of his breaks, in his immaculate white car with the leopard print blanket tucked carefully over the seats. In the back window stood a plastic figurine of *Christo Negro*, the black Jesus, extending his divine ebony arms as if embracing the entire contents of the car including me, a heavenly flasher flaunting the joy of his flaming, thorn-encircled heart, promising His protection.

When Ignatio drove away, the *Christo Negro* traveled with him, herding him home to some impoverished little apartment packed with tight-knit, quarrelling, hugging, singing, loyal-hearted family members. I watched *Christo Negro* retreat from me, giving me his stiff blue back, forgetting me already. Then I trudged back to the dismal motel room that was the stuttering understudy for the home I never had, to face the hailstorm of accusation, intimidation, and pleading pep talks that was my Mother. I clung to her rocky bosom and promised her the moon: fame, fortune, and all my leftover scraps of adoration. And for the first time, I knew beyond a doubt that I was lying to her, leading her on. I had just experienced my first prize of affection, from Ignatio, and it had been so meager that there was none left over for her. I was never going to overflow with adulation, would never become her healing fountain. What would she do if she discovered that I shared her deficiencies? "Just don't turn your back on me," I prayed silently to her. "Don't drive off without me."

Ignatio is the only secret I've managed to keep from my Mother. I never became Ignatio's girlfriend, he never even kissed me again, but for a long while, every time I pushed open the door to the burrito counter, his plastic-gloved hands would pause in the rice vat, he would tilt his chin toward me, and look at me as if he knew me.

***

ACKNOWLEDGMENTS

Unending thanks to my family, who have graciously tolerated my insolvency and vampiric schedule while offering steadfast encouragement: Stevie Steve 8K Owens, Amanda Owens Caetano, Rebecca Owens Ervin, Jerry Caetano, Reagan Ervin, Ann and Lee Whitney, Mary and Kevin Tubbesing, Paul and Carol Owens, Sister Mary Bryan Owens, Terrance Owens, Joanne Durnbaugh, Dr. Dean and Rina Eyre, and Virginia Owens.

I have benefited from the wisdom and guidance of many remarkable teachers, especially Anne Bechtel, June Coleman-Harris, Sister Mary Joan Eble, Marietta Gregor, Lorna Mathison, Sister Paulette Kirk, Sister Mary Barbara Wieseler, Sister Rosemary Kolich, Aishah Rahman, Nilo Cruz, Paula Vogel, Mary Gaitskill, Carole Maso, Keith Waldrop, Gale Nelson, Dennis De Pauw, Buck Wong, Dale Moffitt, Lou Salerni, and Paul Walsh. Thank you for your generous mentorship.

To my colleagues at Brown University who inspired me with their prodigious writing talents: Sarah Ruhl, Laura Zam, Sawako Nakayasu, Nic Kelman, Emily O'Dell, Christine Evans, Charlotte Meehan, Quill Camp, Kamili Feelings, Rose Weaver, Paul Foster Johnson, E. Tracy Grinnell, Mark Tardi, Sherry Mason, Jim Higdon, Michael Hayes, Elen Gebreab, Anna Joy Springer, Marc Robert, and J. Thraves.

To my friends who appreciated my writing long before it ever appeared in print: Jeanne Goodnow Matthews, Rosemary Snow Jacobs, Christina Shirel Lively, Teresa Runyon Barry, Julie Heim Beying, Heather Locke Schreiber, Krista Loy Onofrio, Charlie Riordan, Sean Quinn, Bill Hess, Colleen Savage Shamburger, David Colclasure, Tina Parker, Tim Johnson, Wilson Michaels, Jose Dominguez, Niki Davis White, Gina Lewis, Steve and Amy Krajewski, Joel Juarez, Anthony and Joe Russo, Jerome Seven, Leah Wysong Spellman, Debra Brennan Tagg, Lynda Lester, Joshua Wolf Coleman, Amy Lynn Budd, Felix Pire, Sunday Kurtz Cook, Martina Tkadlec Strong, Ali Liebegott, Dan Delaney, Houston Curtis, Julian Fletcher, Radek Palinowski, Joanne Runyon, and Barbara Smith. Special thanks to my most ardent advocates: Robin Larsen, Erin Ryan Burdette and Stephen D. Tomac.

To my colleagues at Harrow College, whose erudition and dark British humor greatly influenced my stories: Wendy Burt, Sarah Carnegie, Jo Dooley, Mary Ling, Rob Brown, Sue Rogers, Laura Pasternack, and Carol Hayes.

To the visionary John Saddler, the first in the publishing industry to take an interest in my work.

To my father, Tom Owens, who read me *Great Expectations* aloud when I was an infant in my crib.

To Joe Taylor and Livingston Press for their artistic integrity, professional enthusiasm and support of new writers.

In loving memory of Blanche Pauline Ayers, a lady of lettters who was far ahead of her time.

Most of all, to my partner, Dean Louis Eyre, a truly exceptional person whose intellectual stimulation, elegant articulation, and tireless championing made this book possible.

***

"Little Miss Might-Have-Been" was originally published in *The Massachusetts Review*. "Once Removed" was originally published in *Southern California Review*. "Inheritance" was originally published in *Wisconsin Review*.

Stacia Saint Owens grew up in Leavenworth, Kansas. She holds an MFA in Creative Writing from Brown University, and a BFA in Theatre with a Playwriting concentration from Southern Methodist University. While at Brown, she was awarded the university's Weston Prize in Writing, and studied under Pulitzer Prize-winning playwrights Paula Vogel and Nilo Cruz, and acclaimed fiction writers Mary Gaitskill and Robert Coover.

In the late-1990s, Ms. Saint Owens co-founded The Pig Latin Embassy— An Artists' ColLaboratory. Located in Hollywood, the resident company mounted interdisciplinary, experimental premieres by West Coast writers and artists. Ms. Saint Owens served as Artistic Director and produced three seasons of performance events, including plays, musicals, improv comedy, performance art, and a short film festival.

Ms. Saint Owens' plays have appeared at La MaMa Experimental Theatre Club, The Working Theatre, Cherry Lane Theatre, New Dramatists, and regional theatres in Dallas, Chicago, Providence, and Los Angeles. Her writing awards include The Princess Grace Foundation Award in Film, George Burns and Gracie Allan Comedy Writing Award, Slamdance Film Festival/ Sci-Fi Channel Horror Writing Award, and quarterfinalist for The Academy of Motion Pictures Arts and Sciences Nicholl Screenwriting Fellowship. She has written two short films, "OUT OF HABIT" and "PELEA DE GALLOS" ("THE ROOSTER FIGHT"), which have been selected by an extensive list of international film festivals and broadcast on television.

Her fiction and creative nonfiction have appeared in *Southern California Review*, *Willow Springs*, *Wisconsin Review*, and *The Massachusetts Review*. *Auto-Erotica* is her first book.

Stacia recently lived in London, England, for four years, where she served as Lecturer in English Literature at Harrow College. She now lives in Los Angeles and is writing a novel.

She can be reached at www.StaciaSaintOwens.com